ADAM WINN

KILLING A MESSIAH

A NOVEL

Academic

An imprint of InterVarsity Press
Downers Grove, Illinois

InterVarsity Press
P.O. Box 1400, Downers Grove, IL 60515-1426
ivpress.com
email@ivpress.com

InterVarsity Press® is the book-publishing division of InterVarsity Christian Fellowship/USA®, a movement of students and faculty active on campus at hundreds of universities, colleges, and schools of nursing in the United States of America, and a member movement of the International Fellowship of Evangelical Students. For information about local and regional activities, visit intervarsity.org.

All Scripture quotations, unless otherwise indicated, are taken from The Holy Bible, New International Version®, NIV®. Copyright © 1973, 1978, 1984, 2011 by Biblica, Inc.™ Used by permission of Zondervan. All rights reserved worldwide. www.zondervan.com. The "NIV" and "New International Version" are trademarks registered in the United States Patent and Trademark Office by Biblica, Inc.™

Cover and image composite: David Fassett
Interior design: Daniel van Loon
Images: madaba map: © WitR / iStock / Getty Images Plus
    palm tree leaf: © joakimbkk / E+ / Getty Images
    asphalt texture: © Pongasn68 / iStock / Getty Images Plus
    cardboard texture: © Katsumi Murouchi / Moment Collection / Getty Images

ISBN 978-0-8308-5277-2 (print)
ISBN 978-0-8308-4381-7 (digital)

Printed in the United States of America ♾

InterVarsity Press is committed to ecological stewardship and to the conservation of natural resources in all our operations. This book was printed using sustainably sourced paper.

Library of Congress Cataloging-in-Publication Data
Names: Winn, Adam, 1976- author.
Title: Killing a Messiah : a novel / Adam Winn.
Description: Downers Grove, Illinois : Apollos, IVP an imprint of
  InterVarsity Press, 2020. | Includes bibliographical references.
Identifiers: LCCN 2019041673 (print) | LCCN 2019041674 (ebook) | ISBN
  9780830852772 (paperback) | ISBN 9780830843817 (ebook)
Subjects: LCSH: Jesus Christ—Fiction. | Bible. New Testament—History of
  Biblical events—Fiction. | Antisemitism—Study and teaching. | GSAFD:
  Christian fiction. | Biographical fiction.
Classification: LCC PS3623.I66285 K55 2020 (print) | LCC PS3623.I66285
  (ebook) | DDC 813/.6—dc23
LC record available at https://lccn.loc.gov/2019041673
LC ebook record available at https://lccn.loc.gov/2019041674

P 25 24 23 22 21 20 19 18 17 16 15 14 13 12 11 10 9 8 7 6 5 4 3 2 1

Y 37 36 35 34 33 32 31 30 29 28 27 26 25 24 23 22 21 20

"For centuries, Christians have been taught that the only possible reading of the Gospels was one in which the Jews, the enemies of Christ, are responsible for his death. Winn, using those same sources and informed by the best of contemporary scholarship, has produced a plausible alternate narrative of what might have occurred during that famous Passover week and demonstrates that anti-Jewish interpretations of the New Testament are not inevitable."

David Fox Sandmel, rabbi, director of interfaith engagement for the Anti-Defamation League

"*Killing a Messiah*—this is an easy read, but also a highly informative one that displays Adam Winn's solid grasp of the social, political, and historical realities at work in the complex of events surrounding Jesus' execution. The Gospel accounts leave so many questions unexplored— sometimes about who did what, but especially about how and why Jewish and Roman leaders acted as they did. What motives led to Jesus' crucifixion? How was the Jewish council able to determine so quickly that Jesus deserved death? Why weren't Jesus' disciples rounded up along with Jesus when he was arrested? How do we explain Judas's role in these affairs? And so on. Winn's delightful and well-crafted story imagines what was going on behind the scenes even as it respects the Gospel accounts and the historical issues they raise."

Joel B. Green, professor of New Testament interpretation and associate dean for the Center for Advanced Theological Studies, Fuller Theological Seminary

"As a filmmaker, I gravitate toward page-turning tales of complex characters caught in high stakes, political intrigue. Adam Winn offers readers a fresh take on the crucifixion of Jesus through rigorous research and astute imagination. *Killing a Messiah* is a brilliant exploration of the ultimate historical hinge point."

Craig Detweiler, cofounder of the Windrider Film Forum, author of *Into the Dark: Seeing the Sacred in the Top Films of the 21st Century*

"With a sure grasp of first-century religious and political realities, Adam Winn brings the events surrounding Jesus' execution vividly to life. What emerges is a story of manipulative authorities, greedy informers, severed friendships, but ultimately hope in the figure of Jesus himself—all told with the verve and panache of a novelist."

Helen K. Bond, professor of Christian origins, head of the School of Divinity, University of Edinburgh

"Adam Winn uniquely and subversively contributes to historical Jesus research through this compelling story about the events leading up to Jesus' death. Through the eyes of a varied cast of characters, Adam illuminates Jesus' historical, social, and political world and challenges some conventional understandings of the Gospels. If you are interested in engaging your theological students, pastors, or congregations in issues and questions surrounding the study of Jesus and the Gospels, you should get this book."

Elizabeth E. Shively, senior lecturer in New Testament studies, University of St. Andrews, Scotland

"*Killing a Messiah* is, first and foremost, an engrossing read. Once I started it, I resented having to put it down for other tasks or for sleep! But it is also a highly informative read. Dr. Winn immerses his readers in a web of plots plausibly driven by the complex political dynamics at work in Judea in 29 CE, dynamics often lost on the casual reader of the Gospels. He advances, in narrative form, a bold hypothesis concerning the backroom maneuverings behind Jesus' arrest, trial, and condemnation that does justice both to the public view of these events preserved in our Gospels and to the character of the authorities known from other sources. Perhaps his greatest achievement is his stunningly well-rounded and sympathetic portrayal of figures like Caiaphas and Pilate. This novel will certainly enrich, and quite possibly challenge, your understanding of the most critical week in human history."

David A. deSilva, Trustees' Distinguished Professor of New Testament and Greek at Ashland Theological Seminary, author of *Day of Atonement: A Novel of the Maccabean Revolt*

To my mother, Kemi Winn,
who cultivated in me a love for the Bible
from a young age.

CONTENTS

ACKNOWLEDGMENTS

This project began fourteen years ago as an idea for a lecture on the passion narrative in one of the first courses I taught. I was a green adjunct professor trying to find my way in the complex and challenging world of academia. For the students that heard this idea for the first time and received it well and for all subsequent students who bore with me as the idea evolved and matured, I am thankful. I thank Dan Reid, former academic editorial director at IVP, who first accepted my proposal for an academic book on what has become the central thesis of this novel. And I thank Anna Gissing, also at IVP, for not scoffing at the idea of transforming that academic book into a novel! To trust an academic to write a work of historical fiction is surely an act of bravery by any measure. Thank you for believing in me and this project, Anna! I also thank the editorial board at IVP, who also believed in this project. I thank my mother-in-law, Syl Field, who saw the first draft of this novel, with its many warts, and proofread every page. Thank you to David Wilhite, Amy-Jill Levine, David Sandmel, and Tim Brookins, all of whom read early drafts of this project and provided invaluable feedback. Their wisdom led to a much-improved final product. I thank my wife, Molly, and my daughter, Brennan, for their daily love and support, even when writing projects like this take up precious time. You both are the loves of my life! Finally, I thank the God and Father of my Lord Jesus Christ, through whom I have received blessing beyond measure. May this book play even the slightest role in the ongoing establishment of your kingdom.

PROLOGUE

JUDAH

As he looked around the room, Judah saw the faces of his closest and most trusted friends, all young men like himself, none older than twenty-five. He had known most of them from childhood. A paradoxical mixture of pride and humility filled his heart. He was proud of their commitment to this, the greatest of causes, and humbled by their commitment to his leadership to see that cause through.

Tonight, God's kingdom would be one step closer. Tonight, God's enemies would bleed. Tonight, Israel's oppressors would taste the pain they so eagerly delivered.

Each man had experienced Roman oppression firsthand. When Simeon was only twelve years old, a childish game disrupted a group of Roman soldiers who were throwing dice. Simeon paid dearly for the disruption. His right cheekbone was crushed, and his once handsome face was permanently deformed. Joseph's mother, who ran a small tavern, regularly fed Roman soldiers. They thanked her service by refusing to pay, due to complaints about the food—a dishonesty betrayed by their repeat visits. And now their bluster and vulgarity drove away other customers. There were whispers that she could not keep the doors open much longer.

At one time or another, Roman soldiers had forced each of them to carry heavy equipment for a mile, often to their personal detriment—a sale lost, an appointment missed, or a commitment unkept. And while all had paid the heavy price of Roman taxation, Jacob and Nathaniel, the sons of John, had lost long-held family businesses because of unmanageable financial burdens. But Samuel, Judah's closest friend and Joseph's cousin, had been victim of the worst transgression of all: Roman soldiers had raped Samuel's sister just two weeks before. The mere thought turned Judah's stomach and filled him with rage. The elders of Jerusalem were seeking justice, but everyone at the table knew there would be no justice—no Roman soldier would pay for this crime. Pain and anger now distorted Samuel's once boyish and handsome face. Pain and anger marked every face that looked back at Judah. While each man here believed that his God had called him to this cause, it was that pain and anger that fueled their desire for the blood that would be spilled that night.

Judah's voice broke the silence. "I see the pain in your faces. I know the lives you have lived under the thumb of these Roman blasphemers. I know the trouble they have brought to your families. Tonight we enact God's justice!"

The room exploded with a guttural roar that would have possibly drawn unwanted attention if they were not secluded in the underground scriptorium of a prominent Pharisee.

Judah continued, "Tonight our hearts are true, our zeal for God and his promises pure, and our plans are blessed by God's good fortune."

All of them at once began to whisper prayers of thanksgiving to the God of Israel.

For God's good fortune had certainly fallen on them. Several months ago, Joseph overheard two drunk soldiers in his mother's tavern. Apparently, each week a small group of Roman soldiers arrived in the city from Caesarea carrying important correspondence from the governor and a small chest of gold and silver. With this news, Judah and his friends had spent the last two months trying to determine which night these soldiers arrived and at which gate. Three weeks ago, they had found out both: the first day of the week at the Joppa gate. With this knowledge they began to monitor weekly activity, and a clear pattern had emerged. A group of five Roman cavalry arrived at the gate at approximately nine o'clock. Each time they carried a small scroll, which the guard noted but did not inspect, and a small chest, which the guard always opened. After this brief interaction with the gate guards, they proceeded through the city to the Antonia fortress, the Roman military headquarters in Jerusalem. They used the same route every time—a route that gave Judah the perfect place for an ambush.

"We have planned, we have trained, and we have purified our hearts before God. As he did with our ancestors before us, God will surely match our faithfulness with his own. He will meet us in the battle and give us victory! Tonight Rome will bleed, but it will not be the last time. Tonight we deliver a mere flesh wound, but it will be the first of many. In the end our resolve will drive these vile Romans from our holy city!"

Again a roar filled the hall.

"The time has come. You know what to do. God grant us strength and victory."

They left the scriptorium, made their way through the house above, and scattered through a variety of exits into the cool Jerusalem evening. They had planned the routes to their stations to avoid attention or suspicion. Each concealed a small bow and a quiver of arrows beneath a heavy cloak. Roman authorities did not allow the inhabitants of Jerusalem to possess such weapons, but one could procure them with the proper connections. Judah and his nine companions had been secretly training with the bow for a little over a year. It would be the best way to ambush and kill Roman soldiers, who were virtually unbeatable in close combat.

As Judah made his way to his assigned station, he thought of his father, Isaac. It was his father who repeatedly told him the stories of Joshua, Samson, Jonathan, David, and his own namesake Judah, called Maccabeus, who smashed the pagan Greek armies like a hammer and led the Jews to independence just two hundred years ago. "These are men of true faith," his father would say. "They did not sit back and wait like cowards for God to move on their behalf. They stepped out in faith, met God's enemies head on, and God rewarded that faith with victory!"

His father despised the Pharisees, a sect of Jews who opposed any violent resistance and taught the people that they could only obtain God's promises through patience and purity. Such ideas were laughable—as if the proper washing of hands or strict forms of Sabbath observance would have the Romans shaking in their boots! Though the Pharisees were certainly no friends of Rome, their teaching was rendering the people powerless. It was this system that allowed Rome to exercise its pagan authority in the holiest of cities.

But things were starting to change. There was a growing unrest in the city. Judah could feel it. The patience called for by the Pharisees was wearing thin, and the desire for deliverance was beginning to grow greater than the fear of Roman power. Judah knew all they needed was a spark, something that would turn the embers of discontent into the fire of revolution. His deepest desire was to be that spark.

Judah came to the place of the planned ambush. Here the road made a sharp ninety-degree right turn, and then after about sixty feet it picked up its original direction by making a sharp left turn. This created a small space in which they could easily hem in the five mounted soldiers. Judah had placed his men on the surrounding rooftops, which were relatively low, giving each a good angle on his target but also providing cover from which they could shoot. He placed three archers, including himself, facing the approaching soldiers, and a single archer each on the soldiers' right and left flanks. The goal was for these five archers to do the most damage. They would have the element of surprise, and if their arrows flew true, they had a chance of taking out all the soldiers. Judah knew this was unlikely, but he hoped the initial attack would eliminate at least three. Judah placed the remaining five bowmen at the two exit points so that a volley of arrows would meet any soldier attempting to break out of the trap. If all went according to plan, there would be no survivors.

Judah was first to arrive at his station, but Jacob and Nathaniel soon joined him. He then heard one low whistle, followed by an additional three signifying that the others were in place. Judah's heart was racing, and he could hear the nervous tension in the short quick breaths of his friends. While they had all trained with the bow, they had never engaged in live combat. Would they be able to overcome their nerves in the face of Roman soldiers? Would fear paralyze them? Would it overwhelm their training? Their aim?

The sound of hooves in the distance interrupted Judah's thoughts. His muscles tensed and he fought back the lump in his throat. His long, low whistle signaled the others to draw their bows. No one was to fire until all the soldiers had made their first turn into the trap. As the sound of the hooves drew closer, Judah and those with him drew and strung their arrows. In the light of the torches that lined the streets, Judah saw the first soldier round the corner. He felt a calm come over him. His grip on the bow was firm. There was no tremor in his hands.

Another whistle signaled that all the soldiers had rounded the turn and that the time for action had come. Judah took aim at the lead soldier; he released his arrow and watched it rip a hole through the neck of its target. With a guttural cry the soldier clutched at his bloody throat and fell. In an instant the strum of bowstrings and whir of arrows filled the air, bringing the cries of soldiers and panicked horses. Chaos ensued. Horses reared, throwing their riders to the ground. Soldiers scurried for weapons or to help the wounded. Judah had caught them unawares, but it seemed the first volley had only killed one soldier. Had it even wounded another?

He felt his courage weaken as the surviving soldiers began taking defensive positions behind their shields. He signaled a second volley and then a third, but the arrows fell harmlessly against Roman shields. The full weight of fear seized him and a million thoughts flooded his mind at once. How had their training failed so badly? Would God not grant them victory? Should he call the retreat now, while they could still get away? Could they get away? Would the soldiers pursue them? If they stayed, how long would it be before the reinforcements arrived and his men were trapped? Had he doomed them all?

But then a break! The soldiers were retreating backward behind their shields—right into his trap! The sound of whirring arrows again filled the air—not Judah's arrows but those of his men set to block off a retreat. All fear vanished as the arrows hit their marks. Shrieks of pain pierced the air again, and the wall of shields melted away. Without need of an order, his men let loose another volley of arrows, most of which found their marks. Three of the four remaining soldiers were down, but one remained standing! The soldier charged forward under cover of his shield, and with deft agility jumped on one of the remaining horses. Momentarily, Judah feared the soldier's escape, but an arrow struck the horse in the hindquarter. It shrieked, reared, and threw the soldier to the ground. Within seconds, Judah and his men filled his back with arrows and he lay motionless.

At last, all five Roman soldiers were down. One was clearly dead, and perhaps a second, but the movement and groans of the others made it clear they were only wounded. Both groans and movement ceased after a final volley of arrows. With that, a chilling silence replaced the chaos that had filled the last several minutes. Three short whistles—the signal to disband. They would regroup at the scriptorium.

But Judah had one more job to do. With a nod, he gave his bow to Joseph, who quickly departed. Judah climbed down the back side of the building to the street level. As he passed by the side of the house into the street where the Roman soldiers now lay, he pulled out a short dagger. Fear engulfed him. If any of these soldiers were not actually dead and could still fight, Judah knew he would be outmatched. Even a wounded Roman soldier was deadly.

He quietly approached the leader of these soldiers, the one he had taken down with an arrow through the neck. Shock and dread still filled the soldiers' dead eyes, a sight that brought Judah a surge of pleasure. He knelt next to the body, lifted up the scarlet cloak, and there he found what he was looking for—the small scroll! He had hoped to get the small chest of coins, an infusion of financial support for the movement, but in the chaos the horse carrying the chest had fled.

But after unsealing and reading the scroll's contents, he realized he had found something far more valuable: the names of two Roman informants. He recognized one of the names. Further bloodshed would come soon.

ONE

A FRAGILE PEACE

CALEB

The streets of Jerusalem were quiet and empty this late at night. Though he rarely walked them at this hour, Caleb enjoyed the peacefulness that was absent during the day. It was not simply absent because of the hustle and bustle of a large city; it was absent because the heart of the city and the hearts of its citizens were restless with longing. Jerusalem—the name itself meant "city of peace"—had not known peace in Caleb's lifetime. Rome, the current foreign occupier of his beloved city, claimed to be the bearers of peace, and in a sense the claim was true. By its sword Rome had brought the entire world to heel, and "peace"—the mere absence of war—was the result. The city had not seen war in a long time. But the peace Rome claimed for Jerusalem was a thin veneer under which restlessness, resentment, and desperation boiled in the hearts of a people longing to be free from tyranny.

Caleb had just come from a meeting of shopkeepers in which such longings were palpable. He owned and operated a middling sized pottery shop in Jerusalem, a shop he had grown up in and had recently inherited from his late father. His father had been instrumental in organizing a network of shop owners and artisans in the city for the purpose of navigating the complicated economic problems created by Roman occupation with the idea that economic survival in this atmosphere would be better accomplished if the many worked together. They considered pricing, trade, taxation, and any number of issues that had a bearing on economic success. They sought to adapt as a group to ever-changing Roman policies, a strategy that on the whole had been quite successful. They kept these meetings as well as the names of all who attended secret since Roman authorities would likely perceive these meetings as dangerous. Sedition was not their purpose, though seditious sentiments occasionally found their way into the meetings.

Tonight the group had discussed a rumor that the local Roman officials planned to introduce a new tax during the upcoming Passover celebration. Passover saw a great influx of people to Jerusalem as Jewish pilgrims from all over the empire came to celebrate the sacred festival in the capital city of the Jews. The population of the city regularly grew fivefold during the Passover celebration, reaching upward of three hundred thousand people. With this influx of people came increased success for local businesses, many of whom relied on this boom to carry them through year's end. The threat of a new tax that might significantly reduce their gains had many feeling anxious and angry. Perhaps if all agreed to certain price adjustments, they could survive.

Perhaps *they* could. But Caleb doubted whether *he* could. Since his father's death, his shop had seen a slow but steady decline in customers. His father was well loved, a gregarious man with a personality that effortlessly drew people to him. People told Caleb he was much more like his mother: quiet and analytical, kind but private. Not that Caleb could confirm such a comparison; his mother had died giving birth to his sister when he was only three years old. While these traits from his mother had served him well in his education and study of Torah, they had not served him well in the daily operation of the pottery shop. The quality of the pottery, made primarily by his sister, Miriam, and one of his cousins, had not changed, yet sales had declined. It was clear to Caleb that the sole factor was a change in the personality people encountered when they came to shop. At first, customers had remained loyal. They came to shop and also brought gifts, food, and stories of what a wonderful man his father had been. But in time, their loyalty waned. The man they loved was gone, and so was the experience they so closely associated with the shop. Of course, close friends and family still came, but their business was barely enough to keep the shop running or put food on the table.

Caleb was uncertain how long he could keep the doors open—and even more about what he would do if he had to close them. How would he support his little sister? Amid these anxious thoughts, his mind drifted to the mysterious visitor who had appeared in his shop as he was closing that evening. Could his offer be the way out?

Lost in thought, Caleb almost walked past his own front door. He entered to see Miriam kneading a loaf of bread. Everyone said she looked like his mother: she had long dark hair that framed an oval face, with big dark brown eyes and olive skin. She had an innocent appearance that did not bear the hardship their family had endured. His arrival brought her usual bright, warm smile and a question about his day. Though she looked like their mother, her personality was just like their father: eternally optimistic and endlessly kind. Caleb usually tried, but today he could not match her warmth and cheer. She quickly read the anxiety on his face. "Caleb, what is wrong? Has something happened?"

"No, my sweet sister, everything is fine," he lied, knowing it would not convince her.

"I know something is wrong, Caleb; I can read it in your face. What has happened?"

"The Romans!" Caleb snapped, though he quickly restrained himself. "The Romans have happened."

"Yes, I am aware," she said playfully, "but they didn't *just* happen. What have they done that is troubling you now?"

"There is a rumor they are looking to impose a new tax, one that may significantly cut our profits during the coming festivals. They see the influx of those making pilgrimage as an opportunity to profit, but that profit comes at our expense. And now, of all times!"

"We have handled these sorts of taxes before, Caleb. We can handle them again," she replied calmly. "Are not the other shopkeepers making preparations for such a tax?"

"Yes, yes, they are. But my concern is with our own shop, Miriam. Things are bad—worse than you know." Caleb couldn't hide his worry and dejection.

"We have faced hard times before, Brother," she reassured him. "We will survive these hard times as well. Keep faith. God will provide."

"Will we? Will he? I don't share your confidence, Sister." It was not the first time such exchanges had taken place, and they exhausted Caleb.

"I fear for your faith, Caleb. It was once so strong, like father's. Father believed in God's promises. He trusted God. You used to trust as well." He could hear the disappointment in her voice.

He shook his head. "You don't need to remind me of father's faith, Miriam—I know it well. But look around this city. The common people struggle to survive under heavy taxation.

Those who farm the countryside live on land they once owned but lost to wealthy landowners because of unjust loans they could not repay. Most struggle to feed their families after they send the profits to Rome. Wealthy merchants control the price of materials and make deals with those in power so that they can maintain that control. As long as Rome is in control, *nothing* will change, Miriam."

"But Rome won't control this city forever. We must be patient," Miriam said confidently. Caleb sighed—he knew what she was going to say, and he could barely stand to hear it one more time.

"God *will* send his Messiah, Caleb. Father said the day was near, that the Messiah was likely already alive, perhaps in our midst, and that God would raise him up and reveal him to us all. When he comes, he will drive the Romans out. He will bring justice, righteousness, and peace to our land. You know this, Caleb!" Then she said quietly, "Or at least you used to."

"Father said a lot of things, Miriam, but Father is dead now!" He saw sorrow and shame fill her face, and he felt guilty. "I am sorry, Sister. I shouldn't have said that. But I can't have this conversation again. I am going to bed." He kissed her forehead and left the room.

He lay on his bed pondering his sister's words: "The Messiah will come." The people of the city were obsessed with the idea, though few could agree on what this figure would be like. The writings of Israel's prophets promised an age in which God would restore Israel to her former glory. It would be an age of peace, justice, and righteousness. Israel would no longer be the victims of oppressive foreigners; instead, their God would raise them to a place of power and glory. These same prophets seemed to allude to a figure through whom God would bring about this new age, but they only provided bits and pieces, and how to assemble them into a coherent whole was anyone's guess.

Many agreed this figure would be a descendant of King David, though the fact that at one time many Jews were willing to see Judas Maccabeus, who had no ancestral connection to David, as a Messiah demonstrated that even this marker was negotiable. Some thought there would be two Messiahs: one a priest, one a king. Some thought the Messiah was someone whom God had appointed from the beginning of time. Some thought the Messiah was one whom God would raise up because of his faithfulness. Some thought the Messiah was a human warrior who would lead the people in a successful revolt against Rome; others thought the Messiah would be a heavenly or even angelic figure who would bring heavenly armies to destroy Rome and raise Israel above the entire world. Some thought the Messiah would come as result of faithfulness to God's covenant with Israel, the Torah—that a pure and obedient Israel would move God to action. But for others, a minority to be sure, the Messiah would only come when the people showed faith in God's deliverance by taking up arms against Rome—only when people showed such faith would God raise up his Messiah from among the people. Caleb's own cousin Judah, two years younger than himself, was a passionate advocate of this view, and was relentless in his efforts to bring Caleb into the fold.

For much of his life, Caleb had engaged in such speculation and lived with a passionate messianic hope. This was in large part due to his father, a man who diligently studied the Scriptures and steeped his son in these studies from the time he was a toddler. But in the past two years since his father's death, that hope had been all but extinguished. It wasn't merely the loss of a father that shook Caleb's faith, though perhaps that played a role. It was the bleak outlook for so many of his people and the unshakeable Roman power that lay heavy not only on Jerusalem but also the entire world. It had become quite clear to Caleb that the expectation of overthrowing Roman power in any significant way was nothing more than a fool's hope. He had seen many "messianic" claimants rise, but they all met a swift and violent end at the hands of the *Pax Romana*—the Roman "peace."

Most recently a prophet named John, the one called the baptizer, had rallied a large number of people around him, proclaiming that God's new age was about to dawn and that all people must ready themselves through cleansing. Caleb himself had even gone out to the wilderness to hear him speak. This John was charismatic, passionate, and compelling. His words even began to plant hope in Caleb's heart. But the Roman-appointed ruler of Galilee, Herod Antipas, had arrested and executed that prophet, again confirming for Caleb that hope was foolish.

Nevertheless, the faith of many remained unflappable. Most of his Jewish brothers and sisters had a deep hope in a coming Messiah. That hope was the ultimate source of tension within his city, whose Roman occupiers were committed to the reign of Caesar and whose inhabitants were committed to the coming reign of another king. How long could such conflicting commitments coexist? Caleb did not know the answer, but he was confident that when that conflict came to a climax, it would be Rome that reigned supreme. Rome would win. Rome always won.

That thought turned his mind back to this evening's mysterious visitor and the hope he had offered.

ELEAZAR

Eleazar reclined on his bed, admiring both his wife, Joanna, and the plate of fresh dates he was sampling. He had told her he would not be present for a private dinner party they were supposed to attend that evening, so she pouted as her slave girl painted her face in preparation. But he had more pressing matters to attend to—and, if he was honest, these dinner parties were incredibly juvenile. The gossip about the young aristocrats of Jerusalem was mind-numbing.

"I don't know why you can't miss this *one* meeting with your father," she started. "You know how long I have been looking forward to this party, and how much I have wanted you to attend. Both Salome and Bernice will be there, together with their husbands. Am I to be all alone? Will they not laugh at me when my head is turned?"

"My darling, you know I would come with you if I could, but this meeting is of the utmost importance," said Eleazar. "The Passover is coming and preparations must be made."

"But *he* is the high priest, not *you*," she protested. "Can you not miss this meeting and receive word of its results after the party?"

"You know better than this, darling. My presence is imperative, perhaps not for the plans to be made, but for learning how they are made and who helps make them. If I am to be high priest one day, I will need knowledge—not only knowledge of how to rule but also knowledge of what it takes to rule. As my father says, 'Successful authority is not founded on policies and procedures but on knowing those who surround you better than they know themselves—in this way you will always stay two steps in front of them.'"

Eleazar was the eldest son of Caiaphas, the high priest of the Jerusalem temple. The high priest was the highest ranking non-Roman in all of Judea, and practically speaking he was *the* governing authority within the city of Jerusalem. The Roman governor lived in Caesarea, and he delegated authority in the city to the high priest.

Caiaphas hoped Eleazar would succeed him whenever his own tenure as high priest ended. The position carried great authority and prestige, and thus was highly coveted. There was no guarantee of succession from father to son, since the Roman governor appointed the high priest, though there was precedent for it. The problem was that other powerful priests would go to great lengths to prevent that from happening. A particular threat came from Annas, Caiaphas's father-in-law and Eleazar's grandfather. He had opposed Caiaphas's appointment from the start, and Caiaphas knew that even now Annas was maneuvering to secure the position for one of his own sons.

"I am sure you are right, my love," Joanna said. "But your cousins Jacob and Mattathias will be there; perhaps it would be beneficial to speak with them. You could learn from them more about Annas's plans or the ideas held by your uncles. Would that not be worth your while? A political investment, perhaps?"

It was a nice attempt, but it had no hope of persuading Eleazar. Yes, Annas and his uncles, Annas's sons, were political threats that required close observation. But Jacob and Mattathias were imbeciles, with less knowledge of the political landscape than his own dear wife.

"My cousins are useless. They know more about the newest Roman dinner party fashion than they know about threats facing our city. My dear, these are troubling times. Just last week, archers in the street ambushed five Roman soldiers. The talk of new taxes only increases people's anger, and this bloodshed increases the chances that Rome will mete out violent justice in the city. In addition to all this, Passover is coming, which you know will bring further threats to peace. I *must* attend tonight's meeting!"

"I understand," she said, dejectedly and unconvincingly. "But people will certainly ask where you are. What would you have me tell them? That you are in a private meeting with your father and a few select priests discussing the safety of Jerusalem?"

"Don't joke, darling," he said firmly. "You know you must not speak of this meeting to anyone, particularly my cousins or their gossiping wives." Eleazar's cousins might be as dense as a sack of flour, but they would rush to their fathers immediately if they had even one whiff of a secret meeting of high-ranking priests. "Tell them I am not feeling well and am sorry to miss the festivities."

"I don't know why such secrets must be kept," she said in mild frustration. "You are all of the same family, and you are all priests. Doesn't everyone want peace?"

"If only that were true, my dear," he said in a tone that verged on condescension. "But Annas and his family *do not* have the best interests of this city or its faith in mind. It is their *own* interests they are concerned about. If a disruption of the peace would unseat my father, they would seek it for the chance to regain their power. They are the worst kind of priests, my dear Joanna—they treat our sacred faith as a tool for gaining power and prestige. They care little for the heritage of their ancestors, the covenant, or the God of Israel, and they are willing to sacrifice any of these things for political gain—though, to be sure, not to the point that it will cost *them* political gain. They certainly have their use for our faith."

Eleazar's father was nothing like his grandfather or uncles. From a young age, Caiaphas had taught his son the value of his Jewish identity and heritage. As a boy, Eleazar had learned to read Hebrew by reading from the sacred covenant, the Torah, the stories of the patriarchs and Moses, and he regularly spoke with his father about their significance and meaning. His father taught him to revere the Creator God of Israel, who had given the covenant to the Jewish people so that they might be a light to the nations. His father had not only taught but modeled the importance of these realities. Among the Sadducees, his father had a reputation as a man of true and sincere faith, which had earned him the respect of many within the party. In fact, this reputation had even earned him the respect of many prominent members of the Pharisees. This had ultimately led to his appointment as high priest.

"I have heard this opinion of your family many times before, Eleazar," said Joanna, "but it seems overly harsh to me. Your grandfather has always been kind to me, as have your uncles. And your cousins and their wives have become my friends. I do not like keeping secrets from them. They are *family*, and that should be more important than political gain. But out of love for you, I will do as you wish, and not speak of your *secret* meeting tonight."

Joanna was well-meaning but naive. She did not know that at the time of his father's appointment as high priest, Eleazar's grandfather had secretly betrayed him. Caiaphas had learned that Annas had gone to the Roman governor himself and claimed that Caiaphas's fidelity to his Jewish faith made him a poor candidate for the position of high priest. He argued that a man with such convictions could not be successful in a position that required compromise with Rome. Despite such claims, Caiaphas received the appointment from the Roman governor Valerius Gratus, who believed there was value in a high priest whom the people of Jerusalem respected and perceived as incorruptible. Annas had not taken defeat well, and his scheming to place one of his own sons as high priest was ongoing. Of course, Annas was outwardly kind to Joanna, as he was to the rest of his family. But Caiaphas constantly reminded Eleazar not to trust this kindness.

"You are as innocent as you are beautiful, my dear, but you must trust me in this matter," Eleazar said. "My grandfather does not have our best interest at heart. Please be mindful of what you say. My cousins might not be as friendly as they appear."

"You worry too much, my love," his wife said. "I wish you would worry less and enjoy life more. I'm afraid I must leave you now."

She gently kissed his cheek and exited gracefully through the door.

Less than a second later, she stuck her head back through the door, smiled, and said playfully, "Enjoy your *secret* meeting."

This drew a smile from Eleazar. He loved his wife, and only hoped she would use discretion.

His thoughts returned to Annas's claims that a pious man like Caiaphas could never successfully be the high priest in Jerusalem. His father had quickly proven this false, as he demonstrated the ability to work well with the Roman governor—particularly the most recent governor, Pontius Pilate. In fact, it was this relationship with Pilate that kept the political maneuvers of Annas at bay. As long as Pilate was in control, Caiaphas's position was relatively secure.

While Caiaphas's aptitude for political life came as a surprise to many of his opponents, it did not come as a surprise to Eleazar. He had long known his father to be a pragmatist who, though devout in his Jewish identity and faith, did not suffer the foolish expressions of that faith that abounded throughout the city. Talk of Israel's restoration, the dawning of a new and glorious age, the destruction of Rome, and an anointed Davidic King were utter nonsense to Caiaphas. Such beliefs found their origins in people's blind commitment to the words of ancient "prophets" who had claimed to hear from God and had visions of a glorious future for the people of Israel.

Many Jews regarded these prophetic texts as sacred Scripture, but not the Sadducees. From his earliest days, Eleazar could remember his father deriding such expressions of Judaism: "Don't listen to such fools, Son. They are blind at best and deceivers at worst. God has indeed spoken to us, and his words can be found in the Torah. It is fidelity to Torah that reveals God to the world, and we must be faithful to that charge." Caiaphas always claimed that a human king was never God's desire for Israel. According to Torah, God alone should be king of Israel.

It was this rejection of a Messiah-crazed Judaism that allowed his father to work so well with Pilate. They shared the goal of keeping the peace in Jerusalem, a goal that required constant vigilance against extreme expressions of Judaism that might threaten the peace. Unlike Annas, Caiaphas was not motivated by power and prestige but instead by the good of his people. He knew that messianic zeal and the hope for Rome's destruction would only lead to Jewish suffering.

But although he worked well with Pilate, Caiaphas knew what this Roman governor and the power he represented was capable of. He had seen far too many crucifixions of those suspected of sedition to know that any substantial threat to the *Pax Romana* would bring swift retribution on the city. Caiaphas worked tirelessly to avoid such a fate. And, should he ever become high priest himself, Eleazar would devote himself to the same goal.

A knock at the door interrupted his thoughts. Philip, a head slave in his house, informed Eleazar that his guests had arrived.

PILATE

After an unseasonably warm day, Pilate sat on the balcony of his private chambers, letting the cool sea breeze wash over him. He could taste the salt in the air and feel it on his skin. From this balcony, he could see virtually the entire city of Caesarea Maritima, with its massive temple devoted to the worship of the Great Augustus, its impressive amphitheater, its hippodrome, and, perhaps most impressive of all, its man-made harbor that rivaled any other in the world in both size and beauty.

The harbor was forty-one acres in size and enclosed by impressive concrete walls on which were massive storehouses used to facilitate the significant trade of the city. Also on the walls were six massive bronze statues and a light tower that burned with fire twenty-four hours a day. To approaching sea vessels, this harbor was truly a wonder to behold. A client king, Herod the first, the father of the current ruler in Galilee, Herod Antipas, had constructed Caesarea at the behest of the emperor Augustus, and the beauty of the city matched his reputation as a master builder. It seemed the late Herod had built all the structures worth admiring in this region, with this city on the Mediterranean being second only in beauty to the great temple in Jerusalem.

At times while walking through Caesarea, Pilate could almost imagine he was back in his home city of Rome instead of this godforsaken backwater of the illustrious Roman Empire. Aside from Caesarea and Jerusalem, there were few other cities of note in the province of Judea. Small villages dotted the region, the farms of which produced little in the way of significant wealth for the empire. To his peers back in Rome, the assignment seemed menial and of little value, but Pilate knew better. Judea controlled both land and sea routes to Egypt, the fertile bread basket of the empire. It also provided a crucial buffer between the empire and one of its most threatening enemies, the Parthians. But such importance didn't make the snide comments and jokes about his assignment any easier to take—perception created reality for those in Rome.

The physical location was not the worst part of the assignment, despite what his friends back home might think. It was the job of *ruling* this province that was truly detestable. Throughout the Roman Empire, provinces thrived under the oversight and protection of Rome. The cities of Greece and Asia Minor had truly prospered through their identity as loyal provincial capitals under Roman rule. The peace and stability Rome brought allowed trade to boom, which resulted in the amassing of great wealth throughout the empire. Most who benefited from such wealth were deeply thankful and held both Rome and its rulers in high regard.

This was not the case for most of those living in Judea. Judea was the home of the Jews, a people that were as odd as they were ancient. They were devoted to one god and refused to worship any other—they wouldn't even make an image of this god or speak his name. Pilate had discovered this the hard way, of course.

Central to their religion was a set of ancient writings that outlined the laws this god had given them. For many Jews, the writings of their prophets were also quite significant. Most Jews believed their god had spoken to them uniquely through these writings, and the prophetic writings seemed to be the crux of the problem. They promised a time in which these Jews, this small and powerless group of people, would rule over the entire world. Their capital city, Jerusalem, would be the center of a new world, and their god would live in the temple that sat on top of a mountain there—as if this mountain would be the new Olympus! All the nations would serve them and come to worship this god.

How preposterous! Could these people not see that this was impossible? They had no army, no weapons necessary for military victory, no siege equipment to tear down city walls, and most of all, no resources with which to procure any of these things. They were living in a fantasy. It didn't help that they had had military success almost two hundred years earlier against the Greek Seleucids. But this was no reason for optimism, since the Seleucids were fighting on other fronts and could not devote the necessary resources to destroy these pesky Jews. Such was not the case with Rome.

The foolishness of this hope did not make it harmless, however. No, this hope bred hate—deep hatred of Rome and its occupation. While cities like Ephesus and Thessalonica built temples and threw massive festivals as a way of thanking Rome for its many benefits, the Jews of Judea openly despised all things Roman. They refused to allow a temple honoring Rome and its gods to be built in Jerusalem. They refused to give such gods any semblance of worship. They wouldn't even permit any Roman image within the capital city—again, something Pilate discovered the hard way. There was no gratitude for the great wealth that Roman power had brought the region, nor even a "thank you" for the freedom of worship the Roman rulers had allowed.

The most difficult part of Pilate's regional assignment was negotiating the complicated realities brought about by this hate. Every day felt like a constant battle to keep the peace. It often kept him up at night. Of course, the Jews could never truly threaten Roman power, but they could threaten the stability of the region. They could riot in the streets and kill

Roman soldiers . . . and governors. And riots could certainly turn into open revolt. Pilate was aware of such possibilities, and was particularly aware that he did not have the military power to stop them. He had at his disposal roughly eighteen hundred Roman soldiers in the region, along with some cavalry. These forces, less than one third of a legion, were hardly enough to stop a people deeply committed to revolution. The bulk of Rome's military power in the region was under the control of the Roman governor of Syria, who had three entire legions at his disposal—approximately eighteen thousand soldiers. If open rebellion broke out, it would take these reinforcements at least two weeks to arrive in Jerusalem. At that point, there was a good chance Pilate would not be alive to care.

With such little military support, keeping the peace often required the ability to work with local rulers and power brokers, some level of diplomacy, a cunning instinct, will, some acumen, and on top of all of that a bit of sheer luck. It was a constant struggle, and Pilate envied those who governed in friendlier provinces—where governing was not only easier but also appreciated!

But as difficult as this job was, Pilate had become quite good at it over the previous five years. He had certainly made his share of mistakes in the beginning—painful and embarrassing ones. Even now, his faced reddened when he recalled the pomp and arrogance he brought with him from Rome when he first took this assignment, and the shame he had quickly incurred because of it. Before coming to this backwards region, many warned Pilate about the difficulties he would face and the people who would hate him. A foolish young Pilate politely listened to such warnings, but ultimately ignored them. He was brashly confident he could corral these people with a dramatic display of Roman power. Who would not fall in line once they had truly tasted Roman steel or watched a beloved leader cut down or crucified for insurrection? Pilate's opportunity for such an exhibition came quickly.

Not long after his arrival in Judea, he made a visit to Jerusalem to see this important city and introduce himself to both the common people and leading officials. Advisers had told him that these people were very particular about displaying images or any sort of likeness of a living creature, and his predecessors had been very careful to not bring any such images into the city. They stripped soldiers' uniforms and military banners of any such images, be them of animals or the emperor, when they entered Jerusalem. But Pilate felt that such decisions showed weakness and decided it was time for these Jews to embrace the Roman power over them—images and all! Out of what Pilate believed was sensitivity, he brought the soldiers in at night so as to not cause a disturbance.

The following day it did not take long for the people to realize what had happened, and protests began outside the former palace of Herod the Great (the home of the governor when he visited Jerusalem). The crowd was shouting and yelling, but for the most part Pilate could not understand them; they were not speaking Latin or Greek. Instead of facing the mob, Pilate decided to meet with the leading officials: the high priest Caiaphas and his councilors. They explained to Pilate the gravity of his offense; if he wanted to keep the peace (something they wanted as well) he should remove the image-bearing shields immediately. Pilate responded with arguments about the lack of honor these people showed Rome, which bestowed such blessings on them. He refused to remove the images, but after much pleading, he agreed to reconsider and make a final decision in the coming days, though he had no intention of changing his mind. Pilate anticipated that as the days passed the protesters would tire and go home. While the numbers diminished at night, many stayed—some praying, some shouting. And every morning the crowd seemed larger than the day before.

Eventually, Pilate had had enough. The shouting and wailing had become exhausting, and his frustrations with these ungrateful and obstinate people had reached a breaking point. On the morning of the fifth day, Pilate ordered his soldiers to surround the protestors. After they had done so, Pilate came out and addressed them. He rebuked them for their actions that dishonored Rome, the source of their peace and prosperity, and he ordered them to cease and desist. Any who refused to leave, he would have killed for insurrection. He was quite confident that the threat of real violence would break their spirit. But to his utter shock and amazement, one of the leaders of the group got on his knees and threw his head back, baring his neck. And slowly the rest in the crowd did the same.

In this act, the people conveyed the depth of their conviction. By it, they said, "Do what you must, for we will do what we must." Pilate had not expected such a response. Though many had warned him, he did not believe a people could be this recalcitrant. He was tempted to give the order to execute them all, but he knew that such violence would have reprisals— perhaps the people would riot, and also Rome might not approve. He had only been there a matter of weeks. What would the emperor say if he could not keep a peace that had lasted for over seventy-five years? He ordered his soldiers to sheathe their swords and disband, and the next day the images were removed from the city.

That moment was a terrible embarrassment to Pilate. He felt these Jews had successfully challenged his power, making him appear weak. Although he was angry, he had no one to blame but himself. Despite many warnings, he had pushed these people to the brink of death, and they were willing to go there without any hesitation. He made the grave mistake of underestimating the conviction of these Jews, but never again. He vowed to better understand them—not because he appreciated them, but because he wanted to control them and thus successfully rule over them.

He remembered, perhaps not soon enough, that the former governor Valerius Gratus had advised him that the key to survival was the high priesthood. He had said, "Among a people of zealous conviction, you will find them sensible. And because they love their positions of power, you will find them much easier to control." So before Pilate left Jerusalem to return to Caesarea, he held a private audience with the high priest, Caiaphas.

In this meeting, Pilate projected a demeanor of humility. It was one of the wisest decisions he had made in his political career. He found that Caiaphas was indeed sensible, rational, and easy to converse with. He was a wealth of information about these people, their history, and their religion. These Jews were not as homogenous as Pilate had supposed. While certainly a small number of central beliefs galvanized them, their beliefs and practices could vary widely—and even some of those tenets could be interpreted quite differently. Distinct sects had emerged, like the Pharisees and the Sadducees, each drawing unique boundaries around themselves—and holding distinct values that they would die for. They had different opinions about what texts were truly sacred Scripture, the afterlife of both the individual Jew and Jews collectively, fate and free will, the rules regarding ritual purity, and much more. At any one time, these groups could influence common Jews who were not members of any one of them, though it seemed the Pharisees more often had the greatest sway over the masses.

Pilate also learned more fully about the deep desire among most Jews for independence from Roman occupation, their desire for a leader of some sort to deliver them, and the growing hostility in the city toward anything Roman. But perhaps most importantly, he learned that Caiaphas opposed all such notions and was deeply committed to the cause of peace in the region. In Caiaphas he found an ally who in many ways wanted the same things that Rome wanted; stability, peace, and if possible, growing prosperity. But Caiaphas was adamant that Pilate could not achieve that peace through violence, which would ultimately result in rebellion. Instead, political savvy, manipulation, and—most important of all—information were the tools necessary for maintaining peace and stability.

Information could allow you to identify and neutralize threats before they became problematic. Information allowed you to manipulate important priests, teachers, and artisans who may have sway with the people. Information allowed you to build the right relationships, stroke the right egos, and fund the right special interests. Politics in Judea was complicated, and the person with the most information could navigate those complicated realities effectively. Caiaphas informed Pilate that he had already amassed a significant number of informants. He offered to share information with Pilate if he so chose, but he also encouraged Pilate to develop his own information network.

Pilate's predecessor had also tried to tell him that information would serve him better than brute force. He even left Pilate with a well-developed network of informants. But Pilate's humiliation finally unstopped his ears. Pilate would not prioritize force over information again, and he would also not ignore this high priest again. Valerius Gratus was indeed correct in directing Pilate to the Jewish high priests, but Gratus was wrong about one thing—Caiaphas wasn't motivated by a desire for power. Instead, something much stronger than that drove this priest: a deep desire for peace, grounded in a sincere religious conviction and love for his people. The trappings of power were not the currency Pilate would need to motivate Caiaphas; instead, he needed to play on his commitment to peace and his genuine concern for the Jews.

Pilate's thoughts were interrupted by his chief aid, Lucien. "I have the reports from your informants in the north about Jesus the Galilean, my lord. They are sealed as you requested."

"Thank you, Lucien. You may leave them on the table."

"Is there anything else you need, my lord?"

"Not at the moment, Lucien. After reading these, I may need to send word to Caiaphas or perhaps Herod Antipas. If so, I will need a scribe. In that case, I will send for you."

"Yes, my lord, I will see that a scribe is ready should you need one." With that, Lucien left the room.

Pilate took a long look out his window at the beautiful sea, drew in as much peace from it as he could, and then took up the report of the potential political threat: Jesus, the "prophet" from Galilee.

JUDAH

As if on cue, the traitor left his home and headed in the direction of a neighborhood tavern. Judah and his men had surveilled him for the past seven days. The pattern was always the same. The man left his shop at sundown, went home and ate dinner with his family, and then headed to socialize at the tavern for about an hour.

The man's name was Lazarus, son of Ananias, a Pharisee. Ananias was the most prominent mason in Jerusalem. He had received significant contracts for the construction of the temple, and the excellent work he had done greatly enhanced his reputation. He was favored by the Jerusalem elite for the construction of buildings, homes, and significant remodels. However, in the past year, Ananias had experienced health issues that prevented him from working. His son Lazarus had taken over the family business, and from all reports the business continued to thrive under his management. But ever since Judah had learned that Lazarus was working as an informant for Rome, he suspected that his financial success was in some way tied to his treacherous service.

Little caused Judah's blood to boil more than traitors. Rome was this world's great evil, but worse even than Rome were Jews who betrayed their own people for financial gain. They would burn in the hottest fires of Gehenna on the great day of God's judgment. Not only did they enable the continued enslavement of their own people by foreign occupiers, but they took financial reward that would otherwise go to those more deserving. Judah knew of two other masons that faced financial hardship because they consistently lost bids to Lazarus—despite claims that their bids were more competitive! How could such men hope to survive when the game was rigged? This treachery and injustice made the planning of the ambush all the more satisfying. Tonight, Lazarus would pay dearly for this betrayal.

At first, Judah thought eliminating Lazarus would be simple. When he made his way home from the tavern, stumbling from too much wine, he would be an easy target. Judah's men would grab Lazarus, pull him into an empty building, question him, and then end it. But things got more complicated two days into the surveillance. Those watching Lazarus noticed that everywhere he went, two large men seemed to also be following him. Were they surveilling him as well, or protecting him?

In order to find out, Judah paid two boys with reputations as ruffians. The first boy rounded a corner and ran into Lazarus, almost knocking him down. While Lazarus was getting his balance, the other boy planned to trip him. But as soon as the first boy ran into Lazarus, both of the men bolted forward, coming to the falling man's aid.

Now what was originally the simple task of grabbing a drunk man off the street suddenly involved eliminating the hired muscle that was protecting him. But Judah was undaunted. He had eliminated five Roman soldiers. Compared to that, dealing with these two meatheads would be no trouble at all.

TWO

AN APPROACHING STORM

ELEAZAR

Eleazar departed from his private chambers and crossed the length of the estate to his father's study. As he expected, the group in the room was small. Only three high-ranking priests were present: Caiaphas's two brothers and a cousin. Each of these men had an attendant with them, all of which were blood relations. Caiaphas trusted everyone in this room implicitly. While Annas and his sons were often present for formal gatherings of the high-ranking priests, they were never invited to or even aware of these secret meetings in Caiaphas's home. It was here that the true business was carried out and where they set the agenda for what they needed to accomplish in the formal priestly meetings.

His father greeted him with a kiss, then quickly called the meeting to order. "My thanks to you all for meeting with me tonight. As you know, the Passover is coming, and as usual, preparations cannot begin too soon. Discussion of priestly responsibilities during the days of preparation for the festival itself can wait. We have well-established practices and routines that we can review in the coming months. What is most pressing is the issue of keeping the peace throughout the week. Passover always raises concerns for the peace and stability of Jerusalem and the entire region of Judea. We try our best to focus the celebration on the faithfulness of God, our sacred traditions, and ways of life that resulted from Moses leading our people out of Egypt. But such efforts are often futile against the populist desire for deliverance from Roman power. Our brothers in the Pharisaic party continue to take the Passover celebration as an opportunity to remind people of prophets who promised a second deliverance from foreign oppression, and a time of the prosperous reign of a sovereign and fully restored Israel. Of course, they reject all violent opposition to Rome. But they fail to see the danger in their talk of Israel's glorious future. Impostor prophets or zealous revolutionaries may water those seeds with thoughts of violent revolt."

Eleazar had heard this speech many times. While the priestly party, the Sadducees, were regularly at odds with the Pharisees on many other issues, they were both by and large opposed to violently resisting Roman power. But despite the Pharisees' commitment to nonviolence, his father saw them as dangerous because of their talk of a glorious future for Israel—a future that implied the destruction of Rome. For Caiaphas, there was little difference between ideological resistance to Rome and physical resistance: the former would always be the fuel that fired the latter.

The speech continued in its usual pattern: "Every Passover we must deal with a blind and foolish people who, at the slightest provocation, might be led to engage in hopeless violence, never considering the greater violence that would no doubt crush them. Thus, we must be eyes for the blind and help to protect them from themselves. We must do our best to promote this sacred celebration and to keep it pure from political unrest. As with every Passover, my deepest desire is for our people to forget about their perceived political plight and focus on their identity as God's chosen people—people granted the gift of Torah, a divine covenant that shows them the way to walk before the God of creation. Walking in such a manner is the only way to reveal this God to our Roman overlords. This is what it means to live out the Torah's call that all of Israel be a nation of priests. But of course, I am preaching to the righteous here! Tonight, we must discuss strategies for addressing any known threats of civil unrest and keeping the peace. No doubt the proverb is true that 'plans fail for lack of counsel, but with many advisers they succeed.' What counsel might you, my most trusted advisors, provide?"

The first to speak was Aaron, Caiaphas's older brother: "Regarding impostor prophets, we certainly have some good news. The troublemaker John, styled as a prophet by the people, has finally met his just end. Last year at this time, he posed a serious threat. His call for people to receive forgiveness of their sins through some wilderness baptism challenged not only our priestly authority but also the authority of the temple itself. How could a true prophet of God undermine God's very dwelling?"

Ezra, Caiaphas's cousin, interrupted: "While we doubted he had political ambitions, he certainly made Pilate nervous. His proclamation of the coming kingdom of God, along with the massive crowds that went out to him, had Pilate making preparations to send soldiers to arrest him and disband his followers."

Aaron continued, "Yes, and if that fanatic hadn't gone back to Galilee to harass Herod Antipas, it is likely we would have had another violent outbreak on our hands. The arrest of a popular prophet is all the zealots need to whip the people into a frenzy and engage in armed resistance."

Though Eleazar's father had a good relationship with Pilate, neither Aaron nor Ezra had forgiven his early mistakes. They were dubious of Caiaphas's claim that the governor had indeed learned from his brash and reckless behavior. Any time they felt they saw evidence for their beliefs, they were quick to point it out.

His father calmly interrupted, "Indeed, such risks were real, my brothers, but let us not detract from our esteemed governor. I acknowledge that in the past, he has too often reacted with haste rather than wisdom. And these violent reactions have had a negative impact on our cause for peace. But as you know, over the last several years, my relationship with the governor has grown quite strong. I have been given opportunities to educate him on the intricacies of our delicate situation here in Jerusalem and Judea. He is learning that wisdom, and dare I say, cunning, is needed to keep the peace. While John certainly made Pilate anxious, he was not as close to violent suppression of the prophet as you suppose—though he did consider it."

At this concession from Caiaphas, Ezra exchanged a smug look with Aaron. Caiaphas ignored it and continued.

"But at my guidance, Pilate opted for a different strategy, namely, covert observation of the potential threat, along with various strategies for neutralizing the threat without the risk of violence. I convinced him that the clever use of spies can be quite helpful in these situations, as they can provide information regarding the true nature of a threat. A well-placed spy might even be able to redirect the potential threat in a more favorable direction. I can't say with certainty why John moved to Galilee, but there is a rumor that a Roman spy within his inner circle was quite vocal about Herod's unlawful marriage to Herodias, his sister in-law. Whether that spy was the reason John turned his attention to Galilee, who can say—but his attention was turned nonetheless, and our secured peace was the result."

He gave a knowing look to Aaron and Ezra, both of whom shook their heads to show they remained unconvinced. Persuading them that Pilate had become a capable ruler and trusted ally was a hard sell indeed.

With a minor look of frustration, Caiaphas continued. "Thankfully, Herod has solved the problem of this fanatical prophet for us. As disgusting as his debauched life might be to us, we can occasionally rely on him to serve the cause of peace. Apparently, he is not happy that Pilate did not deal with John when he was in Judea. He suspects that Pilate somehow pushed the problem his way, making him the scapegoat for the prophet's death. Thus, what was a strained relationship between the tetrarch of Galilee and our governor seems to have grown worse. Regardless, we will not have to worry about this so-called prophet causing a disturbance during the coming Passover."

Even Ezra and Aaron had to acknowledge this was true.

JUDAH

The bravado and confidence of Judah's men emerged as they formulated a plan for how to deal with Lazarus's new protection detail. Several thought grabbing three men wouldn't be much more difficult than grabbing one. Simeon and Joseph were confident they could execute choke holds to incapacitate the men. Judah was far less confident. These men were big— bigger than anyone in their group. And they were likely assigned to their task because they had skill and experience at fighting—far more than any of Judah's men. Much could go wrong in hand-to-hand combat, and victory was never certain. Such combat was also likely to draw attention.

In the end, Judah's argument for the bow won the day. Arrows involved far less risk and far less noise. Additionally,

Judah felt that use of the bow created a sort of calling card for his group of freedom fighters, one that would strike fear and uncertainty in the hearts of any Roman or Roman sympathizer. Judah wanted all such people to know that in his city they were never safe, and deadly arrows could find them at any time.

Though more complicated than simply grabbing a drunk man off the street late at night, the plan was quite simple. Six bowmen would eliminate the two guards. Three men would grab Lazarus and drag him to a vacant shop that sat close to the man's route home. One would serve as a lookout and watch for possible problems.

That evening, Lazarus entered the tavern as usual, and his protection followed. Judah knew that he would be there for at least an hour, perhaps more. He departed and traveled three blocks to meet his men in the vacant shop where they would question Lazarus. They were all present when he arrived. Though it might have simply been Judah's imagination, it seemed that to a man they seemed more confident than they had been prior to their attack on the Roman soldiers. Instead of wide-eyed anticipation, he saw resolute composure. This time there was no speech from Judah. It didn't seem necessary. They all knew why they were there and what they had to do. They quickly rehearsed the plan and each man departed to his station.

The hour passed slowly, but finally Lazarus exited the tavern. His inebriation was clear, but he didn't seem to be as bad off as he was most nights. *Taking it a bit easy tonight, are we?* thought Judah. Not even a minute after the man had entered the street, his protection followed. As usual, they remained about twenty yards behind him. Lazarus never once took any notice of them. Judah followed at a distance. The streets were quiet and empty this late at night, just as Judah had anticipated. All was going as planned.

Lazarus passed the first block. After he passed the second, the archers would take out his protection. Judah heard a low whistle, the signal from the lookout that Lazarus had passed the second block and was approaching the third. Judah heard the twang of bowstrings. Almost instantly three arrows hit one of the targets: two in the chest and one in the throat. He slumped to the ground without making a sound.

They were not so lucky with the second target. One arrow missed him completely, one struck him in the shoulder, and one in the thigh. He cried out loudly in pain and fell to the ground. Hearing the cry, Lazarus spun around and froze as he saw one of his guards dying on the ground, and another stuck with arrows, trying to regain his feet. The surviving guard yelled, "Run!"

Suddenly recognizing the danger he was in, Lazarus turned to run. As he did, Simeon and Joseph emerged from the alley and wrestled him to the ground as he yelled and fought for his life. In a tremendous show of strength and determination, the surviving guard got to his feet and was stumbling forward in order to protect Lazarus. With another volley of arrows, he was struck twice but continued to advance.

Judah decided it was time to take matters into his own hands. He drew his dagger and sprinted toward the guard. An arrow whizzed above his head, making him alert to the danger of friendly fire, but he charged forward. He reached the guard, and with one move he grabbed the back of his head and plunged his dagger into the man's neck. As warm blood sprayed over his hand, he felt the life drain from the man's body and let it fall limp to the ground.

He looked up and saw Simeon and Joseph struggling with Lazarus. Simeon had Lazarus in a choke hold and was trying to drag him into the alley, but he was still fighting wildly. Lights were starting to appear in surrounding houses, and Judah realized they need to get this man into the vacant shop before anyone started to investigate. He ran to help Joseph restrain Lazarus's kicking feet. Together they subdued him and carried him down the alley and into the shop. There they bound and gagged him and tied him to a chair. Quickly sobered by the ambush, Lazarus looked at his captors with wide and panicked eyes. He clearly feared for his life, and Judah knew he would do anything to save it.

Eleazar

While all were thankful to be rid of the troublemaking prophet John, Ezra's words quickly sobered the room. "I share in thanksgiving at the removal of John but remind you that these prophets are like cockroaches. As soon as you kill one, another appears. I am afraid such is our current plight. Since the death of John, a man named Jesus has become incredibly popular with the people. Many report that he heals the sick and drives out demons. I have even heard a story of him feeding a massive crowd of Galilean peasants through some sort of miraculous production of food. People are comparing him to the storied prophets Elijah and Elisha. From what I understand, he has limited his movements to the region of Galilee, and to this point has posed no threat to Jerusalem. My sources tell me that Herod is quite nervous about this Jesus and is watching him closely. But because Herod has already killed one popular prophet, he is reluctant to shed the blood of a second."

Eleazar had yet to speak, but the mention of the prophet Jesus triggered a memory. "I believe I have seen this Jesus before. The man I am thinking of was certainly a Galilean. It was a year or two ago, at a festival. Perhaps Purim? But from my memory he was nothing more than a self-appointed Torah expert who had gained a small following. He would teach in the outer courtyards of the temple or at a popular gathering place such as the pools of Bethesda—I think it was at the pools that I saw him. From what I heard, he seemed innocent enough, though the prophetic tradition strongly influenced his interpretation of Torah. He had much to say about the treatment of the poor, if I remember correctly, and he was haranguing some Pharisees about their meticulous tithing but failure to care for their own parents—or something of that nature." A slight smile spread across Eleazar's face as he remembered the incredulous look on one Pharisee's face after this peasant-turned-teacher had accused him of violating the fifth commandment of the Decalogue.

"Yes," Caiaphas responded, "he has been in Jerusalem before, numerous times from what I understand, usually for festivals. And in all past visits, he has drawn relatively little attention to himself. Your description of him as a self-appointed teacher accurately describes his persona on his visits to Jerusalem—at best drawing small crowds, interpreting Torah for them through a prophetic lens, and squabbling with low-level Pharisees or scribes. I believe on one visit there was a rumor that he had healed a blind man, but it gained little attention, and many regarded it a stunt to grow his audience. But it seems in the last year, things have changed significantly. Ezra's assessment is closer to the present reality, though I am afraid not close enough. While some indeed view this Jesus as a prophet, the rumor is quickly spreading that he is presenting himself as a messianic figure. He proclaims that the kingdom of God has drawn near or is indeed present in his own activity. Many now interpret his so-called powerful and miraculous deeds as signs that the long-awaited inbreaking of God has come, and that the glorious future of Israel is right around the corner. Apparently, this Galilean peasant is going to bring it about. Of all the damned foolish beliefs!" Caiaphas shook his head in disgust and frustration. "Apparently, he has even appointed twelve among his group of followers to be leaders, a symbolic restoration of the twelve tribes of Israel!"

"What is the source of this information on the prophet Jesus?" asked Simeon, Caiaphas's youngest and overly cautious brother. "We often hear odd rumors from Galilee that are without substantiation. You know how the imaginations of those uneducated villagers can run wild. Could it be that rumor and speculation have grown up around a simple peasant teacher, and that he remains no more than what was witnessed in Jerusalem on his previous visits?"

"At first I wondered the same thing, Simeon, as the only information I heard about Jesus came second- or third-hand from Galileans visiting the city," replied Caiaphas. "But as the rumors grew, I sent some of my informants to gather what news they could. I could not spare many, as most are involved in important duties here in the city. But I sent three to different parts of Galilee: one to Capernaum, which is supposedly the current home of this man; one to Sepphoris, by way of nearby Nazareth, which is presumably his place of origin; and lastly to Tiberias, the capital city. The latter two were largely unsuccessful, as it seems this Jesus never visits these large cities. Instead, he prefers to teach in the countryside around the lake of Galilee, only entering small villages."

At these words, Simeon raised his hands to the rest of the table, as if this information confirmed his suspicions about the uneducated villagers of Galilee. Eleazar gave his uncle an affirming nod.

Ignoring the exchange, Caiaphas continued, "These informants would often hear rumors of where Jesus might be, but when they tried to find him at such locations, it turned out he had already moved on. None of them saw Jesus, but they heard from virtually all of the local population exactly what I have reported to you. Many said they had seen Jesus, but stories about the nature of what he taught conflicted. Some said he presented himself as a powerful prophet, others as a humble teacher of Torah, and others as the deliverer of Israel.

"However, the informant sent to Capernaum had better luck. He saw Jesus on one occasion and listened to him teach. He was charismatic, and the people were hanging on his every word. His preaching certainly focused on a coming kingdom of God, but much of what he said was in parables, making it hard to fully comprehend his meaning. The informant claimed he even witnessed Jesus exorcise a demon from a homeless villager, though little can be drawn from such testimony. The informant is a man given to believe in such absurdities."

Another look of vindication from Simeon, which Caiaphas again ignored as he continued.

"He tried to follow Jesus, but he and his followers got into boats and sailed across the lake. After this, he never saw Jesus in Capernaum again. He questioned many in the city about him, and many there were convinced that Jesus was the indeed the Messiah whom God has raised up to deliver Israel. But others also reported that Jesus remained ambivalent about such an identity—neither explicitly discouraging nor encouraging such an identification."

Eleazar spoke again. "Surely Pilate is aware of this man, as he has his own spies and informants. What information has he been able to gather?"

"Yes," Caiaphas answered. "Pilate is aware and has sought to gain information about him through his own spies, but they have had little more success than my own. When we compare notes, they are quite similar. One of Pilate's informants heard teachings my own informants had not. He heard Jesus speaking of the need to love one's enemies, which at first seemed counter to any sort of political subversion. But in the same breath, he would speak of not bringing peace but a sword, one that would divide families. Such talk has made Pilate nervous indeed, but for now, issues of jurisdiction force him to see Jesus as a problem for Herod Antipas to deal with."

"But surely he is aware that this man could quickly become a problem in Jerusalem as well as Galilee?" asked Ezra, further evincing his frustration with the governor. "He has already been in the city numerous times, and no doubt will return. In light of these developments in his teaching and practice, the next time he arrives in Jerusalem could be problematic indeed—particularly if rumors of his messianic identity begin to spread through the city. I am quite sure that is not far away."

"I am afraid your assessment is correct," Caiaphas answered. "And this is the very situation that concerns me. My informants tell me that talk of Jesus as a possible Messiah is already present in the city, though not at a level to cause alarm. And as he has regularly come to Jerusalem for festivals, I have no reason to doubt that he will come for the Passover. I will address this with Pilate in our next correspondence. As always, I will consult with him soon regarding the festival and our usual plans for maintaining peace and stability. Every year presents unique challenges, and this year is likely to be no different. Certainly, Pilate will have his own ideas for keeping the peace, but we must begin our own preparations."

At the mention of Pilate's "own ideas," Aaron and Ezra gave each other concerned looks and shook their heads in frustration.

"It seems to me," said Simeon, "that increasing our number of informants would be a prudent move."

"Indeed," Caiaphas replied. Turning to Aaron, his older brother, he asked, "Where do things stand regarding the recruitment of new informants?"

"Today I initiated contact with two new potential recruits. One is the son of a prominent innkeeper. The other is the son of the deceased Pharisaic teacher Saul, who, as you remember, was quite popular among the people. The son now runs his father's pottery shop. The inn is a bustling place where one can easily acquire gossip, and rumor has it that a group that style themselves as zealous insurrectionists meet there. They identify themselves as *sicarii*, as stabbing with a dagger is their preferred way of attacking isolated Roman soldiers. If I can recruit this innkeeper's son, he could be quite useful to us. The son of Saul has a cousin, Judah, who is rumored to be the leader of a secret resistance group, one that is far less conspicuous than the *sicarii*. We know very little about them at this point, but I have heard whispers that the group includes two or three prominent Pharisaic teachers—one who may even be a member of our esteemed great council. If we can win over this son of Saul, he may be able to join this secret group and provide us with valuable information. Apparently, he is facing financial hardship, so his services might be easily bought."

Eleazar had heard of the *sicarii*, though there hadn't been an attack on a Roman soldier by these "dagger men" in over a year. But the mention of a second resistance group caused Eleazar to wonder. "Might this second group have something to do with the ambush of the five Roman soldiers by archers here in the city? The *sicarii* have never used the bow and arrow, nor have they ever been so bold as to take on five Roman soldiers."

His father responded, "It is certainly possible. The attack is extremely troubling, for it was well planned and well executed. Luckily, I heard about it early in the morning after it occurred and gained an audience with the commander of the Jerusalem cohort, Brutus, before he did anything rash. As you can imagine, he was livid and was about to begin breaking down doors, dragging people to the dungeons, and torturing any Jew who was known to have sneered at a Roman soldier. I urged him not to take such actions, warning him that they might lead to even greater reprisal from the people. I asked that he first contact Pilate before he took such extreme steps, and that for the time being he pursue more subtle steps of investigation. I even offered our own informants to gather information and identify possible suspects. He agreed, reluctantly at first, but in the end was thankful for my offer of assistance. Unfortunately, it has been almost a week and my informants have found nothing useful. Perhaps Aaron's new recruits might prove helpful in this matter. The potter's son seems particularly promising."

Caiaphas paused. The weight of keeping peace in the city was heavy, and Eleazar knew that threats from insurrectionists kept his father up at nights.

After a moment, he said, "The peace of this city is built on such well-placed informants, though convincing them is becoming harder given the harsh retribution that has come to those who have been discovered. We must be more discreet than ever and constantly assure them of protection."

With these words, violent and gruesome images gripped Eleazar's mind. Just two months prior, authorities had found the mutilated bodies of two informants, each stabbed over one hundred times. These murders, the obvious work of the *sicarii*, were meant to send a strong message to any Jew who would work for the enemy.

"Fear of retribution is certainly an obstacle that must be overcome when recruiting informants," Aaron replied, "and assurance of anonymity and protection is often necessary to overcome it. We feared that the identity of one of our informants was revealed in the recent attack on Roman soldiers. Pilate had carelessly included our informant's name, along with the name of one of his own informants, in a written report that went missing in the attack. Luckily, nothing has yet happened to this informant, and we have now provided him with constant security to protect him from any possible threat. But while all such measures are important, I still find the best way to overcome an informant's fear of reprisal is a generous financial offer. Most men are willing to risk their lives if the price is right."

While Aaron sounded confident in his ability to protect his recruits, Eleazar knew that he had assured this very protection to both stabbing victims from two months prior.

JUDAH

Judah knelt in front of Lazarus, looked him in the eye and said in a calm voice, "Do you understand that at this moment your life is in grave danger?"

Lazarus nodded, his eyes filling with tears.

"How this night ends is entirely up to you," Judah said. "If you speak truthfully and tell me all I want to know, your life will be spared. But if you lie, even one time, you will die. Do you understand?"

Again Lazarus nodded, this time more vigorously. Judah's words had seemingly given him some hope of survival.

"Let me be clear," Judah said. "I am going to ask you a number of questions, many of which I already know the answer to. Should I catch you in a lie, you will not get a second chance. Are you sure you understand?"

Again, a vigorous nod.

"I am going to take off your gag now, but you are not going to scream, are you? If you scream or in any way call for help, you will die. Will you cry out for help once I have removed your gag?" Lazarus shook his head.

Judah took off the gag and Lazarus remained silent. He seemed to have calmed down and the panic was no longer in his eyes. The hope of life Judah had placed in front of him was serving its purpose.

"First question: Are you an informant for Rome?" Judah asked.

There was a long pause. Finally, Lazarus said, "I am an informant, but I am not an informant for Rome."

This caught Judah off guard. If not an informant for Rome, then for whom? "What do you mean, you are not an informant for Rome?"

"The person who recruited me was a Jew. He assured me I would not be gathering information for Rome but for my own people. He told me I would be keeping the city safe!"

"And you believed this, that you were gathering information about Jews for other Jews?" Judah asked.

"Yes," Lazarus replied sheepishly, as if hearing Judah's question out loud made him realize how foolish it sounded.

"Did it never occur to you that the Romans might use Jews to recruit their informants? Or that they would tell such a story in order to convince you?"

A long pause. Then finally, "Perhaps the thought occurred to me . . . but . . ."

"But the money was too good to pass up?" Judah asked scathingly.

Realizing he was making things worse for himself, Lazarus blurted frantically, "The man said I would be helping our city! He . . . he wasn't a Roman!"

Judah shook his head. "You are a fool! No, you are worse. You are a greedy, treacherous fool!"

Lazarus cringed, and panic returned to his eyes. "Don't kill me! Please!"

With calm returning to his voice, Judah replied, "I told you I would not kill you unless you lied. Have you lied to me yet?"

"No! I swear it! Every word has been the truth." Lazarus began to cry.

"Then you have nothing to fear," Judah said, "as long as you continue to tell the truth."

"All right! All right," Lazarus said, slowly calming down. "I promise I will tell the truth."

Judah continued, "How long have you been an informant?"

"I was recruited a little over a year ago."

"And how much are they paying you?"

Lazarus looked down. "They pay me in contracts," he said quietly.

Judah had expected this, but he pushed further. "Explain that. What do you mean that they pay you in contracts?"

"As long as I provide them with information, they ensure that I get the majority of the major masonry contracts in the city, and at times even contracts in other cities."

"So not only do you betray your people by passing on information to the enemy, but you also cheat the other masons of their livelihood by taking contracts you have not earned?"

Lazarus hung his head and said nothing.

"And why would you need to make such a deal?" Judah asked. "Your father has been one of the most successful masons in the city, and I dare say he achieved this success without having to betray his people. Or was your father a traitor as well?"

"No!" Lazarus blurted. "My father is an honest and good man. He earned all he had." Tears returned to Lazarus's eyes, but these seemed shameful tears rather than fearful ones. "I am not my father. And when my father took ill, I wasn't as successful as he was. The business started to fail. We began to lose contracts we would have never lost before—many contracts. I was afraid I would lose the business. That is when my contact approached me. It was a way to save everything, a way to save my honor."

"The irony," said Judah. "In seeking to save your honor, that was the one thing you lost."

Again, Lazarus said nothing. Tears streamed down his cheeks.

"How would you pass on information?" Judah asked.

Lazarus took a moment to compose himself before he spoke. "I always gave it to my contact, usually once or twice a week. He would find me, usually in my shop. If I ever had anything urgent to report, anything that might jeopardize the city's peace, I was to signal my contact. But it never came to that."

"What was the signal?"

"I had a pot in one of my shop windows. I was told to simply turn it in the opposite direction."

Judah nodded. "We are almost done. You are doing well," he said in a kind voice. These words put Lazarus at ease. It seemed he could see a light at the end of the tunnel.

"What sort of information did you pass on?"

"Not much of importance. At least, it never seemed that important to me. At times I would report on conversations I heard in the taverns or in my shop. Sometimes they had me entertain certain guests to find out more about this or that political issue. For a short time, they even had me go out to the baptizer John and report on his teachings and the tenor of the crowds around him. *Did he speak of violent resistance? Did the crowds?* I was only there a handful of times before the prophet went to Galilee."

"Did you ever give information that led to a person's arrest or death?" Judah asked.

"No!" Lazarus declared. "There was not a single instance in which information I gave led to the harm of a fellow Israelite."

"That you know of," said Judah.

"Yes . . . yes, that I know of."

"Good," Judah said. "You have told me all I desired to know, and I do believe you have told me the truth."

"Then you will let me go?"

"Of course," Judah said. "I am a man of my word. I just need to unbind your hands."

Lazarus gave a sigh of relief and released the tension from his body. Judah moved behind him, drew his dagger, and in one quick move, slit Lazarus's throat.

As blood poured out onto his hand, he looked into Lazarus's stunned eyes and said with a cruel smile, "Treachery is a fickle mistress."

In a matter of moments, Lazarus was dead. Judah signaled to his men to take his body outside. They sat him up against the alley wall, and with the mason's own blood, Judah wrote the word "traitor" above him. He turned to look at his men.

"May every Jew hear of this and know the risk of conspiring with the enemy!"

PILATE

The beauty of Pilate's balcony view had brought him little peace. He had been brooding for the past several hours over the news from his Galilean informants.

Jesus the Galilean prophet.

How could such an insignificant man from such an insignificant town cause the most powerful man in Judea such distress?

A nasty byproduct of the Jewish hope of ruling the world was the occasional lunatic who presented himself to the people as one appointed by God to bring these hopes to fruition. Such figures were never men of means, privilege, or power. Rarely did they even have an education. They usually offered no evidence to support their claims, yet, because of a charismatic personality, a desperate people would believe them and rally around them. These men were unlikely to bring down Rome's empire, but they could certainly cause trouble—a lot of trouble—if not properly dealt with. They were like a splinter in your finger: unlikely to kill you, but if left unattended, could cause a nasty infection. Diligence was crucial. You had to be adept at identifying and neutralizing these figures quickly.

To date, both Pilate and his predecessors had been quite successful at both. It had been almost thirty years since one of these figures had presented a serious threat to the peace and stability of the region. When the Roman emperor had removed the client king Herod Archelaus and placed Judea under direct Roman control, a certain Judah from Galilee rallied a larger number of people together to revolt. The threat gained ground quickly, but the new governor Varus put this rebellion down and killed Judah. To send a message, he crucified thousands of Jews. This act brought the region a good measure of peace, which allowed the governor to create an effective network of informants and spies that could identify potentially dangerous figures and neutralize them before they became a problem. Over the last two decades, no significant "messiah" had disrupted the peace. A few fanatics had certainly emerged, but Roman diligence had nipped them in the bud.

Pilate himself had had a recent scare with a figure named John—the "baptizer," they called him. John had challenged the authorities of the Jewish Temple and summoned the common people out into the wilderness for purification of their sins—as if dipping them in the dirty Jordan River could cleanse the soul. It couldn't even clean a cup! Crowds of people had gone out to John, and many stayed with him and listened to his teaching. This initial popularity had set Pilate on high alert and his first inclination was to send soldiers to arrest John and disperse his followers. The high priest Caiaphas had cautioned against such measures. He argued that arresting a popular prophet might spark the very rioting that Pilate was trying to avoid. Besides, from all he could tell, John seemed more interested in the greater well-being of Jews than in an anti-Roman agenda. Instead, the priest suggested he use informants for close observation and perhaps even infiltration.

Learning from his past mistakes, Pilate decided to listen to the priest, though he soon feared it may have been a mistake. As John's popularity grew, the political rhetoric began to grow up around him and infiltrate his followers. There was more and more talk about the coming "kingdom of God" in which Israel's God, through his appointed king, would overthrow all oppressors. Some of John's closest disciples were trying to convince him to take violent action against both the temple authorities and Rome. When Pilate heard these reports, he prepared to dispatch soldiers. He had listened to the priest long enough and sensed that the flower of rebellion was about to bloom.

But one of Pilate's informants, a Jew named Zechariah, had gained John's ear and began to direct his attention to the illegal marriage of Herod Antipas to his brother's wife, Herodias. Despite strong voices calling for violent action against Roman occupation of Jerusalem, they could not dissuade John—as a prophet of God, it was his responsibility to call the rulers of the land to account for their sins and demand repentance.

Thus, just as soldiers were leaving Caesarea to deal with this zealous baptizer, he went with a small group of followers to Galilee to do battle with the infidelity of Herod. The great crowds that had followed John disbanded quickly, and the threat to Judea was gone. Pilate had celebrated long and hard the night he received that news! In the end, the priest had been right again.

Only a few months later, Herod had John arrested and not long ago executed. For a brief time, there appeared to be no zealous prophets on the horizon. But now there was this Jesus. As far as Pilate could tell, he began as a popular teacher among the people of Galilee, with some claiming he performed miracles. Apparently, he had come to Jerusalem on a number of occasions, for festivals primarily, but during these visits he had never caused any disturbances or drawn much attention to himself. He did nothing that would draw attention from the local ruling elite or Pilate himself. Pilate had certainly heard his name before in the reports from his informants, but all reports on Jesus were innocuous. He was a religious teacher, perhaps marginally controversial to his own people, yet seemingly apolitical. Ultimately, he gave Pilate little cause for concern.

But in the last year, things had changed. Pilate's informants in the north had noted a quick increase in Jesus' popularity, and with it, rumblings that Jesus was the long-awaited deliverer the Jews had been waiting for. Though surprised by these reports, Pilate had acted quickly. He sent additional spies to gather more information. Of these, he instructed a handful to get close to the prophet. He would employ the same strategy that worked so well with the baptizer.

Locating Jesus took some time, but after doing so, joining the large group that traveled with him was easy. It seemed anyone who was willing to leave their home and family to follow this man could do so. But gaining access to him, learning of his plans, and winning his confidence proved to be much harder. He had surrounded himself with twelve men whom he had personally selected, and who had been with him for at least two years. While Jesus would teach the crowd of disciples that followed him, and was certainly friends with many of them, he shared nothing of his plans, intentions, or purpose with them. He was affable with them, and even seemed genuinely concerned about their lives and needs. Such concern, combined with his magnetism and charisma, no doubt drew them to Jesus. But Jesus took none from this larger group into his confidence, nor did he seek their advice or confide in them. Presumably the twelve men he had hand selected had such access and privilege. Jesus and his chosen twelve would often separate from the crowd, only to rejoin them later. It was clear that following them or even asking questions regarding their plans or destination was not acceptable. Such secrecy alone worried Pilate. Drawing conclusions from lack of evidence was always dangerous, but Pilate had no choice but to fear the worst of these secret meetings.

Without direct access to Jesus, all Pilate's information came from Jesus' teaching to the larger group. In reading reports, Pilate found himself sitting on the edge of both terror and relief. Aspects of Jesus' teaching seemed anti-Roman. He spoke frequently about the "kingdom of God" being at hand, clearly a reference to the hopes of Israel to one day rule the world. This kingdom would bring woe to the rich and powerful—no doubt Rome and its allies—and empower the impoverished (the image of peasants trying to rule the world always amused Pilate until he thought about the dangers of them attempting to do so). This kingdom would start out small, like a mustard seed, but grow into a massive tree—no doubt a reference to this small and insignificant group one day ruling the world. Jesus even critiqued the temple, a building he claimed was built with unrighteous wealth, and spoke of God destroying the current temple and establishing a new and righteous one in the kingdom of God. The people hung on these words that resonated with their deepest hopes. Such rhetoric was certainly cause for concern.

But at the same time, Jesus never spoke of violent revolution—at least not openly. In fact, he often spoke of nonviolence, directing his followers to pray for their enemies and to not return their slights or insults. And perhaps most confounding was the fact that Jesus resisted any clear identification with a political deliverer or messianic figure. Speculation ran rampant not only among those who followed him, but throughout the towns and villages of Galilee as well. While many were convinced he was indeed the one whom their god had raised up to bring about the promised kingdom, others were unsure.

It wasn't that Jesus said nothing in this regard, but that he seemed purposefully equivocal. He frequently identified himself as the "son of man." One of Pilate's Jewish informants told him that the designation was ambiguous, that it could indeed be a reference to the messianic figure found in some prophetic writing, but that it could also simply be an innocent form of self-address. On the rare occasion that someone openly identified him as a messiah or king, Jesus never denied it, but he did instruct them to be silent. Was he denying the title? Was he merely being humble? Or coy?

Pilate was having a hard time putting all the pieces together. He could not be sure whether Jesus was a political threat or not. But ultimately, in such cases, certainty is not necessary—security is. By exciting the masses, this Galilean prophet was playing with fire, and his inner intentions mattered little. Whether he intended to be or not, this Jesus was a threat that must be dealt with swiftly. Waiting for him to make his purposes known could be disastrous.

But when it came to direct action, Pilate's hands were tied. Galilee was under the authority of Herod Antipas. The thought of the pretentious and pampered tetrarch turned Pilate's stomach, but he had no other choice than to rely on him to deal with this problem. He would send copies of his reports to Herod and request that, for the security of the region, he neutralize and eliminate the prophet as quickly as possible.

As Pilate called for his secretary to compose a letter to Herod, he had little hope that it would accomplish the task. And if this Galilean Jesus set his eyes on Jerusalem, Pilate must be prepared to deal with him.

CALEB

It was a slow day in the shop, and Caleb was having difficulty focusing on his responsibilities. His thoughts shifted between concern for his failing business and the meeting he might have that evening.

Caleb had thought about the proposal all night. Information —that is all the man said he wanted, and that he would pay well for it. He didn't say who wanted the information, or what kind was wanted, but in his heart Caleb knew enough. Information was wanted by those in power—by Rome. And no doubt the Romans would use it to maintain their ongoing occupation of Jerusalem. He didn't need to know any more than that. This man was asking Caleb to be a traitor to his people. The thought made his stomach turn.

But there was an offer of money, and Caleb needed money badly. The thought of his family losing the shop and their home was more painful than the thought of treachery. He would at least listen to the man's offer. It couldn't hurt to listen. How much information did these people want, and what kind of information were they looking for? Would the information directly hurt anyone? And how much money was it worth? No, it wouldn't hurt to listen, to learn more.

The mysterious visitor had met him again early that morning as he was making his way to the pottery shop. It was still dark outside, and he was startled by the hand on his shoulder. All he said was, "If you are interested in my proposal, meet me in the alley behind your shop as soon as you arrive."

So before opening the shop, Caleb made his way to the alley and saw the man standing in a dark corner. He was clearly trying to remain unseen. Caleb approached and said, "I am interested in your proposal, but I have questions." The man placed a finger to his lips. In a low voice he said, "Not here." He handed Caleb a small piece of broken pottery with a bit of writing scrawled on it. "If you are interested, be at this location at the first watch of the night. Find a table in the back where the light is low. He will find you. Wait until he does." The man quickly turned and walked away.

Confused, Caleb called out, "Wait, who will find me?" The man did not turn around and soon disappeared around the corner. Caleb looked down at the piece of pottery. He had heard of the location, a tavern on the edge of the city, but he had never been there. It had a poor reputation, and few devout Jews would ever darken its doors. Would he be so bold as to do so tonight?

His recollection of the morning's earlier events was interrupted by someone calling his name. "Caleb." "Caleb?" "Caleb!" Caleb turned to see his cousin Judah standing close by. "What are you so lost in thought about, Cousin?" Judah asked.

"Oh, sorry, Judah!" Caleb answered. "I was just reviewing the month's profits in my head—or, uh, lack of profits. Forgive me."

"No forgiveness necessary. How are things?" Judah asked. "I have heard rumors that business has not been good as of late. I hope you don't mind me asking."

Caleb shook his head, indicating he did not mind the question. "Things have been slow, but that is not too unusual this time of year," he lied. "Things should pick up as we approach Passover." Perhaps this was not a lie, but it certainly communicated a confidence Caleb lacked.

"Ah, the festival!" Judah replied. "That should give you a good boost, to be sure! That is, if the new tax is not too high." He uttered these last words with an air of disgust, and Caleb perceived them as bait. He did not take it.

"Yes, such a new tax could be problematic, but as you know, we shopkeepers are seeking a way to navigate it, should it come about."

"Yes, of course," replied Judah, "but it is a shame you should even have to. Price adjustments to overcome taxation only hurt the people, those who come on pilgrimage as well as those in the city. Everyone loses, except the damned Romans!"

There it was. It always came to a rant about the "damned Romans"—he had heard these rants many times.

"They are killing us, Caleb!" Judah exclaimed. "Not with the sword, though they are happy to do that when given the opportunity, but by crushing the life out of us slowly. How long do you think the people will stand for it? How long will they tolerate high taxes, abusive soldiers in the streets, privilege of the elite, and the pagan pollution of our holy city? The tensions in the city are high, Cousin; you know this as well as I do. They are bound to reach a breaking point soon."

"Yes, times are indeed hard," Caleb granted. "And yes, tensions *are* high. But what can really be done?" He regretted those last words as soon as they left his lips.

"Much more can be done than you think, Cousin. Even now, people in the city prepare to take action against our oppressors. Resistance is on the minds of many, and action will soon follow. You heard about the five slaughtered Roman soldiers—that is action, and proof that Rome can bleed! There are far more of us than them, Caleb. If we could join together and organize, we could drive them out of this city!"

"Yes, I have heard of the attack on the soldiers," Caleb replied, "but it does not bring me the hope it brings you. I fear retribution will come of it. People will suffer. And perhaps you are right that we could drive them out of the city, Judah, but what then? Do you honestly believe Rome will stand for that? There might be very few soldiers here now, but open rebellion will bring countless legions. What price do we all pay then? I think you know."

"You of little faith, Cousin!" Judah exclaimed.

Caleb would have quieted him, but seeing no one else in his shop, he let it go.

Judah continued, "Do you forget that God is on our side? Have you not read the stories of old—the stories of God joining his people in battle and routing his enemies, and against far worse odds than we face? If we reclaimed this holy city, surely the Lord would help us defend it! His dwelling, the temple, rests on Mount Zion, and as he has promised, he will not abandon his faithful ones."

"Not all see violence against Rome as faithfulness, Cousin," Caleb replied. "Many see it as presumption—an attempt to force God's hand."

"The path of cowards," Judah snorted. "The proclaimers of faith who have no true faith!"

"Men of devout faith see things differently, Judah." As Caleb said these words, thoughts of his father came to his mind.

Judah shook his head in discouragement. "It seems circumstances have not changed your mind, Caleb. The beliefs of your father still grip your heart. He was a good man, to be sure; I don't mean to slander him or his faith. But perhaps increased injustice and difficulty will change you. When your anger grows great enough, you may see things differently. When that day comes, Cousin, you must find me. You would be an excellent asset to the cause. Action might come sooner than you think, and you will want to be on the right side when it does."

"What do you know, Judah?" Caleb asked. "Do you know of plans that will bring violence?"

"Not exactly," Judah answered, "but Passover is coming. The city will grow to five times its size, and all minds will be dwelling on God's deliverance from Egypt. What better time could there be? I also hear rumors that Jesus, the popular prophet from Nazareth, will likely be coming. From what I hear, his teaching has turned more and more to talk of the coming kingdom of God. Many are wondering if he might be God's anointed, the Messiah. It hardly seems likely to me, but in him and his followers, our movement might find allies—and he might prove to be a catalyst to move people to action."

The plausibility of these words gripped Caleb with fear. "God help us all if what you say is true. I am sorry, but I must get back to work—and I can't have customers hear us talking of these things."

"You know where to find me, Cousin. You are always welcome at my side." With these confident last words, Judah turned and left the shop.

Caleb generally assumed talk of violent resistance against Rome was just that—talk. But the way Judah spoke had awoken him to the reality that a violent response to Roman occupation was possible—perhaps even probable. That thought truly terrified him; he knew how such resistance would ultimately end. But at the same time another thought entered his mind. This conversation with Judah had provided Caleb with new information—information that might prove profitable at his meeting later that evening.

The day passed slowly as Caleb anxiously thought about the meeting. The day's lack of customers made it so there was little to distract his mind. He closed the shop a bit early and told his sister he had an important business meeting and was uncertain when he would be home. Thankfully, she didn't ask any questions. She told him she would have dinner ready for him when he got home and kissed him on the cheek as he walked out the door.

Sweet sister, he thought, *If all goes well tonight you will never have to know of the dire financial hardship we face.* As the sun was setting, Caleb made his way toward the edge of the city.

It took Caleb a bit longer than he thought to reach the tavern, as it had been many years since he had ventured into that part of the city. By the time he arrived there was little light in the sky. Thankfully, he had not seen anyone he knew along the way. Any questions they might have asked would either require him to lie or face embarrassment and further explanation. That was a choice he didn't want to make.

The tavern was poorly lit, and there were no windows. The air was stale, and the odor was a combination of sweat and sour wine. The tavern's owner was a big man, bald headed with hairy arms. A large scar ran across his right cheek. He looked suspiciously at Caleb, then waved his hand toward the tables, indicating he could sit anywhere. Few tables were occupied, which relieved Caleb. The appearance of those present suggested an unsavory identity, which made Caleb feel ill at ease. As instructed, he took a seat toward the back of the tavern, and a young girl soon appeared to take his order. Upon hearing the few options available, Caleb ordered a barley stew and red wine. Almost immediately after the girl had departed, Caleb was startled by a hooded man who slipped in across from him. In a firm but calm voice, the man said, "Be at ease, I am the one you are here to meet."

The cloak cast a shadow over his face, but Caleb could tell that man was older than himself, perhaps in his late forties or early fifties. His skin was smooth and well cared for, and his beard was well groomed. Caleb also noticed that the man did not smell bad, and in fact carried a very faint odor of flowers—a pleasant reprieve from the dominant odors of the tavern. These features relaxed Caleb a bit, and he said, "I am Caleb son of Saul, may I ask your name?"

"I know who you are," the man replied, "and you will call me Aaron, as I am only the mouthpiece for one greater than myself." Caleb perceived the obvious reference to the brother of the great prophet and lawgiver Moses. There was a brief pause. Finally, the man spoke: "I am assuming that your coming here indicates you are willing to aid us with information."

"Not necessarily," Caleb replied, though he knew this was largely a lie—and he suspected the man knew so as well. "I have many questions I must have answered before I agree to help you."

"Questions are expected," the man replied, "and I am happy to answer all that I am able."

"My thanks," Caleb said. "Perhaps my most pressing question is, For whom will I be gathering this information? And only slightly less pressing, For what purpose?" Again this was a bit of a lie, but the answer was indeed important to Caleb. He continued, "I am a loyal Israelite, devoted to my God and my people. I have no desire to betray either." Caleb truly believed this . . . or, he deeply wanted to.

"I appreciate your questions," the man answered, "and I believe I can give you a reply that is more than satisfactory. I too am a Judean like yourself, born and raised in this very city—the same is true of the one who sent me. You can no doubt tell from my accent that what I say is true." Caleb nodded, and the man continued. "Let me put your mind further at ease. You will not be gathering information for the Romans, which I would guess is your primary concern. You will be gathering information for your own people, to protect your own people."

The words gave Caleb some relief, but also confusion. Apparently recognizing that confusion, the man continued, "These are difficult times for our city. Tensions between the people of Jerusalem and our Roman occupiers are nearing a breaking point. Perhaps you have heard of the recent ambush of Roman soldiers." *Of course*, thought Caleb, *who in the city had not?*

"While we have had peace in this city for over seventy years, groups composed of our own countrymen seek to jeopardize that peace by organizing violent resistance toward our occupying guests. While such resistance might have a hope of temporary success, the retribution that would descend on our city would be disastrous." Caleb nodded. It was as if the man was speaking aloud the fears that had struck Caleb earlier that day.

"I represent a group that desperately wants to avoid that fate. We seek from you information that will aid us in doing just that. Thus, far from asking you to betray your people, we are asking you to help us save them, perhaps save them from themselves." These words brought further relief. In fact, they conveyed a sentiment Caleb himself shared.

But he quickly reminded himself that this was a negotiation, and there was financial compensation at stake. An overly enthusiastic response could only hurt him. Instead he coyly replied, "Many of our people would not see things this way. While they might reject violent resistance, they would view your cause as ultimately helping Rome—an act of betrayal against your own people."

The man nodded and replied, "No doubt some would view us in this way. As you know, there are diverse perspectives among us Jews regarding the Roman occupation and the proper response to it. I can only say that our goals are indeed the safety and protection of our city and the people who dwell within it. To this end, we work tirelessly. If you feel aiding us would be a betrayal of your people, you are free to reject our offer. And if you do reject it, you will never hear from us again."

In response, Caleb tried to communicate interest, but also reservation. "I am not opposed to your ideology, and I think I could be persuaded by it. But I fear that in your effort to keep peace, some of our own people might come to harm. I do not want to provide information that might lead to the injury, arrest, or death of my kin. I am not opposed to providing information that undermines plots or frustrates violence, but I refuse to provide information that will itself produce violence." Even as he said these words, Caleb knew there was no way he could control how this man would use any information he would provide—and that he could use it to eliminate potential threats. But he sincerely wanted to distance himself from direct betrayal and bloody hands. To some there may be no difference, but for Caleb's conscience the difference was significant. He felt such a stance was also advantageous to the present negotiation.

"Your requests are admirable and fair, and I believe we can work within those parameters. As long as your information is true and useful in preventing violence in the city, we will not ask you to directly betray anyone close to you." Caleb nodded, and the man continued, "You may be wondering why we identified you as one who might be able to provide us with information?" He nodded again, though the thought had not really crossed his mind.

Before Aaron could continue, the girl returned with Caleb's soup and wine. She looked at Aaron, who dismissed her with a quick wave of his hand. He said, "There are many reasons. First, you run a pottery shop that has long been popular in our city. You have often attracted many customers who talk and share gossip and rumors. At times, you likely hear things that might be advantageous to us. Second, you are the son of the beloved Pharisee Saul. Because of this, many love and trust your family. Through the friendships of your late father, you have strong connections to many respected Jews throughout the city. No doubt these friendships could also produce useful information. Third, you are the cousin of Judah, son of Jonah. His hatred for Rome is a poorly kept secret, and there are rumors that he may be associated with a secret resistance movement. Your relationship with him may put you in a position that is useful to us."

The mention of Judah was not surprising to Caleb. In fact, he had suspected his cousin might come up. But given the reservations he had expressed, he gave a look of reluctance. "I already told you I will not betray my kin. I will not give you information about Judah that might lead to his arrest or worse."

"I understand," the man replied. "You needn't give us any direct information regarding your cousin. But perhaps you could give us information of a general nature that might undermine an attack or allow those targeted to alter their plans. Perhaps in this way you could help the cause of peace without betraying your cousin?"

Both men knew what remained unspoken—even the passing on of such information could easily result in Judah's harm. But the respective goals of each allowed them to push such a possibility aside.

"Perhaps now we should discuss both your security and compensation." While Caleb was eager to talk about compensation, the issue of security startled him. It had not even dawned on him that this venture might be dangerous. But of course it could be! If he was working to undermine the plans of violent men, the discovery of his actions would likely draw violent retaliation from them. It was only a few months before that two men had been found stabbed over a hundred times. Many suspected that the *sicarii* had killed these men for the very thing Caleb was being asked to do. Why had he not thought of this danger yet? Had the opportunity for financial salvation blinded him? Reservation began to grow in his mind.

Perhaps his face revealed these thoughts. Aaron spoke confidently, perhaps overly so. "We can assure you of complete anonymity. We will never leak your name, and no one will know of your association with me. We will have no written correspondence that might be traced back to you. The transfer of information will be planned in order to avoid detection or even suspicion. If at any time you feel you are in danger, we can provide guards that will watch over you from a distance."

This all sounded good, but it didn't alleviate Caleb's growing concerns. "How can you be sure these precautions will work and my safety be ensured? I have heard rumors of great harm coming to informants within the city."

"I will not lie to you, Caleb," the man said with conviction. "Yes, in the past informants have been careless, and it has cost them. But if you are careful and do as we say, I am confident of your security."

This brought a sense of ease to Caleb, as did his following words from Aaron. "Though minimal, there are indeed risks, and that is why we intend to compensate you well for your service. We are aware that business has slowed significantly for your pottery shop." Caleb figured his financial struggles were related to his recruitment—it clearly gave his recruiters leverage. "Your compensation will begin by an increase in business. In the coming days you will notice an increase of customers in your shop, many of whom will be quite affluent. They will bring to you specialized orders, often very large ones for which you will be well paid. As long as you provide useful reports, these well-paying clients will find your pottery shop their shop of choice in Jerusalem. In addition to this boost in your business, once a month we will make a payment to you of 150 drachmas. This should enable you to hire more workers in order to meet the growing demand on your shop. It will eventually be extra profit that will help not only to sustain your family but perhaps to enhance your status within the city."

This amount of money stunned Caleb, as it was far more than he had anticipated. His shop was currently only making thirty to forty drachmas a month, which, after paying his cousin, was barely enough for him and his sister to live on. Even in his father's day the shop rarely made more than eighty drachmas a month. With these numbers in his mind, the risk he was taking seemed to shrink and the confidence in his safety increased. Feeling overwhelmed, he lost all sense of trying to negotiate and blurted out, "This is fair. I will accept it!"

He was instantly embarrassed, but Aaron only smiled warmly. "I am happy to hear this, Caleb. Regrettably, you will likely not see me again. You will pass all your information through the man you spoke with this morning. Do not worry; he will find you when the time is right, and he will explain to you everything else you need to know. For the time being, all you need to do is keep your eyes and ears open for anything that might be important. May our God bless you and keep you as you serve him and his people in this way."

The man rose from the table, pulled his hood further down around his face, and silently exited the tavern. Caleb sat in silence with his stew and wine. The stew was cold and flavorless, the wine cheap and sour. Eager to be rid of this place, he left both along with payment at the table. Twenty minutes later, he was eating fresh bread that Miriam had made. His heart was much lighter, and he and his sister talked and laughed late into the night. It was the first time he remembered laughing in months.

THREE

THE PREPARATION

ELEAZAR

Eleazar sat across from his father in the family library. The room was lavishly decorated with beautiful mosaics covering the floor and ornate colorful tapestries from all parts of the empire hanging from the walls. The back wall held hundreds of scrolls, including works from Jewish, Greek, and Roman authors. His father was a true scholar, extremely well read, and able to discuss anything from the Greek works of Homer and Polybius to Jewish works such as the life of Tobit and the extremely bizarre and misguided oracles of Daniel. But affixed prominently above all of these was a beautiful and pristinely kept Torah scroll, the most sacred Scripture of all Jews. This scroll contained the sacred way of life that God had laid out for his chosen people, and following that way of life was the people's loving response to their divine election. His father knew the Torah as well as any in Israel, and he could debate its proper interpretation with the most learned scribe or Pharisee.

Caiaphas looked up from the letter he was reading from Pilate, the governor of Judea. "It seems our governor is particularly concerned about the coming Passover. He is considering bringing additional soldiers with him to Jerusalem when he comes for the week of the festival. He thinks an additional show of force might serve as a deterrent to any thought of riot or revolt."

"It seems a prudent move, Father," Eleazar replied confidently. "While adding such a small number of troops to the thousand or so already stationed here doesn't really provide additional protection from a rioting mob, appearances do matter. Just the glimpse of Roman scarlet is often enough to make commoners think twice before they pick up a club or rock."

"Perhaps," Caiaphas replied. He paused and stroked his long graying beard. "Or perhaps such a demonstration unnecessarily raises tensions. Some might perceive such a move as antagonistic. Is parading more Roman power in front of a people who are already angry about its presence a wise move? I am not so sure it is. There is far more to peace than a show of force. Pilate has come a long way, but still he seems slow to learn this truth."

The correction stung a bit—it always did. But despite the sting, Eleazar couldn't deny the wisdom that regularly dwelt in his father's words. From this wisdom he had learned countless valuable lesson, each one often a chisel to his own pride. "I hadn't thought of it that way. Perhaps you are right, Father. Will you then write to Pilate and suggest he not bring these troops?"

"I may include a subtle suggestion," his father said, "but it is highly unlikely his mind will change on this matter. There is little point in using all your strength in a fight you are sure to lose. Best to save your energy for the more important and winnable battles—this prophet from Galilee, for example."

"What is Pilate's estimation of him?"

"He is extremely concerned," said Caiaphas. "His informants have told him that Jesus has left Galilee and is headed south. Pilate is convinced he is coming to Jerusalem for the Passover, and no doubt he is correct." He paused, a concerned look on his face. "I am afraid this prophet will be our problem soon, my son. Pilate is considering an attempt to arrest him before he ever gets to the city. He feels that if Jesus makes it to the city, the potential fanfare around him will make the situation incredibly difficult to deal with."

"That seems a legitimate concern," said Eleazar, again seeing the logic in the governor's thinking. "If his popularity here rivals that of his popularity in Galilee, any attempt to arrest him will be challenging. The arrest itself will run the risk of triggering a violent response from the people. And many of our informants have indicated that at least some people are talking about him as a messianic deliverer. There seems to be a growing energy surrounding the rumors that he might come to Jerusalem for the Passover."

Caiaphas nodded. "You and Pilate are right—there is reason for concern. But I still feel we don't know enough about this man's intentions to make such a move. So far, he has made no open declarations of rebellion against Rome, and as far as my informants, as well as Pilate's, know, he has made no claim to be a 'messiah' or 'deliverer' of Israel. If Pilate arrests a popular Jewish prophet right before the Passover, it will greatly raise the anger of the people toward Pilate, making his visit to the city precarious indeed. Can you imagine the reaction when Pilate enters Jerusalem with three hundred soldiers? Even if we were to avoid violence, such action would cast a dark shadow over the week's festivities."

While his father had a point, Eleazar pushed the governor's position further. "But would the danger not be greater if he entered the city and it became clear that he did style himself Israel's Messiah? He himself could be the catalyst of revolt. And trying to arrest him at that point could also be a catalyst for the same."

"Perhaps," Caiaphas acknowledged, "but what if he is only coming to the city as a peaceful participant? What if he has no intention of inciting the people? If that is the case, we would not only be arresting an innocent man, we would potentially be creating the very problem we want to avoid. In my estimation, the only scenario that does not bring the risk of violence and riot is one in which this Jesus comes to the city as a peace-minded prophet. At this point, we don't know whether this is the manner in which he will come. From what we do know, it is certainly possible. His coming to the city as a popular messiah would be the worst possible outcome, as it brings the greatest risk of violence. But arresting him prior to the festival is only marginally less risky. As such, I favor allowing him to come to the city unimpeded. Here we can watch him more closely and better assess the level of risk he presents. I understand this plan of action is risky, but it carries with it the best possible reward—the peace of our city."

Eleazar was not convinced, but it was clear his father had made up his mind. He asked, "So this is the plan that you will suggest to Pilate? Do you think he will listen?"

"Yes, it is the plan I will recommend," Caiaphas answered. "I will urge him to call off any arrest attempt and allow the prophet to come into the city. It is here that I will exert my strength and hope to win. Pilate has proven to be reasonable, and his past failures have certainly made him open to my counsel. But he may still find the safest way forward is to eliminate the threat of Jesus before it becomes a true problem. We must be prepared either way."

The comment about the need for preparation gave Eleazar the entry point to inform his father about another potential threat that faced them. "Father, I think we might also need to be prepared for Annas. Joanna was at a dinner party last night, and my cousins Mattathias and Jacob were holding court regarding Jesus and his potential visit to the city. They spoke of what a threat he was, of how we need strong leadership to handle him, and that they hoped the current leadership was up to the challenge. The entire discussion was a thinly veiled critique of you as high priest. Sadly, their comments raised much concern among the guests, many of whom are important power brokers.

"After a bit too much to drink, Jacob let it slip that Annas intends to meet personally with Pilate when he arrives, and that he would express his concerns regarding the present leadership's ability to maintain the city's security and peace. He was on the verge of saying more, but Mattathias silenced him. Knowing them, I am confident they were parroting what they heard from their fathers, or perhaps Annas himself. They are far too dimwitted to have their own thoughts on the matter. Regardless, it seems clear that Annas is making his own preparations, and we must be ready for them."

These words seemed to bring a sadness over Caiaphas. "This news is not surprising, Son, as your grandfather has been scheming to have me removed as high priest from the day I was appointed. But you are right—we must keep our eye on him as well. We face a battle on many fronts, and we cannot ignore any of them. Sadly, Annas's true concern is his own prestige and power—he cares little for the safety and security of the city. He no doubt sees this Passover visitation of Jesus as an opportunity. Should I misstep, either by dealing too harshly or not harshly enough with this prophet, he knows I will incur political damage with the people, Pilate, or both. Thus, he will surely push me to misstep one way or the other. When I do, like a vulture, he will be ready to swoop in and take advantage."

He paused for a moment, thinking over the challenge his father-in-law presented. "If we can ascertain which direction of a misstep he will favor, perhaps we can use that to our advantage." Then, with somewhat of a change in his mood, he said, "I am very pleased with your marriage to Joanna, Son. She is as wise and as shrewd as she is beautiful—she may end up being one of our most important informants." A warm smile emerged as he said these words.

His father was not generous with his praise for his children, and this praise for his wife filled Eleazar with pride. However, he thought best to conceal it if there was ever to be further praise. "Thank you, Father. I will convey your praise and tell her to continue to be alert for information that might prove useful. She is quite fond of you as well, and will do what she can to help you and our family."

Caiaphas nodded. After a brief silence, he returned to business. "That brings us to the status of our current informants. You met with Aaron about this?"

"Yes," Eleazar replied, "he updated me this morning. We currently have over fifty informants spread across the city. They are aware of how valuable their information will be during the festival. We assigned five to monitor the outer courtyards of the temple, one to each gate. We designated the rest to prominent taverns, markets, and shops. They know how to reach their handlers if any urgent information comes to them, and the handlers will then bring the information directly to us. We can be confident that little of significance will happen in the city without us knowing it quickly."

"Very good," said Caiaphas. "I must thank Aaron for his excellent work in this regard. Jesus or no Jesus, knowledge is power, and thus it is the key to the peace and security of the city. Hopefully these informants will help bring about the results we are paying them so well for."

Their conversation was interrupted by a knock at the door. As if on cue, Eleazar's uncle Aaron appeared. He and Caiaphas exchanged kisses on the cheek. "Were your ears burning, Brother?" Caiaphas asked. Aaron looked confused. "We were just talking about you, and Eleazar was passing along your update on our informants. Well done, indeed!"

"Thank you, Brother," said Aaron. "But I have important news that cannot wait! The Roman commander has arrested three people for the recent ambush and murder of five Roman soldiers."

This was stunning news. "Who was arrested, and when?" Caiaphas asked urgently.

"Only two hours ago," Aaron answered. "They arrested a man named Joseph, the son of a local tavern owner. They also arrested a Simeon, who was at the tavern at the time of the arrest and tried to escape. The soldiers took this as a sign of his guilt and arrested him too. The third man was Joseph's cousin, a man named Samuel, who had accused Roman soldiers of raping his sister. His kinship with Joseph and his strong motive for retribution were the primary reasons for his arrest."

Eleazar saw concern on his father's face. "Surely there were more men involved in the death of these five Roman soldiers. Are more arrests expected?"

"At this time there are certainly suspects, men close to these three, but the others cannot be found," Aaron answered. "The Romans are hopeful that they can extract the names of the other men from those now held in prison." The thought of these men being tortured for information was clearly troubling to Caiaphas, and Eleazar sensed his father was concerned whether they had arrested the right men.

"How did you come to this information so quickly?" Caiaphas asked.

"The Roman commander himself sent me a message informing me of these arrests and thanking me for my assistance. The information that led to the arrests came from one of our informants. The commander also said to pass along his thanks to you for your wisdom regarding how to proceed with the investigation. He recognizes that his original plan for harsh and widespread interrogation would have likely driven the assailants into hiding, while your advice of a subtle and quieter investigation has produced great fruit."

Caiaphas nodded thoughtfully. "Well, if these men are indeed guilty, I am thankful we were able to assist in their arrest. However, I am concerned about how these arrests might affect the Passover. No doubt they will only add to current tensions."

Eleazar broke the silence he had maintained since his uncle's entrance. "I understand your concern regarding rising tensions, Father, but I wonder if these events might be helpful as you seek to persuade Pilate not to arrest the prophet Jesus. He was reluctant to instruct the Roman commander to take a light hand in the investigation of the murders, but now your advice has proven prudent. Perhaps this might induce Pilate to consider your advice regarding Jesus?"

The look on his father's face made it clear that this idea had not yet occurred to him, which gave Eleazar a degree of pleasure. After a thoughtful pause, Caiaphas replied, "Perhaps you have identified a means of leverage, Son. But one must be careful in applying pressure to a Roman governor." As usual, his father was not generous with acknowledgment of Eleazar's own wisdom. The earlier praise of Joanna was likely enough for one day. All the same, Eleazar took pleasure in the knowledge that he too could take a chisel to his father's pride.

CALEB

A few weeks had passed since his recruitment as an informant, and the shop was again buzzing with customers. The influx began just two days after Caleb had met with Aaron, before he had even delivered any information. On the second day after the meeting, a wealthy merchant had come in and placed a large order for oil lamps—and, shockingly, paid half of the cost up front. The next day, a small but expensive order came in from a prominent priest. In just two days Caleb had made almost as much as he had made in the past year!

With this dramatic change in fortune, he noticed a change in his mood and attitude as well. His anxiety had all but disappeared, and with it his fear, anger, and despair. He found himself smiling often, even engaging customers with what might border on charm and wit—nothing like his father, of course, but he was displaying a sociability that was surprising to even himself. He actually felt happy for the first time since his father had passed away.

But he was keenly aware that this newfound success did not come without a cost. He knew that he needed to be useful, to pay attention to the conversations of the people around him and gather information that would be useful to his new benefactor. Just days after being recruited he began to frequent popular taverns—reputable ones, of course. He paid attention to the political climate of the room and listened for any bit of information he might be able to pass on. Perhaps most noteworthy was the talk about the popular Galilean prophet, Jesus, and his possible visit to Jerusalem for the Passover. There was much excited speculation about his potential messianic ambitions. Apparently, the prophet himself was quite circumspect with any sort of messianic identification, but the things he did and taught had convinced many he was indeed God's anointed one. Caleb felt this sort of information was somewhat beneficial, though it was not specific enough to be particularly valuable. For more valuable information he was going to need a different strategy, and his cousin Judah might just be the answer. Fortunately, Judah came by the shop just three days after Caleb's meeting with Aaron. As always, Judah spoke of the evils of Rome and the need for the people of Jerusalem to rise up against them. This time, Caleb gave subtle indications that he might be more open to Judah's way of thinking than he had been in the past. He didn't want to come on too strong, but he wanted his cousin to sense there might be an opening.

Judah did press that opening three days later on his second visit to the shop. Before he left, he told Caleb he recognized a potential change of heart and wondered if he might be more favorable to the cause of liberty for Jerusalem. Without seeming too eager, Caleb admitted that he might be. "Give me time to think more about this," he told Judah, who left with more hope than he ever had in the past.

It was almost a week later when Judah came by the shop a third time, seeking to gauge the temperature of his cousin's interest. This time Caleb moved a step further, saying he was intrigued but didn't know what he should or could do. As he already knew, his cousin was ready to help; on the spot he invited him to a secret dinner! Things were going better than Caleb could have hoped. The dinner would be the following evening, and there would be many there that he already knew. It would be held in the home of Solomon, a prominent Pharisee. Caleb knew both the home and its owner well; Solomon was one of his father's closest friends, and Caleb had dined in his home many times. To Judah's great delight, Caleb accepted the invitation.

When Caleb arrived the next evening, a familiar slave greeted him. To Caleb's surprise, the slave led him past the dining area and down into the basement, a large room that was used as scriptorium. It was well lit with torches and a table was set up with foods of a wide variety, including loaves of fresh bread, dates, grapes, figs, and dried fish. In addition to this bounty, it was clear there would be no shortage of wine.

A number of guests had already arrived, and Caleb recognized many of them. There was Simeon, a childhood friend of both Caleb and Judah, but he was always much closer to Judah. Simeon's face still bore the vicious scars and deformation from his beating by a Roman soldier. There was also Joseph and his cousin Samuel, again childhood friends with whom Caleb had not remained close. Samuel was Judah's best friend, and from the time they were children everyone had recognized their special bond. The rape of Samuel's sister by a Roman soldier, just months ago, had hurt Judah deeply. He couldn't speak of it without tears, and Caleb had heard him speak countless times of exacting justice for this great evil. Over the next half-hour the rest of the guests arrived, numbering a total of twelve. Solomon was not among them, and Caleb never saw him that night.

Over the course of the meal, it became clear to Caleb that nine of these men had been a part of this group for some time, while three, including himself, were newcomers. It was also clear that this meeting was social in nature. They made no plans and discussed no strategies. There was much talk about the hatred of the Romans, the need to drive them from the city, the growing anger of the people that was bound to break out soon in violence, and potential catalysts for just such a popular action. There was some talk of the popular Galilean prophet, Jesus. One had it on good authority that he was making his way to Jerusalem for the Passover, which was only weeks away. Some saw this as a great opportunity to find an ally in the fight against Rome, while others were skeptical that this prophet's aims aligned with their own. Judah claimed that whether he was an ally or not, his presence alone would create the potential for chaos. "A popular prophet, dead or alive, can move a people to act," he said. They only needed to be prepared for whichever way the wind might blow. It was decided that when he arrived, he would need to be monitored. One suggested the possibility of meeting with him and discussing his intentions or their common goals. All agreed this was a good plan.

Caleb thought the discussion surrounding Jesus was interesting and might be useful to pass along. But when the discussion turned to the recent ambush of five Roman soldiers, he thought he had truly struck gold. Joseph raised his glass and toasted to the first strike in the war against Roman oppression—the five Roman soldiers that fell to Jewish patriots. This led to a roar of cheers, which Caleb joined. Most of those present believed this victory demonstrated that devout and faithful men with a well-made plan could overcome the vaunted Roman soldiers. While no guest claimed to have participated in the ambush, Caleb perceived a sort of pride in the discussion that seemed strange for those who were not actually a part of it. Additionally, the guests exchanged glances that suggested they knew more about this attack then they were letting on. It was almost as if these men were both distancing themselves from the event and taking credit for it at the same time. Something was going on that Caleb couldn't fully perceive.

Clarity finally came from a comment made by Joseph. Someone pointed out the carelessness that came from Roman arrogance, and said that a vigilant people could use such carelessness to their advantage. Joseph then said loudly, "True words, my friends, and to think this recent attack began with drunk Roman soldiers talking too loudly in a tavern!"

Again, a roar of cheers erupted. Again Caleb joined in while his mind quickly connected the dots. Joseph's mother owned a tavern, and he worked there with her. No doubt he was the one who overheard these soldiers. And if he was the source of the news, then he had to have passed it on to those who executed the attack. And then, as if Caleb's eyes had opened for the first time, the whole truth hit him: all of them had been a part of the attack! He looked at Judah, who was quietly smiling around at his friends. It was then that Caleb knew his cousin was not only involved, but he was also their leader.

Caleb's mind reeled as he was walking home that night. He had always known that Judah was zealous for the future glory of his people, but he had never dreamed his zeal would lead him to this level of action. The night's revelations were truly alarming. The question now was what he would do. Surely his benefactor would want to know everything: the names of those at the dinner, who hosted it, their assessment of Jesus and plans to engage him, and especially their role in the deaths of five Roman soldiers. Caleb knew he could not pass along all this information. He would not directly betray his kin and friends—he had told Aaron as much. He must filter all he had learned. He could offer information that was useful, but nothing that would lead to the arrest of Judah or his coconspirators —all of whom were Judah's friends.

He spent most of a sleepless night thinking about what he would report. By sunrise he felt he had reached at a good compromise, though he would present it as the totality of what he had gathered. That morning he switched the order of two pots on display in his front window, the agreed-upon signal that he had information to pass on. Today would be the first time he met with his contact for this purpose.

Shortly after he gave the signal, his contact entered the shop. He asked for a specific prearranged item, which Caleb said he had in stock. He then invited the man to come to the back of the shop to look over his inventory. When they were alone in the back of the shop, Caleb quickly gave his report. The talk of the prophet Jesus was growing in the city, and with it excitement over his coming. There was talk that members of a secret resistance movement were interested in meeting with this Jesus when he arrived, and that they hoped to find allies in him and his followers. Finally, he had heard from a reliable source that the attack on five Roman soldiers originated from information gained from drunken Roman soldiers talking too loudly in a tavern. His contact pressed him for more information about the attack, but Caleb said this was all he knew. He promised he would try to track down more information if he could. Thankfully, his contact seemed satisfied. He then pulled a piece of pottery off the shelf and walked to the front of the store with Caleb. He paid for the pottery, thanked Caleb for his service, and left the shop.

Caleb was surprised at how easy it was. The interaction was simple, had drawn no attention, and had not required him to betray anyone close to him. His contact had pressed a bit, but not excessively, and Caleb felt confident that the contact believed his claim that he had told him all he knew. If this was all his new role as an informant asked of him, he was pleased to do it. The reward was indeed well worth it, and the fact that his efforts were ultimately serving the goal of the peace of the city gave him pride in what he had done. Perhaps God had indeed answered his sister's prayers and shown favor on their house.

Four days after he had passed on information to his contact, Caleb was still planning his next move. Would his cousin have another meeting soon? He was due for another visit, and Caleb could then inquire about how he might become more involved in the movement.

A sharp knock at the shop's back door interrupted Caleb's thoughts. He opened it and was surprised to see his cousin staring up at him from the alleyway. Judah's eyes looked wild and full of panic!

Before Caleb could speak, Judah pushed him aside and shut the door behind him. He then closed the door to the front of the shop. "What is going on, Cousin?" Caleb asked. "Why are you so upset?" Judah was pacing back and forth, his hands grabbing his long curly hair.

"They have arrested Joseph and Simeon, and . . ." For a moment Judah lost his words, his face heartbroken. Finally he uttered the painful words, "and Samuel too." With these words a guttural sob came from his cousin as he fell to his knees.

Caleb placed a hand on his shoulder. "Calm down; it will be all right. When did this happen?"

In anger, Judah slapped Caleb's hand away, "All right? It will be all right? How could it be all right? They have arrested them for killing Roman soldiers, Caleb! They will be crucified for this!"

Caleb stepped back, holding up his hands. "I am sorry, Cousin! You are right; this is a horrible thing. But what do you mean they were arrested for killing Roman soldiers? What are you talking about?" Caleb knew he must not reveal what he had deduced at the dinner with Judah and his friends.

"Are you so dense, Caleb? It was *us*, those you ate dinner with last week. We ambushed and killed those Roman soldiers! I thought you guessed this already?"

Caleb tried to look bewildered. "No! I had not realized! I thought we were celebrating the successful work of others. You were involved in the attack? And Joseph and Samuel too?"

Judah looked back at him, tears still in his eyes. Regaining his composure, he said in a much calmer voice, "No, I am sorry, Cousin. Perhaps it was not that obvious. I had told them not to take credit for the ambush—I was not sure you would be ready for that. Now you know the truth."

"This is shocking news to me, Judah!" Caleb lied. "What can I do to help?"

Judah looked down, shaking his head. "I don't know. I just don't know what to do. It is all my fault. And what of the others? Will they be arrested next? No doubt they will do what they can to pry the rest of our names out of those they have arrested."

Caleb saw that Judah's concern was entirely for his friends, though he too was surely in great danger.

"How did this happen, Cousin? How did they know?" Judah's voice was filled with desperation.

Looking into his confused face, Caleb lied again: "I don't know. Who would have known outside of those involved? Would any of your company betray you?"

Judah shook his head. "No one knew but those involved, and not one would have betrayed our cause—I trust them all with my life." Then Judah asked, "You didn't tell anyone of our dinner, did you? Or of what we discussed?"

Caleb shook his head firmly. "No, Cousin. As you asked, I told no one. But was I the only one at the dinner who was not a part of your company?" Caleb asked, already knowing the answer.

"No," Judah said, "there were two others that were joining us for the first time, just like you."

"Do you trust them?" asked Caleb. "Could they have betrayed you?"

A perplexed look came over Judah's face. "Perhaps it is possible. But I can't imagine it. And now that I think of it, what could they have said? No one claimed to be involved in killing the soldiers—no one could have left with anything more than suspicions. You didn't even know! Would someone have reported on suspicion alone?"

"It is possible," Caleb said, praying his efforts to redirect suspicion would work. "And no doubt Rome would arrest on that suspicion alone."

Judah's head sank. "How could I have been so careless? This is all my fault."

"You don't know the truth yet, Cousin," Caleb replied. "Be careful not to jump to rash conclusions. Is there anything I can do to help?"

"Perhaps," Judah said. "We must warn the others, and quickly. They must have time to either flee the city or hide. Could you warn Nathaniel and Jacob for me? Both should be at their father's home."

Caleb knew the danger in this request, but he could not deny it. "Yes, Cousin, I will warn them. But you must think of yourself as well. Do not return home. Warn the others and hide yourself."

Judah embraced him. "Thank you. I knew I could count on you." The words stabbed Caleb's heart like a dagger as he watched the cousin he had betrayed depart into the alleyway behind the shop.

Caleb stood dumbfounded in the doorway. The happiness, confidence, and renewed faith he had been feeling moments ago had vanished, replaced by a sickening feeling of dread, guilt, and treachery. He didn't know how, but he knew it was his report that had resulted in the arrests.

How could I have been so foolish? How could I have thought I could filter information to protect my kin and friends? He didn't know what other information the authorities already possessed or how they might combine that information with his to deduce the identities of the conspirators. He had played a dangerous game and lost.

But as he was contemplating these questions, competing thoughts arose in his mind. *He* was not to blame for these arrests. *He* was not the one who attacked Roman soldiers. *He* did not engage in violent resistance that was bound to have violent consequences. These men had made their choice, and he had only passed on the basic origins of their plan. How could he be held responsible for what was to happen next?

With these thoughts he tried to push down his raging guilt, but he was not sure it was working. After a few moments, he told his sister he had to run a quick errand and headed to the home of Nathaniel and Jacob. Warning them was the least he could do.

PILATE

Pilate was already in a bad mood as he sat down to read his most recent correspondence. He had just come from the hippodrome in Caesarea, where he had failed miserably with his bets for the day. He was particularly angry because he had received tips on two races—one a two-horse chariot race and another the day's final four-horse race. Because he had done so poorly on the previous races, he had doubled down on the final race, only to see his chariot blow a late lead when one of its wheels came off. Although losing the money was painful, losing it to his arrogant friend Jason made it even worse. He wouldn't hear the end of it until next week's races.

He first read a report from one of his informants who was following the Galilean prophet, Jesus. Jesus had indeed headed south and was taking the eastern route, along the Jordan River. He had left Capernaum three days before and had made his way to the villages near the city of Pella, where this correspondence had been sent from. Pilate calculated that he was covering approximately ten miles a day. At that rate, he would cover the remaining distance in about four days, putting him near Jerusalem about a week and half before Passover. But if he decided to stay in certain cities longer than one night, his arrival would be delayed.

If Pilate was going to arrest this prophet, he was going to have to act quickly. The best plan would be to send soldiers to Jericho and have Jesus arrested there. It would be his last chance to arrest him outside Jerusalem, as most travelers would cover the distance between the two cities in one day.

"Lucien!" Pilate called for his chief aide, who appeared from around the corner and dutifully replied, "Yes, my lord, how can I be of assistance?"

"I would like you to send for Commander Cornelius," said Pilate. "I have an assignment I must discuss with him." Cornelius was the centurion responsible for the single cohort of soldiers stationed in Caesarea.

"Of course, my lord."

In less than twenty minutes, he had returned with Cornelius. Cornelius was thirty-five, only a few years younger than Pilate. He was an accomplished soldier and a well-respected commander. During his time in Judea, he had become quite enamored with the god of the Jews and had recently spoken to Pilate of his growing devotion. Pilate found this strange, but respected Cornelius enough to not interject his own opinion on the matter. Since Pilate's appointment to the region, he had established a good working relationship with Cornelius, and perhaps even a friendship. They dined together regularly and would often discuss both the political and military climate of the region.

"My lord, you called for me?" said Cornelius.

"Yes, Cornelius. There is an assignment I need to discuss with you. Not long ago, we spoke of the Galilean prophet, Jesus, and the potential threat he posed to the region."

"Yes, I know of the man," Cornelius replied. "At the time, you were watching him and had sent a request to Herod to look into the matter. Has the situation changed?"

"I am afraid it has," Pilate said gravely. "As you might have guessed, Herod gave lip service to my request but did nothing—the coward. Now this prophet has left Galilee and is headed south. All indications are that he intends to visit Jerusalem for Passover. If he indeed has revolutionary ambitions, his presence in Jerusalem could be disastrous. Arresting him in the city during Passover might create as much trouble as he might cause on his own. Thus, he should never make it to Jerusalem. I want you to send soldiers to Jericho to intercept and arrest him there."

Cornelius hesitated for a moment, then replied, "Such arrangements can be made. A small cavalry unit could travel to Jericho within a day."

The centurion's hesitation was not lost on Pilate. "Why are you uncertain of my plan, Cornelius? Please speak freely. I count you a friend and have always respected your insights."

"My lord," Cornelius said cautiously, uncertain whether to trust the permission Pilate had granted. "You said *if* he has revolutionary ambitions his presence in Jerusalem would be disastrous. But how certain are you that he has such ambitions? From the reports I have heard, he has not endorsed violence, nor has he publicly proclaimed himself a messiah of any sort."

Pilate paused thoughtfully. "Yes, that is correct, Cornelius, but it is quite clear that he proclaims a new and coming kingdom of god to this region, and the people love him and are enraptured by this teaching. Such talk of a new kingdom is inherently subversive, as it implies the fall of our beloved Roman Empire. We cannot be ignorant of this. And while no talk of violence has made its way into his public teaching, he could no doubt rally these desperate people in revolt at a moment's notice. The threat is real, and we must not ignore it. I was reluctant to arrest the prophet John, and that reluctance was almost costly. I promised myself not to make the same mistake twice."

Cornelius nodded, paused a moment as if composing his thoughts, and said, "These are valid concerns, my lord. But if we arrest a popular prophet mere days before Passover, do we not ourselves risk retaliation? You are set to leave for Jerusalem in a matter of days. How will the city receive you with the shadow of this prophet's arrest hanging over you? It would raise the tension in the city even higher, making the situation extremely dangerous. This is a very difficult decision, my lord— one I do not envy having to make. Both courses of action come with risk, and I will faithfully execute the duty you give me. Of this you can be sure."

"I have no doubts about that, Cornelius, and I appreciate your counsel," said Pilate. "I will need to think on these things. For now, prepare for the mission. I leave the details to you. You will hear from me on this matter within the day."

"Consider it done, my lord." Cornelius quickly left the room to make the necessary preparations.

Pilate turned to his aid, Lucien. Lucien was fifty-five years of age, a true Roman, born in the great city itself and deeply committed to it and the empire it had built. "What is your opinion in this matter, Lucien?" Pilate already knew well what he would say but wanted to hear him say it anyway.

"Permission to speak freely, my lord?" Lucien replied.

"Of course, Lucien, speak your mind."

Lucien straightened himself. A strong, defiant look appeared on his face. "Rome is the greatest empire this world has ever known, my lord. It has brought peace and prosperity to the entire world, even to this ungrateful region of Judea. Any threat of sedition, any attempt to subvert this great work of our people, no matter how great or small, ought to be utterly destroyed. If this man speaks of a new kingdom, then he is clearly not a friend of the current one—and if not a friend, then an enemy. In my estimation, you cannot put him on a cross fast enough, along with any who follow him. Yes, I know this might disrupt the peace of Jerusalem and perhaps the entire region. The people might riot and revolt. But what of it? Why should we fear this result? Such actions are only the manifestation of the truth in their hearts—the hate and ungratefulness they harbor within. Let it be revealed openly to the world, and then let the legions of Rome come and crucify them all! Let their city and their temple burn! Why should we step cautiously around them, always concerned about offending them? We are Rome and they are not! I say arrest this Jesus and let the chips fall where they may." It was clear that the freedom to voice these thoughts brought Lucien deep satisfaction.

And Pilate admired the speech, particularly its passion. Lucien's words resonated with many of Pilate's own feelings and justified his own plan of action, which was why Pilate asked to hear from Lucien; a little self-indulgence is good for the soul every now and then. This was the response of a true Roman, the same that Pilate would have received from many patriots back in Italy.

But unfortunately, its sentiment did not reflect the will of the imperial family. They desired peace and stability in the region. While Lucien might have been right about Rome winning any war against Jewish revolutionaries, it would come at a high cost. War was expensive, and war in one part of the empire meant vulnerability in another. And what if a rebel state of Judea allied with the Parthians? Such an alliance would prove troublesome indeed.

For all these reasons, Pilate could not fully embrace his aid's advice. "I share many of these sentiments, Lucien, and appreciate your honesty. It did my soul good to hear the deep convictions of a Roman patriot. And that is what you are." He could see the pride rise in his aid's eyes. "Unfortunately, the cause of peace is a priority for our great imperial family. I am afraid we must follow a different course of action."

"Indeed, my lord," replied Lucien, nodding firmly. With that, he took his leave.

The next piece of correspondence on Pilate's desk was from Caiaphas. Perhaps it would prove useful in making his decision. He read the letter carefully and was once again struck by what an excellent politician this high priest was. Two objectives emerged from the letter, the first more subtle than the second. Caiaphas implied that Pilate's idea of bringing three hundred additional soldiers to Jerusalem might be misguided. Would the presence of these soldiers ensure greater peace given the tension their entrance and presence would create? Caiaphas claimed to be unsure, though it was clear to Pilate he was quite sure. But Pilate was quite sure as well—the additional show of force was necessary and nonnegotiable. Any deterrent to violent resistance was necessary, and the additional soldiers would accompany him to Jerusalem. Case closed.

On the second objective, Caiaphas was far more direct. He argued strongly, though respectfully, that arresting this prophet would be a mistake that would cast a dark and dangerous shadow over the coming Passover celebration. He shared many of the concerns already expressed by Cornelius, but perhaps his strongest argument was that the best possible outcome would be Jesus coming to Jerusalem as a peaceful prophet seeking to celebrate this great festival. They could not yet rule out this outcome, and as it was the best opportunity for peace, they should take no action against Jesus until it became clear he was a threat. The greatest mistake would be creating a threat to peace where no threat exists. If Jesus did turn out to be a revolutionary, arresting him in Jerusalem might prove more challenging, but the risk of violent retaliation was not that much greater than it would be if they arrested him prior to his arrival.

Pilate found all these arguments compelling, save the last one. He did not believe the danger of arresting Jesus prior to his arrival in the city was about the same as that of arresting him in the city. The latter brought far greater danger. At Passover the city would be a tinderbox, only needing a spark to set it ablaze. Arresting Jesus in the city could be just such a spark. While arresting him prior to his arrival might bring anger, Pilate did not believe it carried with it the danger of arresting him in Jerusalem.

But Pilate kept coming back to Caiaphas's claim that the greatest mistake would be creating a threat to peace where no threat exists. Pilate had created such a threat in the past and vowed never to do it again. It was Caiaphas who had helped him see clearly then. Would he not listen to the wisdom of this priest again? Just recently, Caiaphas had advised a light touch in the investigation of the death of five Roman soldiers.

In the end, he had been right. They had made arrests, with no apparent threat to peace.

This tipped the scales. Pilate would not prevent Jesus from coming to Jerusalem. He drafted a note to Cornelius telling him not to send soldiers to Jericho.

This priest had better be right, he thought.

FOUR

THE CRISIS

CALEB

It had been almost a week since the arrests of Joseph, Simeon, and Samuel. Caleb had not seen Judah again. According to Judah's sister, he had left Jerusalem on an urgent family matter, and it was uncertain when he would return. Caleb knew this was untrue, though he did not know if Judah's sister knew this or if Judah had actually left the city. As far as Caleb knew, there had been no additional arrests, and he had not heard any rumors of soldiers looking around for additional conspirators. The people expected Roman authorities to punish these men soon, though most believed they would not do so until after the Passover.

The arrests had increased the tension in the city. People claimed that such seemingly insignificant men with no history of violence could not actually be responsible for the deaths of five Roman soldiers. Most believed that these men were peripheral at best to the attack, and that Roman authorities had arrested them in an attempt to find the true culprits.

Since the day of the arrests, Caleb's soul had been conflicted. At times he felt extreme guilt, but at other times he was able to justify his actions and assuage his conscience. Today—at least for this moment—he was living in the latter. No doubt this first day of the Passover week, a beautiful spring day, helped. The city streets were bustling with activity, and excitement was in the air. While some pilgrims had arrived earlier, this was generally the day of arrival for most traveling to the city to celebrate the festival. The city with a population of approximately sixty thousand people would swell to almost three hundred thousand. While this influx of people certainly caused headaches for the city rulers and officials, it brought great energy and excitement for the common people. A majority of those making pilgrimage had family and friends in the city, and therefore this was a time of reunion and celebration.

Caleb himself had many friends arriving whom he was eager to see again. He also had family that he would be hosting in his own home: his aunt, Elizabeth, along with her son, Jacob, and daughter, Mary. Jacob was a year older than Caleb, and Mary was a year younger than his sister Miriam. Their families had been extremely close, but Elizabeth and her children moved to Damascus when she remarried after the death of her first husband. They always returned to Jerusalem for the Passover and stayed through the Feast of Weeks, a celebration of firstfruits and the giving of the Torah, held fifty days later. Because of his responsibilities in Damascus, Elizabeth's second husband rarely made the trip with them.

Jacob and Caleb had grown up like brothers and were inseparable throughout their youth. They both worked in the pottery shop, and Caleb's father took care of his sister's family up until her remarriage. When they moved it was hard on Caleb, who lost his closest friend. It also made the death of Caleb's father, only one year later, much harder. Though the distance had been difficult, the two regularly corresponded and usually saw each other at least twice a year. Their relationship was one on which time and distance seemed to have no effect. With this reunion in front of him, he couldn't allow himself to be mired in guilt.

He closed the shop at noon. After a quick lunch with Miriam, they headed out to greet their family. The march of pilgrims into the city was exciting. Many pilgrims would sing and dance, and those at the gates waiting for family usually joined in as a group approached the city entrance—whether they knew them or not! Even for those who did not join in, the sight of family and friends reuniting was a joyous one.

As was their tradition, Caleb would meet Jacob and his family at the Shushan Gate on the eastern side of the city, across from the Mount of Olives. Travelers from the north would usually come south along the Jordan River to Jericho before turning west toward Jerusalem. They would pass through the village of Bethany, come down the Mount of Olives into the Kidron Valley, and then ascend Mount Zion, where Jerusalem's glorious temple sat.

The current temple was the result of a massive remodeling of the one originally built by the Jewish leader Zerubbabel after the return from Babylonian exile five hundred years earlier. The remodel was undertaken by the late Roman client king, Herod "the Great," whose sons, Herod Antipas and Philip, still ruled on Rome's behalf in northern Israel. While he was a paranoid despot, Herod's acumen for building was undeniable. The remodeling of the Jerusalem temple was, without question, his magnum opus. Before Rome granted Herod power in the region, Zerubbabel's temple was nothing special to behold. It was a shell of the earlier temple built by King Solomon on the same site, Mount Zion (at times called Mount Moriah). Both had occupied only a fraction of the mountaintop. But in order to gain favor with the people and recognition for himself, Herod began a massive building program, turning the entire mountain into a platform for the temple to stand on.

While the people of Jerusalem hated Herod, they loved the temple he had built them. Every Jew in the city knew its dimensions. The enormous retaining wall around the Temple Mount was 1600 feet north to south and 900 feet east to west. The walls were a hundred feet at their highest point and sixteen feet thick. And its stones—oh, those great stones of the retaining wall! Caleb could hear the words of his father when he was just a young boy: "Five hundred tons, my son! Nothing could shake a foundation stone that size!"

The retaining wall was impressive, but the true beauty was the temple that sat within it. It was made of marble that glistened beautifully in the sunlight, as did the ornate golden overlays that adorned it. At times the beauty was almost blinding—as if the glory of Israel's God was emanating from within. It was not quite centered on the Temple Mount but sat a bit to the north. It ran 480 feet east to west and 200 feet north to south, standing fifty feet at its highest point.

Most of the Temple Mount consisted of a massive open courtyard that was not technically a part of the temple itself. This courtyard was named the "court of the Gentiles" because it was open to anyone, Jews as well as Gentiles. Separating the court of the Gentiles from the temple proper was a fifteen-foot wall with multiple gates. Only Jews who had undergone proper purification could pass through these gates. The wall was engraved with warnings in both Greek and Aramaic that any Gentile or unclean Jew who passed through the gates would be sentenced to death. For this crime—and this crime alone—did the Roman governor grant Jews the power over life and death.

The Shushan Gate, where Caleb and Miriam were headed, was named after the capital city of Persia. This name honored the nation that allowed the Jews to return to their ancestral home and rebuild their temple. The gate depicted, ever so ornately, the royal palace of that great city. For this reason, it was often referred to as the "Beautiful Gate." Through this gate one would enter directly into the outer courtyard of the temple, the court of the Gentiles. Consequently, to reach this gate from inside the city, one had to enter the western side of the Temple Mount and cross the entire courtyard.

As Caleb expected, the outer courtyard and its beautiful porticoes were bustling with activity. Newly arrived pilgrims were exchanging their Greek and Roman currency for that which was acceptable for use in the temple. That currency was then used to buy animals for sacrifice, food from local vendors, souvenirs from local artisans, and even payment for guided tours of the temple grounds. Some complained that the exchange rate was unfair, a complaint that Caleb knew on occasion had merit. But he was also a businessman and knew that the temple had expenses beyond what most could likely imagine. While some complained, most understood this to be the business of the temple. Priests of varying ranks were also moving about the area directing traffic, answering questions, and facilitating regular temple tasks. The increased number of people meant a need for additional priests.

Making their way through the hustle and bustle took a while. They declined at least five offers for a guided tour of either the temple or city. Twice Miriam stopped to admire the work of another potter and ask about sculpting techniques, both times causing Caleb to think he had lost her in the crowd. After the second time he snapped at her, saying they didn't want to miss their family's arrival. To this she simply smiled, told him to relax, and that they had plenty of time. This response only frustrated him more. He hated when she pointed out how uptight he could be—more often than not, she was right. And she turned out to be right again. They arrived at the gate at least an hour before their family arrived. Thankfully, Miriam didn't rub it in.

The early arrival gave them a chance to enjoy watching the pilgrims coming up the road singing and dancing. They knew each song, and they sang them with all gathered there—songs of God's faithfulness, his holy dwelling, and his deliverance. While Caleb's faith had waned of late, he couldn't help but sing these songs he had known since he was a child. Watching the reunion of family and friends was good for his soul: the kisses and embraces, the old jokes followed by laughter, the grandparents meeting grandchildren for the first time, and the tears of joy that accompanied it all. He loved his people, and he loved how much they loved each other. Caleb even joined some of these reunions as he recognized friends arriving to the city.

While caught up in one of these reunions, Caleb noticed a commotion brewing around him. Many people were speaking excitedly and moving to the front of the gate. Miriam pulled on his arm. "Come on Caleb, we need to see this. The prophet from Galilee is coming!" He suddenly understood, and together they worked their way to the front of the gate—not an easy task.

At first, Caleb saw a large crowd of people on the road moving across the Kidron Valley toward the city. The crowd was at least a hundred, maybe more. It grew as he watched, with some people running down from the city to join it and others catching up with it from behind. They were singing and shouting, but from this distance Caleb couldn't make out what the people were saying.

As the crowd drew closer, he made out a man at the center who was riding what looked to be a horse. The people near him were taking off their coats and laying them down in front of him. Others were waving what looked like palm branches and laying them down along with the cloaks. The striking scene reminded Caleb of the stories he had heard about the great deliverer, Simeon Maccabeus, entering the city of Jerusalem. Was this really happening?

As the crowd drew closer, it became clear that the man was riding not a horse but a donkey. He could finally hear what the crowd was saying. The most dominant sound was the chanting of "Hosanna"—a declaration of coming salvation! But others were shouting, "Hail the Son of David," "Blessed be the coming kingdom of David," and "Blessed is the king who comes in the name of the Lord!" He couldn't believe what was happening! This prophet was entering the city as a king, as a conquering messiah and deliverer of Jerusalem!

While others were rushing to join the crowd, Caleb slowly stepped back. Dread filled him. He looked around and saw four Roman soldiers stationed at the gate, frantically talking with each other. As he watched them, two remained at the gate while two ran in the direction of the Antonia fortress, which was adjacent to the northern retaining wall of the Temple Mount. It was the headquarters of Roman military power in Jerusalem. The remaining two soldiers made no movement but stood tensely, watching the crowd move closer. A number of others looked shocked and afraid, with some deciding to leave the scene altogether.

Caleb's mind was racing. What did this mean? What would be the consequence? He expected at any moment to see more Roman soldiers storming to the gate to bring this display to an end and arrest Jesus. But none came.

The crowd was a mere thirty feet away now, and he could see Jesus clearly. He was smiling and touching the hands of those who reached out to greet him. He wore the common robes of a peasant. He bore no special decoration, nor did he appear to be carrying any sort of weapon. His face was weathered, but not old in appearance. He had an unkempt beard that could not conceal a warm smile. His eyes were kind and his face warm and sincere. He seemed unconcerned about the political gravity of the situation that surrounded him. When he was about ten feet from the gate, he signaled two men to help him dismount from the donkey. They led the animal back down the road away from the city. The crowd pressed in on him and swallowed him up as it moved through the gate into the outer courtyard of the temple.

Caleb was startled by someone grabbing his shoulders and shouting his name over the noise of the crowd. The sight of his cousin Jacob jolted him out of his concern for the Galilean prophet, reminding him of the reason he was at the Shushan Gate. The joy and excitement of seeing Jacob overcame the dread in his heart. They embraced, kissed each other on the cheek, and exchanged warm words of greeting. As they were doing so, Miriam suddenly appeared with Aunt Elizabeth and Cousin Mary. It was a joyful and happy reunion.

"When did you arrive?" asked Caleb. "I didn't see you coming up the road."

"We were in the crowd with the prophet Jesus!" Cousin Mary replied.

"You likely saw us coming, then, even if you didn't!" said Jacob with a smile, followed by a laugh.

The fact that his family was a part of this dramatic entrance quickly sobered Caleb, though he tried not to let his face reveal his concern. It was awkward to suddenly realize that those he loved most dearly held a surprisingly different perspective than his own. Trying to hide his concern and surprise, Caleb replied, "Ah, so you were a part of the dramatic entrance? No wonder I didn't see you in all that commotion!"

"Wasn't it all so exciting?!" asked Mary.

"It most certainly was!" replied Miriam—a response that surprised Caleb, but he wasn't sure why. "Did you travel with him all the way from the north?" his sister asked excitedly.

"Oh, no," said Jacob. "We first saw him with his followers in Jericho four days ago. As you know, we always stay there a day or two with my father's kin. When we arrived, we heard rumors that the prophet Jesus had arrived in Jericho that same day and would be teaching in the synagogue the following morning. We had heard of him even in Damascus, yet he had never been there. We were eager to hear him, so we decided to get up early to go to the synagogue. And it is a good thing we arrived early, as it seemed the entire town had the same idea. The synagogue was filled to capacity with an overflow surrounding it!"

"But it was worth it!" said Mary. "He was wonderful! His words were kind and gracious and spoken with such charisma. He spoke passionately of a new age about to dawn for God's people and a new work that God would soon be doing in this world—work that would bring justice and peace to the poor and the longsuffering. The kingdom of God is near, he said, and people need to prepare their hearts for it by forgiving one another, sharing with those in need, and extending compassion to those on the margins of our community. The kingdom of God is open to all who embrace it, he said!"

"It was truly powerful, my cousin," said Jacob with deep sincerity. "I was not sure what to expect, as I had heard so many different rumors. But the way he spoke and the things he said moved my spirit deeply. He never openly claimed to be the one God had sent, but the way he spoke seemed to claim it with every word. Many who heard him felt the same way, though there were some prominent Pharisees who were deeply

offended by him. Apparently, the night before he had celebrated a dinner at the home of a chief tax collector, which
must have put them off. If I am honest, to hear that he was
the guest of such a person was off-putting to me at first. But
when I heard him the following morning, it all seemed to
make sense."

Caleb's mind was trying to take all this in. "So, did you stay
with him from that point on?"

"No," his aunt replied. "Apparently, he left the city the next
day, early in the morning. We heard he wanted to reach
Bethany before the Sabbath—"

"But we were able to join him and his group when we went
through Bethany this morning," Mary interrupted. "Jacob
asked one of his disciples if we could travel with them the
short distance to Jerusalem, and he welcomed us. And as you
saw, we were not the only ones! Many others wanted to join
us as we were leaving. The group got larger and larger as we
got closer to the city gate!"

"Did he ride on the donkey all the way from Bethany?"
Caleb asked.

"Yes," Jacob replied. "Two men brought it to him right before
he left. I think they were from among his closest disciples."

"So he *arranged* to enter the city on a donkey?" asked Caleb,
incredulity in his voice.

"Yes!" both Mary and Jacob replied.

"Did he also instruct people to wave branches and place
their cloaks in front of him?"

"Of course not!" replied his aunt. "That just, well . . . well it
just started to happen, I guess. Why so many questions, Caleb?"

"I . . . well . . ." Caleb stammered. "I am just curious, I guess.
It was quite a spectacle, and I guess . . . well, I guess I am just
trying to understand it all. What does it mean? This man entered

the city like one of the great Maccabean conquerors to shouts of 'salvation' and declarations that he is God's appointed deliverer." They all looked back at him, nodding and affirming what he had just said. He stared blankly, stunned they were not more worried about what they had just taken part in.

"Isn't it all so exciting?" exclaimed Mary.

"Exciting?" Caleb asked. "Well, it certainly created a lot of excitement yes, but . . . but . . ."

"But what?" asked Elizabeth with a look of confusion on her face.

"But it is also dangerous, isn't it?" Caleb asked cautiously. "As he was coming near the gate, two Roman soldiers ran off toward the Antonia. I half expected them to return with two hundred more, arrest the prophet, and disband the crowd."

There was a moment's pause as his family thought about what he had just said. Jacob broke the silence. "Yes, I guess in the back of my mind I knew that what we were doing, and what *he* was doing, was dangerous in a way. But in the moment, it just didn't seem to matter. After I heard him teach and watched him, escorting him into the city in that way just seemed right, and so . . . so I joined in."

"Yes, I think that says it all quite well," said Elizabeth. "We will do what we must, and the Romans will do what they must!" she added defiantly.

Those words sent a chill through Caleb, who couldn't hide his surprise at his aunt's response. "I am not sure you are thinking this through to its likely conclusion. I fear what the presence of this prophet will do to our city."

Jacob took him by his shoulders and looked him in the eye. "My cousin, have faith. If he is God's anointed, all will be well. If he is not, God will make that clear. Do not fear—rely on your faith!"

Caleb caught a quick glance from his sister, who was aware that he had not yet expressed his recent doubts to his cousin and closest friend. Now was certainly not the time. Caleb sought a way to end this awkward exchange, thinking that perhaps with this visit it would be harder to pick things up where they last left off. "Yes. Yes, of course you are right, Jacob. My curiosity and worry got the best of me. Our God must be trusted," he forced himself to say. He wanted to get them out of temple grounds as quickly as he could. "Now let's get you and your things back to the house. It is time to settle in and take some refreshment. There is much to catch up on!"

As they began to exit the gate, they saw a large crowd gathered and a great commotion in the direction he and his sister had initially come from. Wanting to stay away from any more excitement caused by the prophet, Caleb turned in the opposite direction, saying, "It's less crowded this way. It will make for a quicker route home." The others followed, though they found themselves going against the flow of traffic moving toward the great commotion behind them.

Caleb couldn't get off the Temple Mount fast enough. He would now have plenty of information to share with his contact, though he rightly guessed that the public nature of these events undermined his chance of presenting anything new.

Cheers went up behind him as he and his family finally reached an exit from the Temple Mount. While the others looked back, he did not want to know what had happened and urged them forward.

ELEAZAR

Eleazar was in the temple scheduling priestly duties for the coming week when he was interrupted by loud knocking on the door of his private chambers. Startled and annoyed, he opened the door to see a wide-eyed and frantic young Levite named Malachi standing before him, saying nothing. "Is something the matter, Malachi? Why have you come? What is wrong?"

"It, it's . . ." he stammered.

"What is it, boy? Loosen your tongue!"

"The . . . the . . . the prophet Jesus, sir, he . . . he has arrived!" said Malachi nervously.

"He is here in the city? When did he arrive?" Eleazar was surprised by this news.

"Just now, sir. He hadn't even made it to the gate before I ran to tell you." Malachi still could not seem to catch his breath or gather his wits.

"All right, thank you for informing me, Malachi. Though I am not sure his mere arrival is worth bothering me in my private chambers. If his presence brings about any urgent news, let me know immediately." Eleazar started to turn around, but to his surprise, Malachi grabbed his shoulder. This was not something a Levite would do a high-ranking priest, and it brought a flash of anger from Eleazar.

Malachi recoiled slightly but continued. "But . . . but, it already has, sir! His arrival itself, sir, and *how* he arrived, sir!"

"What do you mean? In what manner did he arrive?" It began to dawn on Eleazar that something serious might have already happened.

"As . . . as a king, sir! His entrance into the city was like that of a king, sir." Fearing another flash of anger, Malachi flinched as he said these last words.

But his words did not bring anger—merely confusion. Eleazar was having a hard time wrapping his mind around what the Levite was saying. "What?! What do you mean he arrived as a king? I don't understand."

Malachi began to calm down. He took a moment to gather himself and then began to explain what he had witnessed. "He approached the city from Bethany, sir, intending to enter through the Beautiful Gate. But he approached the city riding on a donkey, sir, with a great crowd of people—hundreds of people—escorting him into the city. They placed cloaks and palm branches on the ground in front of him, and they were waving palm branches, as they were all shouting and cheering."

The news was stunning. "What were they shouting, Malachi? Tell me!"

"They were crying out 'Hosanna,' sir, and calling this prophet a king, a son of David who would bring the kingdom of David. It reminded me of the stories I have heard about the Maccabees, sir. Jesus entered the city like the great conqueror Simeon, and the people acted like he was one." It was obvious that the event had made quite an impression on Malachi, who remained wide-eyed in his recounting of it.

Apart from an outbreak of violence, this news was indeed as bad as Eleazar could imagine. His mind was racing. How would Pilate respond to this? Did he already know? Was he already preparing a violent response? He would have to get this news to his father, and quickly.

"Where is the prophet now, Malachi?"

"I don't know sir," Malachi replied. "I left the gate before he even entered the city, but I am sure he has entered by now. He may be in the temple courtyard, or he may have gone into the city itself."

Eleazar realized that there was no time to lose; he must inform his father of this news immediately. "Go quickly and take this news to my father! He is at his home. Do it now, and don't let anything delay you. Do you understand?"

"Yes, of course, sir!" Malachi replied.

He turned to leave, then turned back when Eleazar called his name. "You have done well to bring this to me immediately Malachi. I will not forget it."

The Levite gave a nervous smile. "Yes, sir, thank you, sir." He ran to tell Caiaphas.

Eleazar quickly left his private chambers and made his way out of the temple proper to the courtyard of the Gentiles. If the prophet was still here, he wanted to witness him with his own eyes and see what he was doing. As he exited the south side of the temple, he heard a great commotion and a roar of cheers. The source of the noise was a large crowd to his left, maybe fifty feet away. He moved in that direction, staying close to the dividing wall between the temple and the outer courtyard. Although he wanted to see what was happening, he did not want to draw attention to himself.

He saw a stirring in the middle of the crowd. Men were shouting, "Make room! Move back!" Slowly the people responded and the crowd began to part. Then from the crowd a man emerged, and Eleazar recognized him as the man he had seen a year or two before, teaching a small group of people near the pools of Bethesda—it was the prophet Jesus. He was of average height, about that of Eleazar himself. He had on the simple garments of a peasant. His hair was dark and curly, and he had a dark unkempt beard. He was altogether quite plain looking, with nothing in his physical appearance that seemed impressive or would set him apart from any other man in the crowd. *How could such a simple-looking man be such a threat to the peace of this great city?* Eleazar thought.

Jesus walked through the crowd into an open area in the courtyard. He appeared to be surveying the money changers, those selling animals, and those selling souvenirs. It seemed all eyes in the courtyard were upon him. Would he do something? Say something?

Suddenly he moved to the tables where people were exchanging Roman or Greek coins for Jewish or Tyrian coins. The people in line waiting to make their exchange watched Jesus closely, as did the money changers themselves. In one quick movement, he grabbed one of the tables and violently turned it over. Papers and coins went flying! All stared at the prophet in stunned silence, mouths gaping open. Without a moment's hesitation, he turned to his right and flipped over another table.

Eleazar noticed that the local temple guards had gathered nearby and were looking at the scene in shock, not knowing what to do. He hoped they would have the wisdom to do nothing, as any sort of resistance toward the prophet at this point could easily turn this excited crowd into an angry mob. Jesus then turned in the direction of those selling animals. Seeing what had just happened, men stepped in front of their booths to protect them. Jesus stopped in front of them and did not move for what felt like an eternity but was no more than a minute. The crowd stared in stunned silence.

Then Jesus stepped back into the middle of the courtyard, looked around at everyone, and said loudly, "The leadership of this most holy place has failed us and the God they claim to serve!"

He paused as murmurs spread through the crowd, then continued. "Pagans have appointed our leading priests, and they use their appointment to increase their own wealth!"

Eleazar had heard such critiques before, and as such the words themselves bothered him little. The people often complained about the wealth of his family and other leading priests. The envy of the masses was not surprising. But this time the growing crowd and the pall of anger that rested over it was a different matter. His anxiety was rising.

The prophet continued his rant. "They grow fat, eating fine foods and living in luxury while the people of the city, their own people, struggle to survive!"

Now cries of full-throated support broke forth, and a deep fear seized Eleazar. Would this prophet light the spark of rebellion here and now?

He raised his hand, and slowly the din of the crowd faded. Then he looked specifically in the direction of Eleazar and continued speaking:

"As in the days of Jeremiah, these priests are bandits. They hide in this temple, thinking it will protect them from God's judgment. But the kingdom of God is coming, and it will be no respecter of this place!"

The crowd erupted with cheers at these final words. He moved toward them, and the crowd parted to let him pass through. A smaller group, perhaps his disciples, fell in behind him. Eleazar kept on watching them as they made their way back to the Shushan Gate and exited the city.

The entire horrifying scene took no more than five or ten minutes, but it seemed like an eternity to Eleazar. While stunned at what had unfolded before him, Eleazar was also relieved that the crowd had not been turned into a rioting mob.

In his twenty years as a priest, he had never witnessed such a direct affront to the temple and its leadership or a more imminent threat of violence in the city. His mind was racing as he tried to wrap his mind around the political ramifications of the prophet's actions. He had entered the city as a victorious king, an act that both challenged the authority of Rome and jeopardized the peace of the city. Additionally, he had entered the temple courtyards, caused a violent disruption, and not only challenged the authority of the temple and its leadership but also almost brought the people to the point of violence. King Herod had burned men alive for such a disturbance in the temple! In less than an hour this man had, in the eyes of Rome, committed two capital crimes. The peace of the city was indeed at great risk.

Jesus' intentions now seemed quite clear, and these were the very intentions Pilate had feared. They were the reason the governor had wanted to arrest Jesus before he reached the city, but Caiaphas had convinced him not to. Eleazar shook his head at this thought. Pilate would be furious. It was looking like his father had made a rare and tragic mistake in judgment. He could only hope it was not a fatal one.

PILATE

Pilate sat at his private desk, fuming. A messenger from the Antonia fortress had just delivered news about the prophet Jesus' dramatic entry into the city and his defiant act of protest in the temple courtyard. It was a complete and utter disaster—the very thing Pilate wanted to avoid! But this was far worse than he could have even imagined. He thought this prophet might slowly rally the people to his cause, stir them up throughout the week, and finally attempt to lead them in some demonstration against Rome's power. But this man took a completely different approach. He flaunted his ambitions from the very beginning and did so in one of the boldest ways imaginable. *At least secrecy and the element of surprise will not be weapons to fear with this messianic aspirant*, Pilate mused sarcastically.

In a way, the strategy was quite brilliant. In openly proclaiming his ambitions, this prophet put Pilate in a bind. Pilate would obviously need to remove the threat to keep the peace, but how would he do it and *still* keep the peace? From the report he had received, the masses had eagerly supported the prophet's actions in the temple courtyard. The people loved him! Any attempt to arrest him openly might spark a riot and jeopardize peace. Pilate was damned if he did and damned if he didn't! *Well played, prophet,* he thought. Perhaps he was even hoping to force Pilate's hand, inciting a violent military response to his entrance. The manner he went about entering the city certainly seemed like he had a death wish.

But if that was Jesus' plan, no one took the bait. Brutus, the commander of the Jerusalem cohort, had not sent soldiers onto the Temple Mount to arrest him. Brutus had received a report of the disturbance from the soldiers at the Shushan Gate, where Jesus had entered the city. In response, he had quickly organized three hundred soldiers to be ready to storm the court of the Gentiles if things began to turn violent; one hundred of them were archers who could rain down arrows on an unruly mob from the top of the courtyard porticos. From the fortress towers, he could observe the situation easily enough, but it never escalated to the point of mob violence, so he stayed his hand. Pilate was proud of the prudent way Brutus had handled the situation and would have to comment on it in his next letter to the legate of Syria, the supreme commander of Roman military forces in the region.

Why had he not arrested the prophet in Jericho?! Why did he listen to Caiaphas? All his best instincts told him to eliminate the threat before it became unmanageable, but he didn't listen to them. He wouldn't ignore those instincts again. Caiaphas was certainly correct that in not arresting Jesus, Pilate would ensure his own peaceful entry into the city. Just three days prior, Pilate had marched into the city with three hundred soldiers, and it didn't elicit a single peep from the onlooking crowds. But Pilate would have gladly traded such an entry for one with angry jeers and rotten figs to avoid the situation he found himself in now.

What would he do about this Jesus? It seemed the prophet clearly wanted a confrontation, and Pilate knew a confrontation must come. The open flouting of Roman power and claims of messianic deliverance could not go unchecked. But Pilate determined then and there that any confrontation would be on his terms and not the prophet's. This was a latrones match in which both parties were aware that Pilate had the advantage. But if Pilate was not careful, a victory could quickly become a loss. He needed to play out this game, and he knew that Roman power alone could not solve the problem. He was going to need the help of Jewish authorities to succeed. As much as the thought sickened him, he was going to need Caiaphas's help.

He was not only angry at Caiaphas but also saddened the priest had made the wrong call; perhaps he was even sorrowful at his own anger toward Caiaphas. But perhaps the priest who got him into this mess would prove useful in getting him out of it. As grave a mistake as it was, Pilate told himself that it was not beyond the possibility of redemption. All was not lost, and there must still be a way to both successfully eliminate the prophet Jesus and keep the peace. If both goals could be accomplished *and* Caiaphas was able to help him accomplish them, the high priest's error in judgment could be forgiven.

The thought of finding a new high priest certainly didn't appeal to Pilate. He worked well with Caiaphas. He liked Caiaphas. He did not like his alternatives, most of whom were either related to or in some way aligned with Annas, a former high priest. Pilate neither liked nor trusted Annas. He seemed disingenuous, always plotting ways to enhance the wealth and power of his own family.

Pilate did not look forward to his scheduled meeting with Annas the following day. Apparently, Annas had concerns about the way the city was being run by its current leadership, concerns Pilate might not be aware of. No doubt this would be another attempt to undermine Annas's son-in-law. While Pilate was angry at Caiaphas, he was not interested in whatever chicanery Annas might be up to.

On the other hand, a meeting with Caiaphas was both crucial and urgent. They needed to meet that very night. Thoughts of how to deal with this prophet were beginning to form in his mind, but the developing plot would require Caiaphas's help. He would no doubt dislike Pilate's proposal, but he would have little choice. It was Caiaphas's fault they were in this mess, and that gave the priest little leverage regarding how things would move from this point forward. The latrones match was on, and Caiaphas was going to be one of Pilate's most valuable pieces.

FIVE

THE PLOT

PILATE

As Caiaphas entered Pilate's private chambers, he certainly did not seem sheepish or hangdog. Instead, he bore all the dignity and confidence of a priest of his stature. While Pilate didn't expect anything different, it irritated him that there was no sign of contrition for the terrible mistake in judgment this priest had made. Though Pilate wouldn't overdo it, he needed to put this priest in his place.

Caiaphas had quickly responded to Pilate's request to meet and had agreed, without any pushback, to come to Pilate rather than vice versa. In the past, the place of meeting had often involved negotiation, as Jews had qualms about meeting in the homes of Gentiles. They couldn't jeopardize their absurdly precious purity. At first, this notion deeply offended Pilate—as if his very existence was a disease! But in the end, he decided he must move past the offense if he had any hope of successfully ruling these people. In fact, Pilate had gone to great lengths to accommodate any Jews who might visit him in Jerusalem. He maintained Jewish dietary customs, removing one of the great obstacles to Jewish-Gentile interaction. Given his earlier experience with bringing images into the city, he also avoided bringing anything that could be regarded as an idol into the palace. To be sure, no Jew would have gone this far to honor *his* sacred traditions.

Pilate paused dramatically before addressing the priest. "You are obviously aware of today's events. In light of them, it seems quite clear what the intentions of this prophet are. And I think we can now safely conclude that he did not intend a peaceful visit in order to participate in the Passover festival." Pilate's word's dripped with condescension and rebuke.

Looking back at Pilate as if untouched by his words, Caiaphas replied, "Yes, his intentions now seem clear. This was always a possibility, to be sure, but I still contend it was prudent to be certain before acting."

The gall of this man! thought Pilate. Even now he refused to admit his mistake and apologize for his poor counsel!

"Prudence be damned!" Pilate snapped angrily. "Former evaluations of what *might* have happened make no difference now! All that matters is what *did* happen. Rulers are not judged on the soundness of their decision-making process but on whether they made the right decision! Your decision was a gamble. You lost. That is all that matters now. You must own your decision and all the consequences that come with it."

Caiaphas lowered his head. Finally, a sign of contrition. "Your words are true, Pilate. My error was indeed a grievous one, and I will accept the consequences whatever they may be."

"Grievous it was," Pilate replied, his tone softening, "but it doesn't need to be fatal. You will indeed suffer the consequences for this mistake, but they are likely not the consequences you currently envision. At least not yet."

"Then you have a plan?"

"Yes, I have a plan," Pilate replied, "though you won't like it."

"Whether I like it matters little. I am obliged to do what I can to alleviate the problem I have aided in creating. When and where do you intend to arrest the Galilean prophet?"

"I don't."

"You don't?" Caiaphas's face could not hide his shock and confusion. "After what happened yesterday, I can only imagine it will get worse. Surely his boldness will increase rather than decrease. How can you allow this threat to continue?"

"Yes, that is indeed a danger," Pilate replied, "but arresting him might be just as dangerous. It is, in fact, what I think he wants me to do. Entering into the city in that manner was intended to provoke a specific response, would you not agree?"

"Perhaps," said Caiaphas, "but simply leaving such a response unchecked cannot be an option, can it? The signal it sends to the people is a dangerous one. It might even embolden them to follow this man into open revolt!"

"No, his actions cannot go unchecked," Pilate said. "That is certainly not an option."

"I don't understand," Caiaphas said. "If he is not arrested, how will you address the threat he poses?"

"I didn't say he would not be arrested," replied Pilate. "I said *I* won't be arresting him." A knowing smile crossed his lips.

Caiaphas's expression changed from perplexed to startled. Then, with an air of sadness and defeat, he said, "You mean *I* am to arrest him."

"Ah, now you take my meaning." Pilate's smile was still on his lips. "If I arrest this prophet with Roman soldiers, the risk for riot and revolt is indeed great. But if *you* arrest him, and *you* punish him, the risk might be mitigated significantly."

This idea clearly did not sit well with Caiaphas. "You may be right, but the people at the temple were certainly quick to embrace this prophet's critique of us. Many of them perceive us ranking priests as an extension of Rome. You appointed me as high priest, of course. Do you really think the people would be less angry if he were arrested by me rather than you?"

"I do—as do you," Pilate replied confidently. Caiaphas was trying to use the people's response to Jesus' critique of the priests as a shield, but Pilate wasn't fooled. "You and I both know the people's envy of wealth might be used to elicit cheers and jeers, but that it is not enough to lead to violence against the institution of the priesthood. Your own reputation with the people is quite favorable and another deterrent to any sort of significant retribution. On the other hand, I grant that any arrest of such a popular figure will carry some risk, but if planned and executed carefully, I believe it could work. At the very least, it would lower the risk of a violent response toward Rome. Given the current predicament we find ourselves in, that is as good as any other option we have."

"No doubt such a plan of action carries greater risks for me than for you," Caiaphas replied. "It will weaken my position with the people, and that weakness could be used against me by my political enemies."

Pilate nodded. "Yes, your political strength will be at risk, and your popularity with the people will likely take a hit. All actions have consequences, so let's hope this is the worst you face. Besides, what other choice do you have? If you refuse, I would have no choice but to remove you as high priest and find another who will do what I ask. Surely Annas would be willing to offer up one of his sons for the task." Pilate made a disgusted face. "I hardly *want* to do that. I like you, Caiaphas. I trust you. We work well together, and I have no desire to replace you." Pilate paused somewhat dramatically before his next words: "But I *will* if I must."

It was obvious that Caiaphas did not like what he was hearing. It was time to give him a bit of good news. "But what political harm does this really create? Perhaps your popularity among the people will decline, and it might make life a little harder on you in the short term. But I assure you here and now that you have my complete support, and thus your political power will be in no danger whatsoever. If anyone comes to me with complaints, I will continue to support you. Ultimately, I think the cost to you will be rather small considering the magnitude of the mistake in judgment you made."

Caiaphas sat in silence for a while. He clearly did not like the idea, but he had little choice.

When he finally spoke, he said, "I have worked hard to earn the reputation I have with the people of this city, Pilate. Unlike many high priests that have preceded me, most of the people trust and respect me. I do not take jeopardizing that trust and respect lightly."

"I know you don't, Caiaphas," replied Pilate. "And I know what I am asking you is not without cost. But I am also *relying* on this reputation you have with the people. It is this trust and respect they have for you that I am relying on as a buffer between your power and my own. I am counting on this trust to keep the people from seeing the truth: that your actions are a veil that allows me to accomplish my own purposes with limited consequence." These last words brought a genuine smile to Pilate's face.

Caiaphas nodded slowly. "You would use my reputation for your own means?"

"I would use any means necessary to keep the peace," Pilate said with conviction. "I was under the impression that you would do the same. Remember, if this current crisis results in rioting and upheaval, the emperor will remove us both from power—or worse."

Another long silence from Caiaphas before he finally spoke. "You are right, Pilate. Peace is the most important goal here, and it is far more valuable than my own reputation. It is my counsel that has put us in this situation, and it is only right that I do what I can to resolve it. Any cost I might incur, I no doubt deserve. Now let's work together to come up with a plan that will save this city from unrest and violence."

There it was. Pilate knew the priest would finally come to this conclusion. Initial resistance was to be expected, but in the end, reason would win him over. It actually took less time for Caiaphas to come to heel than Pilate had anticipated.

"I am happy to hear you say that, Caiaphas. Yes, let us form the plan. We have already agreed that you and your guards will arrest the prophet, but many issues remain unresolved. I think the most important issue is timing. When should we make an arrest?"

Again there was silence as Caiaphas considered the question. "Since the primary danger of arresting him is the people's protest, then it must take place when there are no crowds, when he is not in a public place, when arresting him cannot immediately ignite a violent reaction. In that case, I think arresting him at night would be our best option."

"My thoughts exactly," said Pilate. "If we are lucky, most people will not even be aware of his arrest, perhaps even that he has been sent to his execution, until after they wake up. Sleepy heads are slow to form angry mobs. This would also give us some time to shape the narrative of his arrest and execution in a way that reduces the danger of protest and rioting."

Caiaphas nodded. "Arresting and trying him in the night is certainly ideal, with his execution to follow in the early morning if possible. But there is one challenge to this plan: finding him. Today, he left the city in the late afternoon surrounded by a crowd of people. Several of my informants tried to follow him, but as the crowd left, it broke into pieces. Some headed on to Bethany, others headed to the northern part of the city beyond the wall, and still others to the east. At that point they lost him. If this man is committed to a public confrontation with Rome and a public arrest that could result in mob violence, he will no doubt make himself hard to find at night."

Pilate had not considered the challenge of finding Jesus at night, or how easily he could get lost in a crowd if he so desired. "Yes, this is indeed a challenge, but one we can surely overcome. You have often told me how helpful your informants are at providing you information to help keep the peace of this city. We need them *now*. Set them to the task of finding out where this Jesus is spending his nights. Without solving this problem, our chances of eliminating him *and* keeping the peace are quite low."

Caiaphas nodded. "I will organize our informants for this purpose tonight. Hopefully we can track down his evening whereabouts quickly, before the situation escalates."

"Good. But we have a little time," said Pilate. "I believe he wants us to be the aggressor, to be the catalyst that ignites the people to his cause. We will need to watch him closely and have a military response ready should things go wrong, but I think we have a number of days before we must act. I believe it is in our best interest to arrest him as close to the Passover feast as possible. All day Friday, people will be devoted to preparations. If we arrest him the night before and execute him the following morning, people's devotion to the feast should provide some protection against a violent response."

Caiaphas paused for a moment and a slight smile formed on his lips. "You are correct that the Passover preparations will offer us some protection. While some might allow their passions of rebellion to override a commitment to the festival, most would not—an astute observation of the Jewish mind, Pilate."

Pilate smiled and nodded. "Then our goals on timing are clear. The arrest must be at night, and if possible, the night before the Passover feast. This will give us the best chance of success."

"Agreed," said Caiaphas. "But I see another problem with your plan. If the idea is to execute this prophet, you are the only one in Judea who can sanction it. *We* can certainly arrest Jesus, but we have limited power after that. Ultimately, must it not be *you* who orders his death?"

Pilate caught a glimmer in Caiaphas's eyes, as if he had just discovered a fatal flaw that might give him a way out. But Pilate was well ahead of him. "Yes," he replied, "you will need my permission. But what you are perceiving as a problem, I would rather see as an opportunity."

Caiaphas looked confused. "I don't understand."

"Your need to ask my permission will give me the opportunity to publicly deny that permission."

Caiaphas's confusion persisted.

"Not *ultimately* deny it, of course," said Pilate. "But it will allow me the opportunity to make grand pronouncements of this man's innocence. Before a crowd of people, I will fight to save this man from the fate you so desire—and desire it you must. You will need a crowd of people demanding his death, and eventually I will wash my hands of the affair and grant your request. In this way, we will pit your desire for his death against Rome's legal finding of innocence. Hopefully my support of his innocence will pour a deluge on any potential fires of rebellion. Why should the people revolt against forces that want to save this popular and 'harmless' prophet? And surely they will not revolt against the leadership of their own priests, especially a high priest as respected as you."

As Pilate said these words, an expression of understanding slowly spread across Caiaphas's face. "This is a shrewd plan indeed, Pilate. It does squarely place the guilt of this man's death on my shoulders—no sharing of the load, as it were. But I guess that is the point."

"Indeed it is," Pilate said with a smile. "For peace, of course. But the ruse itself will only be successful if we are successful in the propagation of its narrative. We will need people waking up to this news in the taverns, hotels, markets, and every other public place. If only those at the trial are aware of our performance, it will be of little use to us."

"This will be challenging," said Caiaphas, "but I will work with my fellow priests to devise a plan for spreading our version of events. No doubt informants will be useful in accomplishing this task as well."

"I have no doubt you will solve this problem," said Pilate. "Now let us discuss the execution itself. I cannot be associated with it. You and your priests must oversee the prophet's death. No doubt he must be crucified, given the charges you will bring against him. You will need to lead the procession so that all know this is your will and done under your authority. I will grant you a handful of soldiers to oversee and perform the nasty task itself of course, but it must be clear that they are acting under your authority. It is attention to these details that will solidify the narrative we are creating."

It was obvious the idea of being so closely involved in a crucifixion was not appealing to Caiaphas, but he could see he had no choice in the matter. He agreed that such a course of action was necessary.

"Is it the prophet alone that we will arrest and execute?" asked Caiaphas. "What of his closest followers? If they are not arrested as well, might not the problems persist?"

Pilate had already given much thought to this question. "I believe we must leave his followers alone. Giving you the power to execute one or two men is believable, but if many are crucified, it will be much harder to distance Roman authority from the executions in people's minds. And while these followers could prove a threat, in my experience the sheep scatter when the shepherd falls. It seems none in the group have the status or charisma of the prophet himself, so it is unlikely they can rally the people in any significant way."

Caiaphas nodded. Undoubtedly he was thankful not to be overseeing the deaths of numerous fellow Jews.

"There is one more thing," Caiaphas said. "For me to convict this man of the crime you propose, I cannot do it on my own. The great council will be required for such a verdict."

Pilate had not considered this. "Will this be problem?" he asked. "You are the head of the council, are you not? And you do exercise significant control over it, don't you?"

"You are right that I am the head of the council," Caiaphas said. "But as you know, the council is composed of a rather diverse group of voices, with diverse commitments. Getting them to agree to convict this man might not be as easy as you think. But I will do all in my power to make it happen."

Pilate nodded. "I have no doubt you will." While this sounded like a vote of confidence, Pilate hoped the priest would hear the underlying message: *You had better, or things will not end well!*

Pilate saw it was time to wrap up this meeting. "I believe we agree on the major pieces of the plan. We will likely need to meet again to go over all the necessary details. Let us set our hands to what can be done between now and then."

Caiaphas nodded, but it was clear that the anticipated course of events laid heavily on him. "I know this plan is not easy for you," Pilate said. "But I think you agree with me that it is our best chance for peace. Perhaps now you see more than ever the challenges that come with power. Heavy is the crown, no?"

The priest said nothing, nodded again, and rose to leave. Suddenly Pilate remembered one more thing. "Caiaphas, before you leave there is one additional item to discuss. Tomorrow I am to meet with your father-in-law, Annas—at his request, not mine, I assure you. I believe he will attempt to undermine your position, but don't let that worry you. As I said before, you have my full support as high priest. But I wonder, to what extent should we make him aware of our plans? Can he be an asset in the preparations you need to make, or will he be a hindrance? I will do as you advise."

Caiaphas thought for a moment. "I think it best that you keep him in the dark. In fact, when the topic of the prophet Jesus arises, and no doubt it will, begin the ruse with Annas. Make him think that you don't feel Jesus is a threat, that you plan to do nothing. I think Annas will be a greater asset to me if he thinks you and I are at odds on this issue."

Pilate looked curiously at the priest, wondering what he planned to do with Annas. Regardless, Pilate admired his cunning. "I will do as you wish—the ruse begins tomorrow with Annas."

With nothing further to discuss, Caiaphas departed. Pilate sat quietly in his office, thinking of how the meeting had transpired and the plan they had formulated. He believed it could work, and that he just might escape this situation after all. Only one thing bothered him: again he found himself relying on the ability of the high priest.

ELEAZAR

A loud knock awoke Eleazar from a deep sleep the following morning. He had stayed up late waiting for Caiaphas to return from a meeting with Pilate, but he had grown weary and fallen asleep before his father had returned. The slave Philip had now come to his door to inform him that his father had called a meeting that would begin in half an hour.

Eleazar quickly dressed and took some breakfast. He then hurried across the house to his father's private chambers, where he found both his father and Uncle Aaron. Uncle Simeon and cousin Ezra had yet to arrive.

As he entered, his father greeted him with kiss. Unable to control his eagerness, Eleazar said, "Father, tell me of your meeting with Pilate. Was it successful? I tried to stay awake until your return last night, but the late hour overcame me. Was he angry? Does he plan to arrest the prophet?"

"Patience, my son," Caiaphas replied. "I will tell all when all have arrived."

"Yes, of course." Eleazar was mildly embarrassed at his impatience, but he did not have to wait long. Both Simeon and Ezra arrived in short order.

After they were seated, his father addressed them. "You are all aware of yesterday's events related to the actions of the prophet Jesus. He entered the city like a conquering king and quickly gathered a crowd, to which he spewed his hatred for us priests. His words against us bother me little; he is not the first prophet or teacher to speak ignorantly about us. Inciting a crowd against our wealth is low-hanging fruit for him, but I do not believe the people would revolt against us or our sacred institution. Most respect it too much, and we have worked hard to establish that trust. But the intentions of this prophet and his popularity with the people are another matter. They are indeed quite troubling and greatly jeopardize the peace of our city. If he can incite the people's anger over our wealth, he can no doubt incite their anger against Rome—and this possibility is truly dangerous. The people have no stomach for a civil war, but I fear their appetite for war with Rome has grown.

"As you know, last night I met with our governor, Pilate, to discuss these matters. Though not entirely pleasant, the meeting was ultimately profitable. We have formulated a plan for how we will handle this troublesome prophet. I warn you ahead of time that it might not seem favorable on first hearing, but in the end I believe you will come to see, as I have, that it is the best way forward."

Caiaphas then relayed his meeting with Pilate in detail. He was right: the plan did not seem favorable to anyone in the room, nor did they like Pilate's treatment of Caiaphas. Ezra and Simeon were indignant that Pilate could fault him for providing what at the time was clearly wise counsel. That the counsel turned out to be wrong hardly made it wrong at the time! They pointed out that it had been Pilate's own choice to listen to the advice.

Aaron was distressed that Pilate would demand Caiaphas take responsibility for both arresting and executing the prophet. This would greatly damage their reputation with the people, and Annas would no doubt use that against them. While Pilate might be promising his support now, would he continue it when the people brought him their complaints or when Annas pressured him to find a "more competent" high priest? How could Pilate be trusted?

All agreed that the prophet was most definitely Pilate's problem. Jesus was a threat to *Roman* stability in the region, and Pilate was the *Roman* governor. Surely, he ought to be the one to deal with him!

Caiaphas graciously and patiently let them all speak their minds. When they had all said their piece, he spoke. "I assure you there is not a thought or concern you have raised here that I have not also had. Heaven knows I have been up most of the night with such thoughts, and much of what you say has merit on one level or another. In fact, much of it I raised with Pilate myself. But in the end, we must keep one priority above all others, and that is the peace of the city. Nothing else matters more than that—not my reputation, our family's power, or the fate of the high priesthood.

"Indeed, this plan will likely weaken our political position, and Pilate might not support me under pressure from the people. But none of you can deny that our arrest and execution of Jesus would bring far less risk to the city than if Pilate himself undertook these tasks. We have goodwill with many of our people, and Pilate is right that such goodwill, even if stretched thin by this plan, likely offers us some protection from violence. If surviving the threat of this prophet costs me the high priesthood, then I am willing to make that sacrifice. I have committed myself to this plan, and I ask that you all commit to it as well. I am sure, after giving it some thought, you will see that it is the best possible way to preserve the peace of our city."

Minor protests followed these words, but gradually those at the table calmed down and with further discussion came to recognize that Caiaphas was right. Pilate's plan was the best possible option for peace, even if it wasn't the best plan for maintaining control of the priesthood.

As consensus among the group emerged, Caiaphas addressed them again. "If we are all in agreement, much preparation is needed. First and foremost, we must find out where this prophet goes when he is not in a public place. Aaron, you must set our informants to this task. All must be listening for information, but some should follow the prophet each evening. Does he always leave the city for Bethany? Does he ever stay in the city? If so, where? If we cannot isolate this man and make the arrest at night when all are asleep, our plan has little hope of success."

"I will send these instructions to our informants this morning," Aaron replied. "And I know a few of them that I can trust to track this prophet down at night. I am quite confident that with our resources, we will be able to find his location in the evenings so that we can make an arrest."

"I hope you are right, Brother. Much depends on it!" Caiaphas replied.

Eleazar spoke, "It seems to me it is also quite important to keep eyes on this man throughout the day. I know Pilate believes he seeks to force Rome's hand into violence, and that he himself will not organize the people to such an end, but what if he is wrong? We must watch him closely and be prepared to act if it appears he is calling for open rebellion."

"I agree," replied Simeon. "Our observation must not only continue but ramp up. While informants will be useful, I think some trustworthy lower-level priests and Levites could also be used effectively. We might even seek the assistance of leading Pharisees. From what I gather, they are not friends of this prophet."

"There is wisdom in these words," replied Caiaphas. "I will delegate this task to you both. Find men you can trust, be they priests, Levites, or even Pharisees, and charge them with watching this man while he is in public. Get regular reports from them throughout the day, and if anything this prophet does appears remotely dangerous, have them alert you immediately. No doubt Pilate will have his own surveillance as well, but the more resources we have the better we will be able to control the outcome."

After a brief pause, Ezra raised a concern. "Surely you have authority to arrest the prophet, but in order to bring him to Pilate and demand his death, you will need approval from the great council, will you not? We must follow our sacred customs."

"Yes," Caiaphas responded, "we will need the council's support, and this is something to which I have given great thought. I have significant influence as president, yet to bring this man before Pilate for punishment of a capital crime I will still need the majority of the council to confirm his guilt. It would certainly be politically beneficial to have the council's support."

Eleazar interjected. "I am quite confident you could get a majority of the seventy-one members, Father. At least a third of the priestly members are loyal to you. We might be able to persuade the Pharisees and scribes to support you. As Simeon said, they are no friends of this prophet and might be eager to get rid of him."

"Yes, it is likely we can gain a majority of the council, but we will have to work to assure it. Ezra, will you begin canvassing those priests who are loyal to my leadership? And Simeon, you have a good relationship with the Pharisee Jonathan. Meet with him, get a sense of his opinion of this prophet. Be discreet about our plans but probe to see how likely it would be for the Pharisees on the council to support the prophet's removal."

"What of Annas, Cousin?" Ezra asked. "Unfortunately, more of the priestly members are loyal to him than they are to you. If he is able to add some of the Pharisees or perhaps flip some of our priests to his side, he could cause a significant problem for us."

"What indeed will Annas do?" Caiaphas asked, as if speaking to himself. "I wonder how he will play this situation. He meets with Pilate today, but the governor has agreed not to tell him of our plan. Pilate will tell him that he does not see this Jesus as a problem, and that he has no plans to arrest him."

Shaking his head, Ezra interrupted, "Surely with this knowledge he will oppose us in order to curry favor with Pilate. It seems to me you have made a mistake, Cousin."

"You may be right, Ezra," Caiaphas replied calmly. "Perhaps he would resist our efforts. But he is more cunning than you think, and another option will be available to him. He could support me for the moment, particularly if he thinks I already have a majority of the council. Knowing that my action will be unpopular with the people, he might be willing to give me what he perceives to be just enough rope to hang myself. Then, when the people oppose me, his support will vanish and my downfall will be his chance to rise."

"I think you are right, Brother," affirmed Aaron. "Annas has never been one to make the obvious move. Subtlety has always been his preference."

Ezra was not convinced. "You both give him too much credit," he replied with mild disgust. "And in case you are wrong, we must be confident of our other allies."

"Yes, of course, Cousin. We will make every effort to establish a majority without Annas. I trust you and Simeon can do so?" Caiaphas said.

"Of course," said Simeon, exchanging a nod with Ezra.

"We must also discuss our role in this ruse," Caiaphas went on. "For it to be successful, it must be convincing. If Pilate is to protest Jesus' innocence, he must face formidable opposition for that protest to be believable. Not only will we need support from the council to vote in favor of the prophet's guilt, but we will need to create a significant crowd to demand that Pilate support the council's verdict."

"The priests on the council that are loyal to you will be easy to convince," Eleazar said. "They, with their attendants and clients, will make a sizeable crowd."

"That is a good start, to be sure," said Caiaphas, "but I think securing a commitment from the prominent Pharisees will also be important—and more difficult. But we could also use the priests that are loyal to Annas—here, again, his immediate support would be useful. No doubt he himself would avoid such a public display, but his loyal priests and their attendants would help amass a formidable crowd."

"Should we then recruit for this purpose as well?" asked Simeon.

"Not explicitly," answered Caiaphas. "We cannot betray our knowledge of what Pilate will do. But tell them we might need their support should Pilate not support the will of the council. Stress that we all must be willing to demand this man's death should the Roman governor's will prove weak. I think such an approach will be successful without arousing suspicion."

Simeon and Ezra both nodded.

"It is also important that our demonstration be public. We need word of the events to spread throughout the city," said Caiaphas. "Selling the narrative is just as important as creating it. No doubt the scene will draw onlookers. We must not push them away or limit their access but let them see all that transpires. We must rely on them for word to spread."

"Informants can also help in this regard," said Aaron. "We can place them strategically throughout the city, in prominent hotels, taverns, shops, and markets. We can instruct them to observe and spread the news of the morning's events. The narrative should spread throughout the city like wildfire."

"Excellent idea, Brother," replied Caiaphas. "Without such publicizing, many might simply assume Rome is responsible for the prophet's death. If so, this entire plan could fail."

After they addressed a few more items, Caiaphas closed the meeting. "You all know your assigned tasks. We will reconvene tomorrow morning to assess our progress."

Eleazar remained behind after the others had left. The meeting had tasked him with nothing more than finding men who would observe the prophet's public actions—a duty he shared with Simeon. Surely, he was worthy of greater responsibilities than this.

As if reading his mind, his father spoke without looking at him. "You feel you have been overlooked in the delegations of duties?"

Eleazar had been planning his words carefully. "I am happy to serve in the way you have instructed, Father, but I had hoped to play a more prominent role in the execution of this plan. I believe I have shown my worth and have earned such an opportunity."

His father looked at him thoughtfully and gave a slight smile. "You have indeed proven your worth, my son. I am proud of you, and perhaps I don't tell you that enough. You hold your own quite well in these private counsels."

He looked admiringly at Eleazar, something he rarely did, then went on: "Not to worry. I have not forgotten you or overlooked your abilities. I have two important roles for you to play. First, in addition to appointing priests and Levites to watch this prophet, I want you to do the same. I want you to be my primary eyes and ears in the temple courtyards, where this man will no doubt be teaching the people. It was you who first saw his demonstration against the money changers, and you who brought me the report. I want you to continue to watch this man. Seek to better understand him and assess the level of threat he actually poses to us. I trust your judgment more than all the priests and Levites combined—I daresay more than even your uncles and cousin."

The pride that filled Eleazar's heart could not be concealed from his face. "I am happy to accept this assignment, and I am honored by it. What is the second task you would give me?"

"The second is greater than the first, and more dangerous." Caiaphas paused, seemingly assessing his son's reaction.

The words "greater" and "dangerous" sent a chill of excitement through Eleazar, causing the hair on his neck to stand up.

"I task you to lead the temple guard in the arrest of this prophet."

Eleazar was stunned. Such a role was beyond what he had anticipated or could have imagined. The thought of a possible conflict with the prophet and his followers was invigorating. "I will do it!" he blurted.

With a weighty look, Caiaphas said, "This is no small task, and it involves an element of danger. We don't know what you will encounter when you go to arrest him. Our plan will likely catch him by surprise, and there is no telling what a man will do in that situation. He and his followers are likely to resist, and there could be bloodshed. You must plan for this and be prepared to overcome it."

His father's words did not dissuade Eleazar in the least. In fact, there was a part of him that hoped his father was right. The thought of combat with zealot revolutionaries excited him! Though he had never faced real combat, he had trained for it since his youth. "I understand," he replied. "I am honored by this appointment, and I will see it through."

His father nodded—the look of pride was unmistakable. Then with great seriousness, he said, "For this assignment, you will wear my ring and bear my authority. This task is an opportunity for you to show your merit and earn great honor.

Successful apprehension of this man will commend you to Pilate. Perhaps it will even give him confidence in you as one who might replace me when my time as high priest is over."

With these words, Caiaphas's purpose in making this appointment became crystal clear. This was more than honoring his son with a significant task; he was giving his son an opportunity to make his claim on the future office of the high priest itself. He had always told Eleazar that with the Romans, one could not count on heredity—merit was essential. Here was a chance for just such merit. Then and there, Eleazar swore to himself that he would not fail.

With resolve in his eyes and conviction in his heart, he said, "I hear you, Father, and I understand. I promise you I will not fail in this task."

Caiaphas moved toward his son, embraced him, and said warmly, "I am confident you will not."

CALEB

A day and a half had passed since the prophet Jesus had entered the city as a conquering king, and to Caleb's amazement, nothing had come of it. No one had intervened to stop this man. No Roman soldiers had entered the temple courtyard. No arrests had been made. It was as if his actions had gone completely unnoticed, at least by the Roman governor.

But the people had certainly taken notice. He was all anyone talked about, and they all seemed to love him. Each day Jesus had come to the temple courtyard, and each day larger crowds gathered around him. They were mesmerized by his talk of the kingdom of God and his call for justice and true peace.

There were also naysayers. The most prominent Pharisees engaged him in debates over the proper interpretation and practice of the Torah, and these debates often ended in their public denouncement of Jesus. But such denouncements seemed to have no effect on the people. They seemed to favor Jesus' interpretation of the Torah over that of the Pharisees—which no doubt irritated these teachers who had long held influence over the people. While priests also stood in the crowd, listening to his teachings, few ventured to engage him. When they did, it often did not go well for them. It was not that they lacked a legitimate viewpoint or argument; rather, the creativity and evasiveness of this prophet caught his interrogators off guard. They were used to certain steps in the dance of argument, and this partner's freestyle movement caused them to look foolish. The antagonism of the crowds certainly did not aid their confidence.

Caleb had a front-row seat for all these interactions, though he would have never imagined he would find himself in such a crowd the day this prophet first entered the city. He was there on assignment, you could say.

The morning after he had witnessed Jesus' entrance into the city, his contact had appeared at his pottery shop and instructed him to go to a private meeting place. Within the hour, Caleb had made his way to a small apartment on the north side of the city. Though it was unlikely anyone was watching or following him, Caleb took a roundabout way to the location. He approached the back entrance to the apartment via a small alleyway and gave the door two sharp knocks, per his instructions. His contact quickly let him in. Caleb was eager to share the news of what he had seen the previous day, but his contact quickly silenced him. Apparently, he was aware of this information; another matter was more pressing. The contact's master was concerned about this new prophet and had ordered that he be watched constantly. This observation would be Caleb's new assignment.

He protested, claiming he needed to run his shop. It was a busy time of year for his business. But his host quickly reminded him that their new arrangement was also important for his business, and failure to accept this task could be detrimental. The man knew that Caleb had hired a number of new workers, one of whom could serve as manager when he was absent. The shop would be in good hands while Caleb stepped away for this assignment, the contact told him.

Caleb was surprised and somewhat unsettled at how much this man knew about his business. It gave him a sense of uneasiness about this arrangement, but ultimately he had little choice. Reluctantly, he accepted the assignment.

He was to observe Jesus throughout the day and give a report on what he saw each evening. If he noticed anything that might cause immediate danger or unrest in the city, he was to report it to a temple guard. Aside from his absence from the shop, he thought his assigned task wasn't overly burdensome. It turned out to be quite convenient, since his cousin Jacob had expressed interest in hearing the prophet again.

Caleb was to begin that very afternoon. He put one of the new workers in charge of the shop, stopped by his house to get Jacob, and they headed to the Temple Mount. The crowds around Jesus made it easy to find him. At first, they had to listen from a good distance away, but because of the constant flux of the crowd they eventually worked their way to where they could see the prophet clearly.

To his surprise, Caleb enjoyed listening to this man and watching him occasionally spar with would-be-detractors. He spoke with passion and simplicity, and had a magnetism about him that easily and furtively drew people in. He talked of a coming kingdom of God in which the powerful oppressors would be brought down, in which equity would again be experienced in Israel. But he urged his hearers not to wait and to be actively engaged in enacting that kingdom now, by forgiving debts, loving their neighbors, and extending hospitality to those of lower social standing.

While Caleb was cynical about any coming new age of God, there was much in this man's teaching that was appealing—challenging, to be sure, but appealing. He also had much to say about the leading priests who controlled the temple. He chastised them for corrupting God's house, for growing rich without properly caring for the poor and the widows, and for valuing political gain over the peace and justice God had demanded through the Torah and his prophets. He spoke clearly of the coming judgment on those who currently ran the temple, and it seemed to Caleb that he may even have envisioned a destruction of the temple itself. The day passed quickly, and that evening Caleb had much to report to his contact.

Caleb and Jacob arrived earlier the next day, but still had to fight through the crowd to see Jesus clearly. Today he talked more about the kingdom, but he also spoke about the ancient prophets of Israel and their call for justice and the inclusion of the marginalized and the outsider. He claimed that faithfulness to the kingdom was more important than one's family, even more important than one's own life.

Again his teaching enraptured the crowd, and again he faced various challengers and detractors. The most noteworthy of these came after Jesus had just finished speaking against the temple authorities. Two prominent Pharisees, men Caleb knew as friends of his father, approached Jesus and praised his sincerity, integrity, and commitment to truth. To Caleb, it seemed false flattery. They then asked a question that was clearly intended to test the prophet: "Should we Jews pay taxes to our Roman overlords? Should we give money to Caesar?"

Anyone could see the implications of either answer he might give. To answer "no" would mean he was anti-Roman. This would be consistent with his dramatic entry into the city and his proclamation of a kingdom that would replace Rome and its rulers. It was no doubt the answer the people would have wanted. To answer "yes" would seem radically inconsistent with his previous actions and teaching. It would confuse the people and perhaps upset many of them.

Caleb could not figure out why Pharisees would ask such a question. Why would they try to push this prophet to one extreme or the other?

Jesus responded with a question of his own. "Do you have a didrachma?" This was the coin used for the temple tax, worth two denarii. The two Pharisees looked at each other, confused. But one finally reached into his garment and pulled out a silver coin and gave Jesus an inquisitive look.

"Who grants the power to mint such coins?" Jesus asked.

"Rome," one Pharisee replied.

Jesus nodded and said to them both, "Give to Rome what is Rome's, and to God what is God's." His inquisitors certainly did not expect such an answer, and it took a moment for those in the crowd to gather its meaning and implication. Slowly Caleb heard audible indications of understanding, but it was clear that many still did not fully grasp the significance of the answer.

But in a way, it wasn't an answer at all. Jesus simply turned the question back on his questioners. He forced them to determine what might belong to God and what might belong to Rome. Perhaps one could say the coin belonged to Caesar, as he granted the power for it to be minted in the first place, and thus it should be returned to him: "Give the pagan emperor back his pagan money." Or perhaps it meant that taxes belonged to Caesar, but all else belonged to God. Or perhaps more radically than these first two answers, one might conclude that all belonged to God and thus Rome was left nothing!

Caleb smiled as the impact of the evasive response fully set in. The two Pharisees, both clearly caught off guard, looked perplexed. They nodded thoughtfully and slowly turned away.

He then noticed that they met what looked like two ranking priests on the edge of the crowd. Some sort of argument ensued, and the Pharisees walked away in anger. At that moment, the reason for the question became clear to Caleb: they were not asking on their own behalf, but on behalf of the priests. It seemed the leaders of the city were the ones behind this trap.

In the early evening, Jesus told the crowd that he must depart. As he did so, his followers closed in around him and they began to move toward the east. While some of the crowd dispersed, some followed the prophet and his entourage to the gate and outside the city.

As Caleb and Jacob made their way across the courtyard in the opposite direction, Jacob was ecstatic about the teaching of the prophet, and Caleb could understand why. Jesus was charismatic and inspiring. There was just something about him. They exited the Temple Mount and parted ways, as Jacob and his family were dinning with friends that night.

Caleb headed toward home and wondered about this prophet. He was hard to figure. He entered the city as a conquering king, to great praise and fanfare. He spoke of a new kingdom of peace, justice, and prosperity. These were the actions and language of a messianic figure who envisioned a new and glorious age of Israel and the fall of Israel's oppressors, the Romans. This was seditious by any measure, and the crowds that hung on his words knew it.

But certain things were missing from his teaching that one might expect. He said nothing negative about Rome or its power. He never said a word about the governor, Pilate, or the emperor, Tiberius. He criticized the temple and its leadership, but not Rome. Not once in his call for people to enact the coming kingdom of God in the here and now did he encourage violent resistance, revolution, or revolt. While many who listened to him thought they heard such a call, he never gave it. Was he being coy and employing the rhetoric of subtlety? Was he enticing his audience to action through his implicit message while creating a veneer of nonviolent resistance? Or did he envision a divine intervention in which God would send his angels to defeat his enemies while the righteous watched with joy?

As Caleb was lost in these thoughts, he felt hands grab him. His feet went out from under him as he was pulled toward a small alley. He fought to regain his feet, but his heels only slipped on the loose dirt. The firm grip around his neck and arm tightened, and as his breath failed, his panic soared. With his one free arm he swung and grasped wildly. His fist finally met something hard and pain shot through his hand. His assailant was unfazed; the grip tightened. His hope was failing, and his mind flooded with the horrors of a traitor's end. Then the light of day vanished, and he realized he had been dragged into a dark room. His heart sank.

As quickly as it had seized him, the grip around his neck loosened. He was spun around and thrown against a wall, with a strong arm pressed against his throat and a hand placed firmly over his mouth. He looked into a face shadowed by a dark hood. With a nod of the man's head, the hood fell back, and Caleb saw his assailant's face—Judah!

"Quiet!" His cousin whispered as he slowly lowered his hand.

Anger flared in Caleb's face, but he followed his cousin's command. "What are you doing?!" he whispered.

"I am so sorry, Cousin, but I needed to talk with you, and I could not risk being seen!"

"You scared me! I thought I was going to be robbed and killed!" Caleb stammered. It was a partial lie. The truth was that Caleb had thought someone had discovered he was an informant—that his treason would cost him his life.

"I know," said Judah, "and for that I am truly sorry. But I had to get you into a private place without anyone seeing me. They are searching for me! I couldn't risk any other way of contacting you. Your house is being watched." Caleb gave a surprised look and wondered if it was true. Had Judah seen Caleb's contact watching the house and waiting for a signal? Perhaps the contact was watching for Judah too?

As Caleb's fear and anger waned, he saw Judah's face more clearly. It was gaunt. Heavy bags under his eyes betrayed sleepless nights. "I understand," Caleb said in a low, calm voice. "Are you okay, Cousin? I haven't seen you in almost two weeks. Your family has told everyone you are on a journey to Tarsus for family business."

"Yes," Judah replied. "That is the story they have told. I have been in hiding, not too far from the city. But I have been away from my family too long and need to tell them I am safe. I also fear that without my ability to work, financial hardship will fall on them. This is why I came to find you. I was smuggled into the city in a wagon this morning and will depart tomorrow the same way, but I need you to go to my family and tell them I am safe. I also ask that you help them with their needs, if you are able. They are too proud to ask, but if you can spare any money, I am certain they will need it. Tell them I gave it to you. They are more likely to take it then."

Caleb nodded and embraced him. "Yes, of course, Cousin! I will go to your family tonight and give them news of your safety. I will give them money as well. Business has been good, and I can spare it. I assure you they will have no need while you are away! You look hungry. I have a loaf of bread if you want it."

Judah's eyes widened. "Yes, please! I have had little to eat in the last week." He eagerly took the bread from Caleb and began to devour it.

"May I ask where you have been? Where are you staying?" Caleb asked.

"There are friends of the cause in many villages outside the city," Judah said. "Some of them have welcomed me in and hidden me. Most recently, I have come from Bethany. A man there allows many enemies of the state to sleep in his secret basement. It is quite large and often crowded. Just last night, the prophet Jesus and his closest followers stayed there."

This mention of Jesus grabbed Caleb's attention. His contact had told him to look for any information that would help locate Jesus' whereabouts at night. "He did?" he asked. "I have been listening to him in the temple courtyard the last two days. What do you make of him?"

"Not much," Judah answered. "It was hard to get close to him with his disciples always surrounding him. They are *quite* protective of him." Caleb nodded and tried not to appear overly interested.

"I did get a chance to talk with one of his disciples, though," Judah went on. "We talked for a bit. He shared my name—and my passion for the cause. I asked him about his master and whether he was a friend of the cause. He was reluctant to talk about it at first; the question seemed to frustrate him. But as I probed, he loosened his tongue. He was beginning to have reservations about his master's ambitions. He came to Jerusalem believing they were on a quest for liberation, but he wasn't sure of that anymore. He said Jesus had been talking a lot about his death, like he envisioned himself as a martyr. 'Martyrdom is not what I signed up for,' he said. He then told me he had said too much and needed to get back to his friends."

Caleb nodded and said as casually as he could, "That is interesting. Dissension in the ranks, then?"

"That was the impression I got," said Judah indifferently, "at least with this one man. I can't really speak to the rest of them." Judah paused and shook his head in frustration. "Fate is a treacherous mistress," he muttered angrily.

"What do you mean by that?" Caleb asked.

"I mean the timing of the events is always fated to frustrate. We had been waiting for something to spark the fire of rebellion in the people. And now this prophet is on the scene, a perfect catalyst—and if he's committed to martyrdom, all the better! But now we are scattered, some in prison and some in hiding, with no power to take advantage of the situation." He shook his head in disgust.

"I am sorry, Cousin," Caleb replied. He wanted to steer the conversation back to Jesus if he could. "Perhaps this man was wrong about Jesus? I have heard him talk of a future kingdom. He entered the city as Simeon Maccabeus once did, as a conqueror! I saw it with my own eyes. Surely it is possible he has ambitions of revolution?"

"Perhaps," replied Judah, "but this disciple of his did not believe so. Who would know better?"

"More time with his disciples might reveal a different purpose. Would it be possible to join them?" Caleb asked.

"*That* would be impossible," Judah replied. "They will not be returning again to the same place to sleep. They never stay in the same place more than one night, and I have no idea where they might be next."

Caleb's heart sank. Judah would be of little help locating the prophet at night. But perhaps there was another way forward. "As I said, I have seen this man and his disciples for the past two days in the temple courtyard. What did the disciple look like, the one you spoke with?" It was a risky question to ask, but he hoped his cousin would answer it without much thought.

Judah looked curiously at Caleb, then answered, "He is shorter than the rest, with a thick nose, sparse beard, and round face." He paused. "Oh, and he has a large brown mole on his cheek. I can't remember which one, but it is hard to miss. Why do you ask?" From the description, Caleb knew instantly the disciple Judah had spoken with.

"No reason; just curious, I guess. I think I have seen that disciple," Caleb said casually. Judah seemed to accept this.

Caleb decided to change the subject: "Where are you staying tonight, Cousin?"

Judah was slow to respond, and Caleb wondered if he had pushed too hard and raised suspicion. But Judah's response relieved those concerns. Looking down, he said, "I am ashamed to tell you, Cousin. It is a place of ill repute. But it is the safest place for me now."

"You will find no judgment here," Caleb said compassionately. "I will do all that I can to help you. And until you can return, I will make sure your family lacks nothing."

"You are kind, Caleb," Judah said, "but that might be a larger promise than you can keep. I am not sure I will ever be able to return." These words pained Caleb's heart, and in that moment he decided he must to something to help. But what?

Caleb embraced him and said, "Things can change, Judah. Until they do, I will care for your family."

Tears filled Judah's eyes as he pulled his hood over his head. In a broken voice he whispered, "Thank you."

He disappeared out the door into the alley, and Caleb wondered if he would ever see him again. In the last few moments a plan had been formulating in his head. If it worked as he hoped, he might be able to save his cousin and make amends for the betrayal that had forced him to flee the city. But there was no time to lose!

He headed directly for his shop. It was closed for the night, but he was scheduled to meet his contact in the back room. It was only a few minutes after he arrived when he heard a sharp knock at the back door. He quickly ushered in his contact and said, "I have important information, but I must deliver it to Aaron directly." This response surprised the contact, who at first seemed flustered by the request and then refused it. But Caleb insisted.

"This is highly irregular," the man said. "I don't think Aaron will be willing to meet you again."

"It is information about the location of the prophet Jesus—his nightly whereabouts. I think he might be willing to meet me on that account," Caleb said smugly.

The man's eyes grew wide. After a moment's pause he said, "I will ask Aaron if he will meet with you, but I cannot promise you he will. You may have to tell me, and I will relay the information to him."

Caleb gave the man a cold stare. "*You* will never hear this information from me. Aaron will hear it from my lips or no one will."

The man's cheeks reddened with anger. "Don't leave the shop!" he said as he left quickly through the back door, leaving Caleb to wait.

After a half-hour that seemed like an eternity to Caleb, the man returned. It seemed his anger had cooled, though there was still irritation in his voice. "He will meet you in one hour at the same place you first met. Don't be late." Not waiting for a reply, he turned and disappeared into the night.

An hour later, Caleb found himself sitting at the same table in the same tavern where he had sat at just over a month before. He was looking into the same hooded face, the face of Aaron.

When they first met, Caleb had believed the name was symbolic, a clever reference to Moses and the brother who served as his mouthpiece. But over the last month, Caleb had given great thought to who he might be working for. There were not many options to choose from. The man was not Roman, and Caleb believed it unlikely that he worked for the Romans. This meant he likely represented a powerful Jewish family, probably a priestly one. The money he could offer certainly suggested this, as did his appearance: smooth unweathered skin, finely groomed beard, and the odor of flowers. It was a familiar smell that Caleb couldn't place at first, but it came to him later. It was the smell of a certain incense burned at the temple. Yes, the man was clearly a priest from a powerful family.

But what family? All the pieces had come together two days before, when Caleb had been on the Temple Mount. The high priest Caiaphas and his brothers had crossed the outer courtyard and entered the temple proper. There was something familiar about one of the high priest's brothers that triggered Caleb's memory. The nose or jawline, perhaps? He asked someone standing close by the names of Caiaphas's brothers, and when the man gave the name Aaron, Caleb knew the truth. Now sitting before the man again, he had no doubt that he was meeting with the brother of the high priest of Israel. The man across from him represented the most powerful man in Jerusalem. It was just such a man that could deliver what Caleb was about to ask.

Aaron spoke first. "This meeting is highly unusual. It is my custom to meet only once. But apparently you have something very important that you can only discuss with me? I am here and ready to listen."

"I recognize that this meeting is irregular," said Caleb, "and I thank you for meeting me at this late hour. The information I have is certainly important and, given your presence here, presumably of great value to you."

Though the priest's face remained impassive, Caleb thought he caught a glimmer of anger in his eyes.

He said nothing, so Caleb continued, "I have information about Jesus' nocturnal movements and residence."

"I am listening," said Aaron.

"I have it on good authority that he never stays in the same place twice," said Caleb. "He knows the authorities are searching for him, and thus he stays on the move."

"This is not news to us," said Aaron, frustration in his voice. "But can you tell me where he will be in the next few nights?"

"I cannot," said Caleb.

Unmistakable anger flashed across Aaron's face. In a voice that worked hard to conceal that anger, the priest said, "Then why did you bring me here? If you have wasted my time, I swear you will regret it."

Caleb remained calm. "I don't know where he will be staying, but I know someone who does—someone who might be willing to help you . . . for the right price."

He had regained Aaron's interest. "Go on," the priest said curtly.

"I have learned that one of the prophet's closest followers is unhappy with him and that his loyalty is wavering. He seems to be a weak link that you could take advantage of."

Caleb noticed the priest lean in closer to him.

"Which follower?" he asked.

He had the priest hooked. It was now time to make his request.

"I will tell you, and I will even help you in approaching him, but I also have something I need from you first."

Aaron looked surprised. "We are already giving you a significant amount of money. Do you demand more?"

"No," said Caleb, "I don't want more money. I want you to protect someone for me."

"Protect someone?" Aaron's tone reflected both surprise and indignation. "What do you mean?"

"My cousin Judah is being hunted by the Romans. He is a suspect in the murder of five Roman soldiers. I tell you that he is completely innocent. He was with me the night of those murders, and he had nothing to do with them. I want the Romans to stop pursuing him. I want them to stop harassing his family. He must be left alone. If you can promise me this, I will give you the information you desire."

Aaron's eyes were wide, and he looked stunned. "What makes you think I can help you with this . . . this extreme request?"

Caleb paused for a moment, looking the priest directly in the eyes. "I know who you are," he said. "I know who you represent. Your brother is the most powerful man in Jerusalem. If he cannot help my cousin, then I am afraid no one can."

These words clearly took Aaron by surprise. He sat silently, looking at Caleb with piercing eyes. It seemed the priest was deciding the best way to proceed.

Finally, he spoke. "There is no need for games here. I am who you think I am, and you are right about who I represent. But granting your request is not as simple as you might think. There are powers greater than the one I represent, and they might not be so willing to grant immunity to your . . . *innocent* cousin."

"I understand," said Caleb. "But it seems to me that the information you seek about Jesus is of the utmost importance to you, to the one you represent, and perhaps even to those more powerful than him. And now that my cousin is known to both you and Rome, he can be monitored and kept in check. I only ask that no one hunt him any longer, that he no longer face the threat of arrest or execution, and that he be allowed to return to his life and family—on my word that he is indeed *innocent*. If he is caught committing a crime in the future, then your promise of protection is void and you may do with him as you wish."

Aaron looked at him thoughtfully. Caleb even believed he may have caught a hint of admiration in his eye. "I cannot make this decision here and now. I do not have that power. I must bring this request to others. But time is of the essence, and though the hour is getting late, I hope to have an answer for you tonight. If we grant your request, we will need to act on this information as early as tomorrow."

"I understand," said Caleb. "Your expediency is appreciated."

"Return to your shop," Aaron said. "You will not see me again. Your usual contact will come to you with an answer. It could be quite late, but do not go home. You will have an answer tonight."

Caleb nodded. The priest got up and left the tavern, and Caleb left moments later.

Just before midnight, his contact returned to the shop. "Your request has been granted," he said. And then, with a smug look, he said, "Now please tell me the identity of the disciple who might betray this prophet." Ignoring the petty jab, Caleb gave him the description of the disciple that Judah had told him about. The contact replied, "This information is greatly appreciated. But for your request to be granted, your assistance will be needed to recruit this man." Without a thought Caleb said, "I will do whatever is needed."

"Excellent," the man replied. "Let us form our strategy." For the next hour, Caleb and his contact devised a plan to recruit the disciple who shared the name of his cousin: Judah.

ELEAZAR

Eleazar awoke to the light of the morning sun. Like the previous two days, today would no doubt be a busy one. In addition to the many traditional priestly duties that came with a Passover week, he was also responsible for observing the Galilean prophet while he was in the temple courtyard—and he seemed to be in the temple courtyard *constantly*. There was a continual need for vigilance as Jesus arrived in the mid-morning, held court with the people all day, and left just before sundown. Although Eleazar had delegated this task to lower-level priests and Levites, given his father's request he felt obligated to keep an eye on this Jesus himself. With so much at risk, he trusted few eyes more than his own.

Just then a slave girl entered with a breakfast of dry fish, warm bread, and fresh dates. The morning meeting with his father would be starting soon.

The time spent observing the prophet had produced little of note. Eleazar had orchestrated efforts to draw out additional information from the man by sending priests and even a couple of Pharisees, but all such efforts had proven futile. There was no need to mention these failures to his father and uncles. The good news was that this Jesus had done nothing yet that demanded an immediate arrest or suggested he was an imminent threat. It seemed Pilate was right in this regard.

Up to this point, Jesus' teachings certainly implied Roman removal, but he had not directly called for such removal or encouraged people to join in it—at least not publicly. And there was the rub. It was easy to observe this man while he was in public, teaching large crowds in the temple courtyard. But locating him at any other time had proven difficult. He entered the city in a crowd and left in the same way. Several priests, Levites, and informants had attempted to follow him, but time and time again he disappeared in an outlying village. One Levite was certain he had tracked him to an inn in Bethphage, but when he entered the inn's tavern, the prophet was nowhere to be found. Eleazar knew this was a problem they would have to resolve soon, as arresting Jesus publicly would be extremely dangerous. Each day that danger grew, along with Jesus' popularity. This lack of progress would certainly displease his father.

His wife, Joanna, entered the room as he ate. She was truly a beautiful woman, and her entrance into any room still took his breath away. Her smile was exhilarating, and her large brown eyes intoxicating. She greeted him warmly, embracing him and kissing him softly on the cheek.

"I had an interesting dinner last night," she said as she moved to recline on the cushion next to him.

"Oh, you did, did you? Of interest to Jerusalem's finest young maidens or to me?" he said with a smile.

She feigned a pouting look. "Do you still think so little of my wiles?"

He leaned over and gave her a light kiss on the lips. "Your *wiles* ought never be underestimated! I would be forever lost without them! What have you learned? Do tell!"

She laughed playfully, nibbled a date, and looked at him suspiciously before she said, "There seems to be much concern about this prophet Jesus among Annas and his sons."

Eleazar's demeanor suddenly changed to one of intense focus. "Really? What are they concerned about?"

"It seems that Annas had a private meeting with the Roman governor yesterday." Though this meeting was no surprise to Eleazar, he shook his head and cursed under his breath.

"Do you want to hear what I have to say or not?" Joanna asked, mild frustration in her voice.

"Yes, of course! Please go on."

"Pilate told him he is not concerned about this prophet and he does not intend to intervene. Apparently, this was shocking news to Annas. It has his entire house in an uproar! As I told you before, they all see this man as a grave threat."

Eleazar could not keep a grin from crossing his face. "Yes, go on."

She continued, "Now he and his sons are telling all who will listen of this failure of Roman leadership, and they are demanding that your father do what the Roman governor will not. He is telling the families of the leading priests that this is the time for Caiaphas to show his strength and remove this threat from the city."

Instead of currying favor with the governor, Annas had instead decided to pressure his father into action that would clearly be unpopular with the masses. His call for strength of leadership from Caiaphas was nothing more than the generous gift of just enough rope to hang oneself. As usual, his professed concern for the city's safety and peace was merely a cover for the political gain of his own family. The irony that this response was exactly what his father both anticipated and desired gave Eleazar great satisfaction.

"It sounds to me that he feels your father is up to the task," his wife continued, "that Annas believes he will show strength and do the right thing! This certainly does not look like the action of the conniving usurper you make your grandfather out to be."

Her continued naiveté was both endearing and frustrating to Eleazar at the same time. He gave her a gentle, though perhaps slightly condescending look. "The trap always looks enticing right before you step into it, my dear. I assure you that things are not always as they appear. Let this fruit ripen before you determine its quality."

She looked at him inquisitively and shook her head. "Always so suspicious!" She kissed his cheek and laid her head on his shoulder.

"I might not agree with your assessment of Annas's response, but I am grateful you told me of it. It is valuable information, more valuable than you could know. My father will be quite pleased to receive it, and I will be sure to tell him that it came from you." This brought a loving smile.

There was a knock at the door. A slave entered and informed Eleazar that the rest of the guests had arrived and were waiting on him. He had lost track of time. Though his father did not like tardiness, he would no doubt appreciate the present reason for it. Eleazar arose quickly, kissed his wife on the head, and made for the door.

As he left, Joanna said playfully, "Good luck saving our city, my love!" He rolled his eyes before he left the room.

When he arrived at his father's private chambers, he found his two uncles and his father's cousin enjoying a plate of figs and cheese. Apparently, they had not yet engaged in any significant discussion. He apologized for his late arrival and assured the group there was a good reason for it.

Caiaphas began, "Since we last met, there was much to do, and much still remains. I won't keep you long, but updating our plan's progress is crucial. Eleazar, you have been responsible for observing the prophet. I assume he has not yet done anything to suggest an imminent threat or I would have already been told. Is there any information you would like to share?"

"Yes, I have had eyes on Jesus every day in the temple courtyard from his arrival in the morning to his departure in the evening. You are correct that he has done nothing to suggest that a threat of violence is imminent. His teaching certainly contains an implicit anti-Roman message, but he says nothing that directly critiques Roman occupation. There has been no call for taking up arms or efforts to organize the people to such ends. He is, however, quite open in his criticism of the temple and our leadership, and has said much to defame us."

"We are the leading priests of Israel," said Caiaphas, "and we should not let such insults distract us from our purpose. Let him rant all he wants. Peace is the priority here. For now, I am pleased to hear there is no evidence of him inciting the people to violence or organizing any sort of opposition."

"At least not publicly," Eleazar said. "Unfortunately, we have not yet been able to find where he spends his nights. We have no idea what he might be plotting with his closest followers. It is the possibility of such plots that scares me."

Eleazar noticed his Uncle Aaron glance at his father.

"On the matter of the prophet's whereabouts at night, we have had a bit of a breakthrough," Caiaphas said. "Last night we were given new information. Aaron, would you share your news?"

"Certainly," Aaron answered. "Apparently there is a close disciple of the prophet who for some reason is disenfranchised with his master. An informant has told us he might be willing to assist us in locating Jesus at night. We would like to recruit this disciple later this morning. If all goes well, a path to a private arrest will emerge."

This revelation brought relief and audible joy to the rest at the table.

"Eleazar," Caiaphas said, "I would like you to take the lead in recruiting this man. I cannot be a part of it, and I think it better that someone less visible than your uncles or cousin facilitate it. Would you be willing to speak with this man on our behalf?"

Though inwardly elated by the request, this time Eleazar remained stoic and calm. "Yes, of course. It will be an honor to serve in this way. Share with me the details of the plan, and I will do whatever is required."

His father looked at him proudly and said, "Thank you, my son. I have complete confidence in you. Aaron will fill you in on the details of the plan after our meeting." He turned to address the rest of the table: "What of other pressing matters?"

"What have we learned about the support of the council, Brother?" asked Simeon. "Will we have enough votes to convict this prophet once he is arrested?"

"That remains to be seen," answered Caiaphas. "I have spoken to the priestly families that are aligned with us, and they have committed their support both to convict Jesus and to demand his death from Pilate should he resist us. They clearly see him as a threat to the peace of the city. I have also met with the Pharisee Jonathan, and here I am afraid the news is not good. While many of the prominent Pharisaic families do not support this prophet, they want no part in his death. Jonathan even believes that some secretly support Jesus and would likely push back against any effort to execute him."

"He likely refers to Joseph, son of Isaac, from Arimathea," said Simeon. "I have heard he has let this prophet stay in his home on previous visits to Jerusalem. We have watched him and his house closely this week, but unfortunately there has been no sign of interaction with Jesus. No doubt he now knows the danger of such association."

Ezra interjected, "Joseph is well respected and has influence over certain Pharisaic families. Jonathan controls the majority, but an objection from Joseph could be a problem. And without the Pharisees, the vote will be quite close. I also worry that without more support we will not be able to get the conviction we desire or form a convincing enough crowd to demand that Pilate execute the man."

"I believe I have good news in this regard," said Eleazar. "While dining with Bernice and Salome last night, my dear wife, Joanna, gathered some helpful news. Apparently, after Annas learned that Pilate did not intend to arrest Jesus, he began spreading the word among the prominent priestly families that Pilate was a weak governor and that you, Father, needed to compensate for this weakness by arresting Jesus. He is painting you as the city's only hope. Father, it seems you were right in your anticipation of Annas's plans."

"Indeed," said Caiaphas solemnly. "It brings me no joy, but if this news is true I think we can count on the support of Annas along with those loyal to him. There is always a chance that this information is inaccurate, but confirming it should not prove difficult. Ezra, can you look into this?" His cousin nodded.

With no further business to discuss, Caiaphas dismissed them. As they departed, he reminded them that time was running short and that they may need to reconvene later that evening.

CALEB

Though he had gone to bed late the night before and had only a handful of hours of restless sleep, Caleb was up early the next morning. He should have felt exhausted, but the events of the night before and the tasks of the day energized him. His plan had gone as well as he could have expected, but there was still more to accomplish. He wanted to arrive at the temple courtyard early, before the prophet and the masses arrived. As he had told his contact the night before, the disciple of interest seemed to hold a special position in the group. Jesus or one of the other prominent disciples often sent him on errands of some sort. For the last two days, he had been responsible for purchasing food for the group, but he also often disappeared from the group for short periods. Caleb was uncertain of all that he did, but he recognized that these errands would give him an opportunity to approach this man. He hoped that perhaps the man might arrive early to make arrangements before Jesus himself arrived.

Caleb left a note asking Jacob to meet him in the temple courtyard if he desired, then set out. He arrived at the temple in time to beat the crowds, but the disciple he was looking for was not yet there. After waiting for a very long hour, it became clear his hope of the disciple's early arrival would not be realized.

Jesus entered the courtyard at about the same time he had the previous two days, again through the Beautiful Gate. His disciples surrounded him, as did a large crowd. He made his way to the same place he had taught before. Caleb, assuming he would do so, was already in place.

Unlike the previous days, Caleb had little interest in the contents of Jesus' message. As Jesus spoke, Caleb was watching the disciple his cousin had described: short, thick-nosed, and with a sparse beard. The mole was on his left cheek. While Jesus' other followers seemed concerned with controlling the crowd, he looked rather aloof, as if he was daydreaming.

About an hour after Jesus had begun teaching, this Judah tapped one of the other disciples on the shoulder and whispered something in his ear. The other disciple nodded, and Judah got up and made his way through the crowd. This could be the moment Caleb had been waiting for. He moved to follow, trying to keep a close distance between them. It seemed he was headed for a food vendor, and Caleb wanted to catch him before he reached his destination. He quickened his pace and closed the gap. As he got closer, he called out: "Judah!" The man turned, looking to see who had called his name. Caleb waved, and Judah looked curiously at him, as if he was trying to determine whether he knew Caleb. Caleb drew closer, and the puzzled look remained.

"Do I know you?"

"No, not really," said Caleb. "But I have been listening to your master, Jesus, for the past couple of days and overheard your name." The man's puzzled look quickly became one of suspicion. Cautiously he asked, "And how can I help you?"

"I am sorry to catch you off guard. I just wondered if I could ask you some questions about Jesus."

Judah's suspicion turned to irritation. He shook his head. "I am sorry, but I don't answer people's questions about him. He is there, teaching. You can learn all you want by listening and asking him your own questions."

Undaunted, Caleb said, "But there are some very important people who would also like to ask *you* a few questions. Perhaps you would have time for them?"

Judah's suspicion returned. He shook his head and turned away, saying, "I don't have time for any of this."

Before he could get far, Caleb said, "They will surely make it worth your while. They have made it worth mine, and I am becoming a very rich man."

Judah stopped, hesitated, and turned back to face Caleb, suspicion still on his face. "Who are these people?" he asked.

"I can't tell you that, but I can tell you that they pay good money for information. They believe you have information they want, and they will certainly pay you well for it."

The man looked up, then down, as if torn over a decision. He finally shook his head and walked away toward a food vendor. As Caleb watched him, he felt his heart sink to his stomach. This man was not going to take the bait. Caleb watched him for a moment longer, then headed back to the crowd around Jesus.

Again he found it hard to pay attention to what the prophet was saying, as his mind was replaying his conversation with Judah. Did he come on too strong? Was he too aggressive? Would another approach have worked?

His thoughts were interrupted by a hand on his shoulder and a voice in his ear. "Don't turn around," the voice said. "Just listen. I will meet your friends. Be at the southernmost gate on the western wall in one hour."

Caleb felt a surge of energy go through him, but he did not turn around. He said nothing. A few minutes later, he saw Judah return to his previous position. He had a sack of bread that he began to pass out to Jesus' followers. For the next hour Judah acted like nothing had happened, and he never once looked Caleb's way.

When the time came, Caleb made his way to just inside the gate, where he waited and watched for Judah. Again a voice almost in his ear said, "Inside the gate." As he turned to see the disciple Judah behind him, he began pushing Caleb into the gateway. Once they were inside, Judah moved Caleb up against one of the walls. He quickly looked around and said, "I must meet your friends soon. I cannot be gone long."

"You can meet them now," Caleb said. "They are waiting for us. Follow me."

162 | KILLING A MESSIAH

They exited the gate back into the temple courtyard. Judah's eyes searched diligently for any who might be following them. They moved north along the western wall until they reached a place in the porticoes where there was a series of storage rooms. Caleb led Judah to the third door and knocked three times. The door opened slowly. Caleb said, "You will find my friends inside." As he watched Judah disappear through the door, a flood of relief washed over him. If all went well with the priests, and he was hopeful it would, his cousin would be safe. The guilt that Caleb had been trying to deny for weeks started to ease.

ELEAZAR

The plan was for Eleazar to wait in the storage room from nine until noon. If the informant did not make contact with Jesus' disciple by the end of that time, he would relay a signal and they would then reassess their plan. With noon approaching, Eleazar was fearing the worst. But not long before the hour, he heard three knocks on the storage room door, the signal that the disciple had arrived.

Eleazar and a temple guard were the only ones in the room. The guard opened the door, and a short man with a scraggly beard entered. He bore the mole on his cheek, just as Aaron had said he would. Surely this was the right man. The guard searched him for weapons and found none, though the man did carry a leather pouch filled with silver and bronze coins.

The man looked nervously around the room. "Be at ease," said Eleazar. "You are safe here and we are free to talk. Thank you for coming to see me."

"I don't have much time. What is it you want from me?"

"I understand you are close to the prophet from Galilee, the teacher Jesus. Is that so?"

"You know it is," the man said gruffly. "Can we skip the pleasantries and get down to why I am here?"

"Of course," said Eleazar. "Before we begin, may I have your name?"

"I am Judah, son of Simeon," the man said. "And what is your name, priest?" He uttered these last words with pure derision. They took Eleazar by surprise, as he was not wearing his priestly vestments.

"Don't look so surprised," the man said. "You may not be wearing your robes here, but I have seen you in the courtyard, watching us from afar. It is my business to pay attention to what is going on. I am no fool."

"Clearly you are not," said Eleazar. "But I am afraid my name is of little consequence. If you are truly interested, you are a resourceful man; I am sure you can figure it out on your own."

Judah raised his hands, indicating he didn't care to know Eleazar's name.

"Then let's get to the reason you are here. We desire to know where you and your master stay each night."

"That is it, is it? Why do you want to know that? If you want to arrest him, he is right outside. Just say the word and you can take him."

"The reason we want this information is no concern of yours," Eleazar said. "Will you tell us what we want to know or not?"

"I know why you want this information," sneered the man. "You are a coward. You are all cowards. You are too afraid to arrest him in public. You fear the people. Nothing could be more obvious."

Eleazar tried to maintain his composure. "I repeat: our reason for wanting this information is of no concern to you."

The man laughed mockingly. "Have it your way, priest. Keep your *secret*."

"Do you know where this man stays each night or not?" asked Eleazar, trying to keep his cool.

"Yes, I know where he has stayed, and I know every place he plans to stay while he is here for the Passover. I am the one who has made all the arrangements. But the real question is, what are you willing to give me for this information? Obviously, I will not give it freely. You are asking me to betray a friend, are you not?"

Now it was Eleazar's turn to laugh. "A friend, you say? If this man was truly your friend, I don't imagine you would even be here."

Anger flashed across the man's face. "What he is to me is of no concern to you, and neither is why I am here!"

Eleazar remained calm. "It makes no difference to me. You no doubt have your reasons. What they are, I do not care. What I want is the information. What do you demand from us in exchange?"

Eleazar knew the man was going to give him the information. That was clear when he first entered the room. Only the question of price remained—and Eleazar was willing to give far more than this man realized.

"I will need money," he said.

"Of course," replied Eleazar.

"Thirty drachmas," Judah said.

Eleazar almost laughed, but managed to reveal nothing but a slight smile. He would have given five hundred.

"That price is agreeable to us."

"You misunderstand," Judah said. "I am not asking for a mere thirty drachmas. I have family in the city: a mother in failing health, a younger sister, and a younger brother. I have tried to care for them, but it looks like my resources will soon be running out. I want them moved into an apartment, one they can live in indefinitely. And I want you to give them a monthly allowance of thirty drachmas a month, *indefinitely*. I will take the first thirty today."

This was certainly a greater ask, but it was well within the amount Eleazar was able to grant. "You are a shrewd man, indeed. But I will grant your demands. Your family will be cared for according to your request."

The man nodded. "There is one more thing that I demand," he said.

"Name it," replied Eleazar.

"You can only take Jesus," he said. "None of his followers can be harmed. If you cut off the head, the snake will die. Once he is dead, they will be no threat to you. I can assure you of that."

Eleazar paused. Pilate had already decided to arrest Jesus alone, and thus this request was easy to grant. But Eleazar wanted the man to feel as if he was successfully negotiating. "That is a significant request, but our primary interest is Jesus. We will grant your request—his followers will not be touched. Do we have an agreement?"

"Yes, I agree to these terms," Judah said. "But I warn you, if you go back on your word in any regard, you will regret it. I know people who can find you, find your wife, and find your children. If you deny me what you have promised, no one in your family will be safe."

This threat took Eleazar by surprise, though he did not think it bore teeth. "There is no need for threats," said Eleazar. "We will keep our word to you, I assure you. But if threats are to be made, realize we are trusting you as well. If it becomes clear that your master is aware of our arrangement or if your information proves false, you and your family will suffer, as will all your friends who are loyal to Jesus. I assure you that we have power as well—perhaps even more than *you*." With these words, a sinister smile crossed Eleazar's face.

"Then I guess the treacherous must agree to trust each other," Judah said sardonically.

"Indeed," said Eleazar.

Eleazar found out Jesus' location for the following four nights. Apparently, his plan was to leave the city on Sunday after the festival. But even more interesting was the fact that the following evening Jesus and his closest followers would gather at the garden of Gethsemane on the west face of the Mount of Olives, across the Kidron Valley from the temple. In an act of good faith, Judah offered to lead Eleazar to the gathering point in the garden the following night. It would be his only opportunity to help them directly, as after the dinner that night he was supposed to prepare Jesus' lodging for the night while Jesus and the others met in the garden. Instead of making those preparations, he could meet the party that would arrest Jesus. Eleazar was uncertain if his father would want to take the man up on this offer, but he thought it an intriguing possibility.

Eleazar had thirty drachmas counted out for Judah and received the location of his family within the city. It was in a notoriously poor and particularly undesirable area. He promised Judah that they would have a new apartment within the week in a much better part of the city. He assured him again that they would be well cared for.

Judah turned to leave, but before he reached the door he turned around to face Eleazar. "You might not care why I would betray this man, a man who I assure you *has* been my friend and more. You might think ill of me for doing so, but I assure you it brings me no joy." He paused and seemed to be holding back tears. "It truly breaks my heart. I can only say that things

I once believed this man would do, I now know he will not. Even so, I would die for him if it was only my life on the line. But I have a family that I must think of. I can't give my life as a martyr when it would mean giving up theirs as well. I can only take solace in my belief that the fate you envision for this man is the same fate he envisions for himself."

With this, he departed.

SIX

THE RUSE

ELEAZAR

In the twenty-four hours since his conversation with the traitor Judah, the plan first cast by his father had taken its final shape. They would arrest Jesus while he and his disciples were in the garden at Gethsemane. It would be far more private than doing it in someone's home, and they wouldn't need to worry about neighbors who might spread word of the arrest.

While Eleazar was leading the arrest, his father and uncles would organize the great council. Because the Pharisaic families had refused their support, they were given only short notice of the meeting to prevent word from leaking either to the prophet himself or to others who would sabotage their plans. The priestly families who were loyal to Caiaphas had been committed to the plan from the beginning and were expecting the meeting. Annas himself had met privately with Caiaphas and had pledged his support. Thus, despite Pharisaic opposition, Caiaphas would have all the support he needed to convict Jesus. All who promised to find the prophet guilty also pledged to demand his execution from Pilate the following day. The governor would draw a significant crowd of protesters indeed.

Plans were also in place to spread the narrative of Jesus' public trial throughout the city. Informants would witness the trial and then, in high-traffic areas of the city, report what had taken place. If all went well, Jesus would be executed by crucifixion the following morning. Given the early hour of the execution, the people's preoccupation with festal preparations, and the narrative of Roman innocence in the matter, there was hope that the prophet's death would not lead to a violent reprisal.

The afternoon passed slowly as Eleazar and the head of the temple guard went over the plan for arresting Jesus. While far less trained in combat than Roman soldiers, these guards were well armed and could surely hold their own against Jesus and his followers. Eleazar had chosen fifty guards to compose the arresting party; from what he had heard, only fifteen to twenty men would likely be accompanying the prophet. The plan was to divide the guard into two groups and surround Jesus and his followers from opposite sides. This should cut off any attempted escape. Eleazar made it clear that they must allow the prophet to surrender peacefully. "You will not initiate any assault against this man or his followers," he said. "But make no mistake. Should they choose to resist, resistance will be met with steel!" Secretly, Eleazar hoped there would be resistance and a chance for greater glory.

As evening approached, Eleazar took a light supper and then met his men under the northern porticos of the Temple Mount. There they were to meet Judah, who would lead them to Jesus' location in the Gethsemane garden on the Mount of Olives. After they had been waiting for some time, Judah arrived, looking nervous and agitated. "I left Jesus over an hour ago," he told Eleazar. "The dinner should be over, and they should be in the garden."

"Where have you been the last hour?" Eleazar asked suspiciously.

"I don't see how that is your business," snapped Judah, a response that surprised the present guards. "But if you must know, I was visiting my family. I gave them money and told them they might not see me for a while, but that all their needs would be met." He gave Eleazar a cold and knowing stare. Eleazar nodded his head—those arrangements had already been set in motion.

Eleazar addressed the company. "It is time to depart. Remember, we approach by cover of darkness. No lamps or torches. The moonlight will be enough to guide us. We are counting on the element of surprise. When we are close enough, I will light a torch, which will be the signal for you to do the same. We will then surround the prophet and his followers and call for his peaceful surrender. If he does not surrender, we take him—but we take him alive."

The leaders of the company nodded. There they divided the company, with one group exiting the north side of the city through the Antonia fortress and Eleazar leading another group through the southern exit of the Temple Mount. They avoided exiting from the Beautiful Gate, as they feared such an exit may be visible to any on the Mount of Olives. They would flank Jesus and his followers from the north and the south to prevent any escape.

Eleazar's company made its way slowly in the darkness. The Gethsemane garden was at the foot of the mount. It was known for its many olive trees and large olive press that produced a great amount of oil for the region. Judah had told him that Jesus and his followers would be praying in the center of the garden, just north of the olive press. They entered the grove from the south, going quietly and slowly. As they approached the center, they heard voices. Judah waved them forward. As they inched closer, they saw an opening in the trees. In the opening there were about twenty men. Some were standing in prayer, but others appeared to be asleep. A small fire gave off a bit of light.

They drew closer and waited. Eleazar wanted to make sure the other company had time to reach the opposite line of trees from the north. After a short while, he lit his torch, which drew the attention of some of the men in the clearing. But it was also seen by the other company, who had successfully taken their position across from Eleazar. Quickly the flaming torches formed a circle and closed in around the men in the clearing.

There was panic among Jesus' followers. One or two fled, escaping to the east where there was still a small opening. Others scrambled to grab weapons from their packs: swords, daggers, and even an ax. One man armed with a sword attacked a temple guard, striking a blow to the helmet. Disoriented, the guard fell to the ground, blood coming from his head. It appeared they would not be able to avoid a fight, and a surge of energy rushed through Eleazar's body.

But then, out of the chaos, a loud voice yelled, "Enough! Put your weapons down!" The followers of Jesus recognized the voice of their master, though his words seemed to shock them. Slowly they lowered their weapons and moved toward him. He stepped forward and asked, "Who is leading this group?"

Eleazar stepped out of the tree line. "I, Eleazar son of Caiaphas the high priest, am leading them. I act with his authority. I am here to arrest Jesus the Galilean for the high crime of treason and disturbance of the peace of the city of Jerusalem."

"I am the man you seek," Jesus said. "I see you have brought a friend of mine. Judah, I had wondered what had kept you so long." Sorrow marked these last words.

Judah stepped out from the others. His presence with the temple guard brought a look of horror and shock to the faces of his former friends.

Eleazar again spoke up. "Our purpose is a peaceful arrest, but should you resist you will be shown no mercy. You are outnumbered and outarmed." It seemed clear to Eleazar that between the instruction of their master and the size of the force they faced, the fight had gone out of Jesus' followers. He seized on this and said, "We are only interested in your master; the rest of you may leave and will not be followed." At this they looked at each other and at their master, uncertain of what to do. In silence, one laid down his sword and walked quickly away from the group and past the guards. That was the first domino to fall. The others fell soon thereafter, each one moving hurriedly away once they passed the line of guards. In a matter of minutes, only the prophet remained.

"I will not resist you," he said. "But I find it odd you come to arrest me at night, when I have been preaching openly each day in the temple." He gave a subtle smile.

"Bind him!" Eleazar commanded, and two guards rushed forward to secure his hands with rope. "Take him to the home of the high priest. The council is gathering there."

As they were departing, Eleazar saw no sign of Judah. At what point the traitor had disappeared, he did not know. He would never see the man again.

The return trip to the city and to Eleazar's home was quick and uneventful. As they passed through the temple courtyard on the way, he dismissed much of the temple guard, taking only four with him.

When they reached the house of the high priest, they entered a large room where the council had gathered. Normally this gathering would have taken place on the Temple Mount in the Hall of Hewn Stones, but the late hour and the urgent nature of the meeting forced an alternate plan. The council was made up of seventy-one men, respected elders of the Jewish people—priests, leading Pharisees, and a number of scribes. The majority had come to the meeting. The room was crowded and buzzing with conversation and activity when Eleazar arrived. As planned, Jesus was to remain outside until Caiaphas could address the council. Eleazar caught his father's eye and signaled that all had gone well—the council's business could proceed. Caiaphas returned a knowing nod.

As his father moved slowly to the front of the room, a Pharisee named Nicodemus said loudly, "Caiaphas, what is the meaning of this meeting? Why have you called us here so late at night? And before the Passover? How long will you keep us in the dark?" After looking around the room he added, "Those of us who are actually in the dark!"

Caiaphas did not respond but signaled for calm. Slowly the din subsided and he spoke. "I know you are all wondering why you have been called here tonight."

Well, at least a few of you, Eleazar thought.

"As many of you know, a great threat to the peace of our city has emerged this week. On Sunday a prophet rode into our city as a conquering king, to the chants and praises of our own people crying out for deliverance. That same day he challenged the authority and power of our sacred institution the temple and its honorable leadership. From that time on, he has daily spoken traitorous words in the temple courtyard, words that stir up the people and seek to incite them to violence. We all know that such violence would bring turmoil and destruction on the entire city. He also continues to denigrate God's sacred temple and those who lead it. The leading priests and I have determined that this man is a significant threat to our city and that we must deal with him quickly, lest he sway the people to violent revolution."

A Pharisee in the crowd yelled out, "A threat he may be, but isn't this Pilate's problem? What business do we have addressing this man's guilt or innocence?"

"Your interruption is not appreciated, Nathaniel, but your question is relevant," Caiaphas replied. "Pilate has decided that this man is no threat and has told me that he will not seek to arrest him."

Annas stood up and interrupted. "Pardon me, my son." Eleazar knew his father despised Annas calling him "son." "But let me affirm for all of my brothers here that the word you speak is true. Pilate has told me this as well. His choice has revealed his cowardice, and thus it falls on us to protect this city from the violence that looms over us. We must deal with this troublesome prophet ourselves. Tonight, we are called to resolve and strength"—he turned to Caiaphas—"which you, Caiaphas, are showing us now!"

Caiaphas nodded respectfully to his father-in-law. "Thank you, Annas. You honor me, and your words regarding our governor are true indeed." This necessary deference shown to his treacherous grandfather sickened Eleazar. "If Rome will not act, then we must! The safety of our city must be our greatest concern, and this Galilean prophet is a grave threat."

Another interruption came from Joseph, son of Isaac, the Pharisee they had suspected of being a sympathizer of the prophet. "If he is such a danger to the city, Caiaphas, why have you waited until now to arrest this man? And why at night? He has been peacefully teaching each day in the temple courts, but you arrest him now, the eve of the great Passover feast. Such a meeting is highly unorthodox. I am inclined to question your motives."

"You will have your opportunity to speak, Joseph, in the due process of our trial. All will be heard that desire to be heard," said Caiaphas. "But as for the timing of these events, I assure you there is no hidden agenda or false motive in play. It was only recently that we learned that Pilate himself would do nothing in response to the threat this man posed, and therefore we have moved as quickly as we can to stop him. It was imperative that he be arrested *before* the feast."

"I would call that convenient," interrupted Joseph. These words brought a rumble from the group of Pharisees sitting behind him, which in turn led to a similar response from many of the priests. A division among the council was evident.

The presence of opposition to the arrest and trial of Jesus bothered Eleazar. He knew they would have enough votes to convict Jesus and bring him before Pilate, but the blindness of these Pharisees who saw something worth protecting in this man was disturbing.

Caiaphas quieted the room again and reiterated that all would have their chance to speak. He then brought out Jesus and read to him the charges of sedition and disturbance of the peace. To these charges the prophet said nothing. "Do you understand these accusations?" asked Caiaphas. Again, the prophet said nothing, but nodded his head.

Eleazar tried to read him. It was hard to put his finger on it. Jesus didn't seem angry or frightened. He seemed . . . sad? Yes, that was it. Sad.

"We will now hear testimony against this man. No charge will be considered for a vote by the council unless supported by the testimony of two or more witnesses, pursuant to the divine mandate of our law."

Several witnesses were brought forward. They testified to Jesus' entry into the city and its seditious nature. "He clearly presented himself as a king," one claimed. "He made no effort to quiet the people who were calling for him to bring salvation to our city," said another. Many testified to Jesus' demonstration in the temple courtyard, his turning over the tables of the money changers and his threat to those selling animals, though interpretations of the significance varied. Some saw it as an act of rebellion against Jerusalem's leadership. Others saw it as symbolizing the destruction of the temple itself, which one person even claimed he had heard Jesus say was impending. Another claimed he heard Jesus say he would destroy the temple, though others contested this claim. Many testified to Jesus' denigration of the temple's leadership and his challenging of its authority, an authority established both by Rome and by God. These teachings were treasonous, and even blasphemous to some. Virtually to a man, the witnesses claimed that Jesus was an imminent threat to the city's peace and that his actions revealed him as guilty of sedition.

After these witnesses had given their testimony, Caiaphas turned to Jesus and asked if he had anything to say in his defense to the charges. He simply shook his head, which brought a surprised reaction from the council members. Caiaphas then asked, "If the defendant will not speak on his own behalf, is there anyone here who would like to speak for him?"

The Pharisee Joseph, who had spoken at the outset of the meeting, rose and slowly made his way to the front of the room. A murmur began, but slowly died down as he stood looking around at his fellow council members. He then addressed them: "Members of this upstanding and long-established council, tonight we are asked to vote on the guilt or innocence of a prophet who is beloved by the people of this fine city. You have heard copious amounts of testimony supporting the charges of his guilt. I speak to his innocence. Of first order, I ask you all, what is this man truly guilty of? Does he speak of a coming kingdom of God? Oh, the shame! On this charge, you would have to arrest each and every Pharisee in this room and those living throughout our land, all of whom look with eager expectation for such a new divine kingdom to dawn in our midst. And we teach our people to look for the same! You Sadducees may reject this vision of our future as well as the prophets who cast such a vision, but we are able to live peaceably enough together. You do not hand us over to the Romans for sedition because of such hopes and teaching. And why not? Because we are deeply committed to nonviolence, and we reject any ideology of violent resistance against our Roman occupiers. I ask you, is this man truly any different? Has he taken up a sword? Has he instructed anyone to do so? I understand the fear that he could, but until this happens, has he truly committed a crime? I daresay he has not!

"And what of his critique of the temple and its leadership, which now fills the seats of this room? He has critiqued the lot of you, but he has said no worse than some of you have said about each other!" He looked slowly from Caiaphas to Annas.

"If the truth be told, some of us Pharisees may have said an unkind word or two about you leading Sadducees from time to time. I don't doubt you have also returned the favor. But are such words, such critiques, truly crimes? If so, then bind your own hands and step forward for the same punishment. It is true that some of you see this man as a threat. And, to be quite honest, I am stunned that our governor does not. But threat or no threat, I see no grounds for this council to convict this man. If Rome finds him guilty, so be it."

A shout came from the audience: "What of this man's entry into the city as a conquering king? That is an act of sedition if ever there was one! You can't deny that, Joseph!"

The Pharisee looked in the direction of the accuser. "I believe the floor is mine until I give it up, Jonathan. But I will speak to this charge by simply asking, are we to condemn a man for his popularity with the people? Can anyone control the masses? Sedition requires more than popularity and palm branches."

It was a weak defense, and it seemed Joseph himself knew it. Although the crowd listened to his earlier remarks, this last statement brought derision. In the face of such a response, Joseph returned to his seat.

Caiaphas again stepped to the front of the room. "Is there anyone else who would speak on this man's behalf?" When it became clear that no one else would come forward, Caiaphas said, "If no one else wishes to speak, as is our custom, we will take an open vote on this man's guilt. All who find this man *innocent* of the crimes of sedition and disturbance of the peace, raise your hands."

As expected, the Pharisees followed the lead of Joseph and raised their hands. But when Caiaphas called for the guilty votes, almost fifty hands went in the air, sealing the prophet's fate. Caiaphas faced Jesus and told him that he had been found guilty of the charges brought against him. Again, he asked Jesus if he had any words for the council. Again, he remained silent.

Caiaphas then addressed the council. "You have found this man guilty of crimes punishable by death, though you yourselves know that we do not have the authority of life and death. We will present this man to Pilate and ask him to honor the will of the council."

At these words, Joseph and his supporters got up and walked out in protest. Caiaphas continued without acknowledging their departure. "It is late, and we should all go home and get some sleep. But I ask you all to meet me at Herod's palace early in the morning. If Pilate stays his current course, he may be resistant to our request. The more members of the council there are, together with those who support its wishes, the more likely we are to persuade our governor." These words brought many verbal affirmations.

The members of the council then departed, and the temple guards took Jesus to a private room in the house. There was a bed where he could sleep if he desired, though he remained bound with guards at his door.

Exhausted after the events of the day, Eleazar went to bed. The next day would surely be another long one.

CALEB

Caleb awoke before dawn after a much-needed night's rest. Today was sure to prove eventful. He had been instructed to go to the open courtyard outside the governor's palace where Pilate administered judicial business. He was told to observe the events that occurred and spread word of those events in a variety of different places in the city. Whatever was going to happen, the ranking priests of Jerusalem wanted it to be known to the masses.

Caleb hurriedly ate a quick breakfast of bread and dry fish before departing for the palace. Built by Herod the Great, the palace was located in the northwest corner of the city. Its western wall was also the outer wall of the city, and three large towers adorned the northern wall. These towers were exquisitely designed, made of white marble and surrounded by white marble columns on the upper third of the towers.

They stood well over a hundred feet tall. Herod had named one after his brother, another after a friend, and the third, the shortest of the three, after his wife Mariamne, a woman he dearly loved but ultimately had executed for suspicion of treason. Caleb had never been inside the palace, nor had anyone he knew. But the descriptions of the palace's inner beauty—its grand banquet halls, gardens, fountains, endless porticoes, grand courtyards, and lavishly decorated bedrooms— were reported throughout the city.

He arrived at first light of day, but it was dark enough that the torches in the courtyard were still lit. A crowd was already gathering. A significant number of priests near the main entrance of the palace had drawn spectators, no doubt curious as to why priests would be outside the governor's dwelling so early in the morning. The courtyard was surrounded by porticoes with large columns, and Caleb made his way forward along the northernmost portico. He wanted to see and hear what was happening, but he also wanted to remain out of the way, so he stayed near the columns. As he stood there, more and more priests joined the group already present.

As he was observing the priests, Caleb heard a commotion behind him. He turned to look and saw the high priest, Caiaphas, leading a procession that included his brothers and other ranking priests. Behind them were at least fifteen temple guards surrounding a man bound in shackles. It was the prophet Jesus! They were clearly bringing him to the governor for trial, but why were there so many priests? And why was Caleb being asked to observe this spectacle and to tell others about it? These things made no sense at all.

As the procession approached the palace entry, the assembled crowd of priests parted to make way. Shortly after, a Roman soldier came through the entrance and spoke with

Caiaphas. After a moment, the soldier departed. For a good ten minutes or more nothing happened in the courtyard, but more and more people gathered around the porticoes to observe whatever was about to unfold.

Then the Roman governor himself appeared at the top of the stairway up to the palace entrance. At the base of the stairs stood the crowd of priests and the prisoner, Jesus. Four Roman soldiers were behind the governor. One brought out a chair, a judicial seat from which the governor would hand out legal verdicts—though Pilate did not sit in the chair.

The governor addressed the crowd in a voice that all in the courtyard could easily hear. "For what privilege do I owe a visit from Jerusalem's leading priests? It seems quite early to be conducting any official business—and on the day of a great feast, no less! What is so important that you find the need to disturb me on such a beautiful and peaceful morning?"

"We have an urgent matter that you must deal with immediately, Governor," Caiaphas replied. "Jesus the Galilean, who has long been regarded as a prophet by our people, now poses a great risk to our city. He presents himself as a conquering king, promotes the replacement of Roman rule with a new kingdom, and defames our temple, its leadership, and the powers that endorse it—*your* power, Governor. Our great council has conducted a formal trial, and it has found this man guilty of sedition and disturbance of the peace of our city. We feel these crimes are capital in nature, and you alone can pronounce a sentence of capital punishment. It is this sentence we ask of you this morning."

"These are indeed serious charges," said Pilate. "And if true, punishment must be enforced. But I am surprised at the number who have come to me this morning. Are so many necessary?"

"Our numbers demonstrate the seriousness and sincerity of our commitment to eliminate this threat to the peace of our city—a threat to the peace of Rome! We come in number so as to be heard."

"Very well," said Pilate. "I will interrogate this man myself and determine his guilt or innocence. Bring the prisoner forward!" Jesus was led up to Pilate, who looked him up and down and escorted him into the palace.

Caleb figured this process would not take long. From what he had witnessed of Jesus, he was surely guilty of the crimes the high priest had charged him with. No doubt the Roman governor would be extremely sensitive to such activity. Jesus would likely be crucified that very morning.

The thought made him both sad and frightened. He had grown fond of the prophet; something about him just drew Caleb to him. Maybe the prophet reminded him of his own father in some way. But he was also afraid: the execution of this prophet seemed dangerous. The people loved him. The chance of violent retribution seemed high.

PILATE

Pilate led the guards and his prisoner through the main entrance of the palace grounds into another open courtyard that surrounded the palace proper. They walked through a garden and then into a small room. Both Pilate and Jesus entered while the guards remained outside the door. There was a small desk with a chair behind it, both of which were facing a larger window that looked out to the garden they had just passed through. There were also chairs opposite the desk, and Pilate motioned for Jesus to sit.

Pilate had known for some time this moment was coming, and he had been ruminating over the best way to handle it.

Did he play coy with Jesus, or did he tell him the truth? He wanted to tell him the truth. He wanted to mock his plans for unsettling the city. He wanted to tell him he had been one step ahead of him the entire time. After all, who could Jesus tell? But Pilate told himself that discretion was the right path. Hubris only opened the door to disaster. He would play coy.

"These are serious charges brought against you," Pilate said. "Are they true? Are you indeed the king of the Jews?" The prophet remained silent, which slightly irritated Pilate.

"You have nothing to say regarding the charges?" he asked. "Do you deny them?" Still nothing. Pilate's irritation grew. To Pilate, the silence communicated nothing but arrogance. Even in the face of death, he plays the king who is in control.

"Why do you not defend yourself?" he asked. "You realize you are facing death?"

At this, the prophet nodded. "Well, there is some reaction," Pilate said, annoyed. "Do you not care if you die?" The man only looked back at Pilate.

"You know I have the power to save you?" A slight smile crossed the man's face. The smile further irritated Pilate. "Do you find that amusing?"

Finally, the man spoke. In a quiet voice he said, "My life will not be spared today by your power. You know this as well as I do." Pilate felt a surge of anger. Was he indicating he was somehow in the know or that he was in control? Pilate took a moment to push back his anger before he spoke again.

"Why do you say this? Do you not believe you will receive a fair hearing? Roman justice is fair."

"Sometimes as fair as it is opaque," the man said.

"What are you hinting at? Is there something you wish to say?" Nothing but silence and a knowing look.

With that, the dam broke—there would be no holding back the anger now. Pilate decided to forge ahead with brutal honesty.

"You are quite right!" he said venomously. "You will certainly die today!" Speaking those words might not have been wise, but it gave Pilate deep satisfaction. He went on, "And it will indeed be justice. You and I both know that every charge brought against you is true. You come into *my* city and present yourself as a conquering king? You are a joke!" Pilate sneered. "A peasant with peasant followers who thinks he will soon rule the world! I have killed your kind before, and I will do so again today!"

The man looked at Pilate blankly. If these words had frightened him at all, he gave no indication. This made Pilate even angrier. "You smug charlatan! You will not only die but you will also feel great pain today. As you feel it, know your arrogance was the cause!" In that moment, Pilate decided to add an additional touch to his punishment of this man Jesus.

"Guards!" he called. "I am ready to return to the priest with my verdict." They opened the door, roughly grabbed Jesus, and lifted him to his feet. Pilate led them back the way they had come to the palace entrance. As he went, he composed himself. The show had to go on, and it had to be persuasive.

CALEB

Caleb was talking with another onlooker when he heard a commotion coming from the crowd of priests. The governor had returned with the prophet Jesus. From the entrance to the palace, he addressed the crowd: "Respected priests of Israel, I have questioned this man thoroughly. I have also questioned my own witnesses, including soldiers who vigilantly watch the happenings in this city. As a result of this process, I find no basis to convict this man of a capital crime or to sentence him to death as you request."

These words shocked Caleb. Innocent!? He felt relief, but also confusion. Surely, from a Roman perspective, this man was a threat. How could Pilate find him innocent?

The governor's declaration immediately brought loud protests from the priests. Many of the other onlookers seemed relieved, but apparently intimidated by the priests, they stayed silent.

Pilate raised his hands to calm the crowd, and the angry din slowly died down. "I understand your disappointment," he said, "but Roman justice must be served. I find no fault with this man, no reason to believe he is leading a rebellion. Perhaps I can still appease you, and we can find some common ground. His rampant talk of a new kingdom is troubling indeed. But if all were killed for such talk, there would no doubt be few Jews remaining! Yet to discourage this talk and the hope it breeds, and to reward your diligence in keeping the peace of the city, I will have this man whipped with the scourge and then released."

Again, the crowd of priests expressed their disapproval. Pilate raised his hands. "This is my decision."

Caleb's heart sank. Scourging was a horrific act, and a difficult one to watch. The victim was not whipped with an ordinary whip but with the Roman *flagrum*. It had a short, thick handle with three or four long lashes attached to it. At the end of the lashes were small lead balls or pieces of bone. These broke open the skin on the first lashing or soon thereafter. It was a gruesome sight, and depending on the number of lashes given, could be fatal in itself.

The Roman soldiers took Jesus to a stone column and bound his hands to it. They bared his back and shoulders. He was slightly bent over, his back facing the Roman soldier who would deliver the scourging. A young slave brought out the *flagrum*, and the whipping commenced.

Most of the onlookers turned away from the scene, but Caleb, along with the crowd of priests, did not. It appeared that the soldier delivering the blows—the lictor, as he was called—was not as aggressive as he could have been. The first couple of lashes brought loud moans from the victim. The skin broke on the third lash, followed by cries of intense pain. With each lash the lacerations grew deeper and the cries grew louder. It was difficult to watch, but Caleb did not look away.

After the tenth lash, Pilate called for the lictor to halt. Though these ten blows had inflicted significant pain on the prophet, stopping at ten was a sign of mercy. This surprised Caleb, but it was consistent with Pilate's claim that he found no reason for executing this man. Had he found him guilty, the penalty would have been crucifixion, and the scourging prior to crucifixion was far more thorough and brutal than what Caleb had just witnessed.

Jesus' garments were placed back over his shoulders, and he was brought back before the crowd of priests. "Surely this punishment is enough to satisfy you," said Pilate. "A man innocent of the charges you brought should endure no more than this." The crowd erupted in jeers, boos, and insults. Their response was clearly escalating, and their anger toward the reluctant governor was growing.

Pilate raised his hands to calm the crowd. "I can see this has not satisfied you," Pilate said, seemingly frustrated. "Very well. I will again question this man, consult with my advisors, and reconsider my verdict." This decision clearly pleased the crowd of priests, but for Caleb and the other onlookers it brought the all-too-familiar feeling of dwindling hope.

PILATE

After announcing that he would reconsider his decision, Pilate led the soldiers and his prisoner back into the palace. He had not originally intended to have Jesus scourged, but the prophet's smugness had forced him to do it. It had taken great restraint to stop at ten lashes. Pilate would have loved to have given the man twenty more, but selling his belief in this man's innocence was paramount. He could not let anger jeopardize the plan. Perhaps now Jesus' demeanor would be less self-assured; the *flagrum* had a way of humbling all men.

There was little more to do now than wait. There would be no meeting with advisors, no more interrogation. The die was cast. The man would be crucified. But Pilate must play this ruse out fully.

The guards took Jesus to a bench in the courtyard where they sat him down. Here Pilate approached him. The smug look had disappeared; only pain remained. Indeed, the whip had broken him. He was breathing heavily and moaning. The pain brought tears he could not hold back and wincing he could not hide. "Did my verdict surprise you?" Pilate asked condescendingly. The man said nothing.

"No need to waste your energy in replying. Save your strength. I already know the answer." Still no response.

Pilate decided to put all his cards on the table. What harm could it do? "I have known what you wanted all along," he said. "You have been trying to force my hand. You wanted me to arrest you from the time you first entered the city. I am sure you were surprised when nothing happened. We are not fools. We know the danger of the masses better than you can imagine. Did you think we would rush in to stop the dangerous prophet only to set the city ablaze with anger? Even this morning you hoped that your arrest and execution at Roman hands would ignite the people to revolt. I am here to tell you that will not happen. Rome *will not* find you guilty. Rome *will not* be the focus of the people's ire. It will be their own leaders, their priests, who will execute you. And that will act as a flood against the fire of rebellion you sought to start. You will die, and your life will be meaningless. Nothing you set out to accomplish will come to pass."

Finally saying these words was deeply satisfying. Yet *still* the prophet said nothing.

"Rest here," Pilate said. "You will need your strength." Pilate turned and began walking away. But as he did, he heard Jesus mumble something.

He turned back. "What? Do you finally have something to say? Speak up. I certainly want to hear it," Pilate mocked. He leaned in close and the spoke again.

In a voice that was clearly trying to draw all the strength it could, the prophet said, "Nothing that happens here today will surprise me. And all that will happen is what ought to happen."

Uncontrollable anger surged through Pilate, and he struck Jesus with a closed fist hard across the face. Pain instantly filled his hand, but it also stung the prophet, who fell to the ground. He found satisfaction in striking him, but it did not quench his anger.

He walked away to gather himself. He would need his composure for the second act.

Caleb

It had been almost half an hour since Pilate had left to reconsider his verdict. The crowd of onlookers had grown, though some had already left. Caleb thought they had likely gone to tell others of the morning's events. Finally, Pilate returned, and the guards had Jesus with them. Blood had soaked through his garments, and he looked weak. His face was full of pain. It appeared there was another man held by the guards as well, but Pilate and Jesus obstructed Caleb's view of the man.

Pilate addressed the crowd of priests that had now regrouped upon the governor's appearance. "Esteemed priests and leaders of Jerusalem, my further interrogation of this man has only strengthened my resolve that he is indeed innocent." A wave of relief washed over Caleb; he had believed a change of the governor's heart was a certainty.

"I find no reason to condemn this man to death, not when others are more deserving. But I see you are committed to the cause of peace today, and that you seek to make a statement against the disruption of that peace. I fully support this notion, and as such I offer you a choice. Would you rather execute this prophet, who it seems clear to me has no intention of committing violence, or a man who has confessed to participating in violence against the Roman soldiers who keep the peace in this city? I am willing to release one and execute the other."

While he was introducing the second man, he stepped aside to reveal him to the crowd. Caleb gave an involuntary gasp. The man was his childhood friend Samuel, who was arrested because of information Caleb had given. His shock was almost instantly replaced with crippling guilt. Samuel looked gaunt, his face pale, and his eyes sunken. He bore bruises that evinced his barbaric treatment in a Roman prison. Caleb's guilt was then accompanied by both hope and anguish. Samuel had a chance to be freed . . . or crucified.

Caleb didn't have to wait long for these conflicting emotions to resolve. The moment Pilate finished his words, the priests erupted in calls to free Samuel and crucify the prophet Jesus! This outburst led to the governor raising his hands in a gesture that seemed to communicate both confusion and frustration. The call for Jesus' execution only grew louder.

Pilate motioned for the priests to quiet down. When they did, he said, "It seems clear to me that you will not be satisfied until you are granted this man's blood. But I in good conscience cannot condemn him to death, as I do not find him guilty of the charges you have brought against him. As you know, Rome grants autonomy to local ruling bodies as much as possible, while still maintaining the peace. It also is committed to justice. I am vexed as to what to do at this crossroads." Pilate's face looked pained. It seemed for him a difficult decision.

In what seemed like almost a minute of silence, he surveyed the crowd of priests and the onlookers gathered around the porticoes beyond them. He finally said, "Because I do not find grounds for charging this man, I will not find him guilty. I cannot. I wash my hands of his fate. But to honor this esteemed body of priests who have led this city with wisdom and honor, I will grant them my power over capital crimes. Do as you see fit with this man. Caiaphas, I grant you the power to crucify, if you see fit."

With these words, Pilate gave instructions to one of the Roman soldiers and then disappeared into his palace.

The morning's events left Caleb's head spinning. Pilate found Jesus innocent? Despite this verdict, leading priests would crucify Jesus anyway? Pilate released Samuel, a known insurrectionist? In his wildest dreams Caleb could not have predicted such an outcome! Looking around, he saw many people running out of the courtyard and suddenly remembered his assigned task: observe and spread the word.

He had quite a story to tell. Would anyone believe it?

SEVEN

THE EXECUTION

CALEB

From the courtyard outside the palace Caleb went to his first assigned location, a prominent marketplace about six blocks east. This market primarily served the middle to lower classes of the city and sold a variety of goods. It was just after eight in the morning, and the market was far from its full capacity. But because the Passover feast was that evening, many more people than usual were there. He quickly found that he was not the first one to share the news.

In the center of a crowd of about fifteen people, a young man and woman were answering the people's questions about the morning's events. Caleb had seen the woman at the trial but not the man. As he drew closer, he saw tears on the faces of some and anger on others. A man asked, "But when did they arrest him? How come we are just hearing about this?" The woman responded, "I don't know when they arrested him. I just know what I saw this morning: he was bound and brought before Pilate by our leading priests—by the high priest himself!"

"He must have been arrested last night," the man said.

"But what were the charges?" another shouted.

"He was charged with sedition. A false messiah who threatened the peace of the city," the woman replied.

"And that Roman tyrant condemned him!" said an angry voice.

"No!" the man in the center said loudly. "You aren't listening! Pilate tried to free him. He said he found no basis for the high priest's charge."

"Horse dung!" shouted the same angry voice. "You said he was being crucified, didn't you? We all know who puts people on crosses!"

"Were you there?" the man in the center shouted back. "Are you calling me a liar? If you don't want to hear what happened I can stop wasting my breath!"

"Calm down!" said the strong voice of the woman. "It was the priests who demanded his crucifixion, not the governor. I was confused too, but that is what happened."

"It makes no sense!" said the angry voice.

"You are right," said the woman, "but it's the truth just the same."

Caleb saw the angry questioner break from the crowd, hands raised in disgust. He joined another group some thirty feet away and unleashed his angry questions on another witness.

Caleb could hear similar conversations going on around him. Some were angry, some were sad, but all were confused.

With the news already spreading like wildfire throughout the market, he went to his next assigned stop, a popular inn and tavern that hosted a large number of pilgrims at the Passover. The tavern was already abuzz with talk of the prophet's arrest and impending execution. Again Caleb saw tears and anger.

One man had the attention of the entire room. "How much longer?" he shouted. "How much longer will we take this tyranny from our Roman oppressors? How long will we let them kill our people, our prophets, without retaliation? And in this holy week! We must take action and drive them from our city!"

A calmer voice replied, "I hear your frustration, Brother, but it seems you have not been listening. The Roman governor found the prophet Jesus innocent. It was our own priests who demanded his death. Do you suggest we take action against our priests? Who among us would be willing to take up arms for such a cause? I fear you seek to turn this tragic event into a cause of rebellion. I am sorry, but I cannot follow you there." Murmurs of support ran through the room.

"Our priests are merely pawns in the hands of Rome!" the man retorted. "Who here can honestly say they believe Pilate's hands are innocent in the arrest and condemnation of this prophet?"

A young woman spoke up. "But I was there! I witnessed Pilate declare the man innocent! He even released a Jewish prisoner to show his sincerity!"

"Nothing more than a charade to fool the masses! Don't be taken in by Roman trickery!" the man shouted in reply.

To Caleb it seemed these words resonated with the crowd; the man might have just gained some supporters. But then an elderly woman stepped forward and spoke commandingly to the room. "Perhaps you are right; perhaps you are wrong. Either way, your call for violence is foolish. I, too, am saddened and confused by this news. Like many here, I believed the prophet Jesus would bring about the long-awaited fulfillment of God's promises. But I won't let my failed hopes be the cause of violence and the bloodshed of my people. If this Jesus is indeed God's prophet, then God will deliver him and us. If he is not, there is nothing you or I can do. Far be it from us to force God's hand!"

Agreement again rumbled through the room. It was clear the man had lost what support he had.

"Cowards!" he yelled. "You embrace weakness and passivity and call it faith. You dishonor your ancestors, who took up iron against God's enemies and with such faith prevailed!" He turned and nodded to a few young men standing behind him, and they stormed out of the tavern. As they left, the room erupted into speculation on the morning's events.

Caleb took his leave. He had one more location on his list, but he could not imagine that news had not already reached it. News was spreading rapidly across the city, and he could not keep up with it. Surprise and sorrow were everywhere, and though anger was present, it seemed like it would not erupt into revolt.

Instead, he decided to head home and check on his sister. Since he had closed the shop for the morning, she should be there with his aunt and cousins. Perhaps they had not yet heard this news—no doubt it would be terribly sad for them. At least they could take solace in the release of Samuel.

It didn't take him long to make his way home. The shades on the windows were open, indicating that all were now awake. He opened the door and was surprised to see no one in the front room. He walked to his room and saw his cousin Jacob sitting with his back to him on the bed. He then stuck his head in his sister's room and saw no one.

"Where have the women gone?" he called out. There was no answer. Irritated at his cousin's silence, he went back toward his room and called, "Jacob!" He entered the room and was shocked to see the face of his cousin Judah turn toward him.

"Judah!" he exclaimed. "What are you doing here? Where is my family?"

"It is good to see you too, Cousin," Judah said with a smile as he rose to embrace Caleb.

Caleb shook his head. "Yes . . . yes of course . . . I am sorry. You deserved a better greeting than that. You just surprised me!"

"I know, Cousin. Not to worry. I was just having some fun with you," Judah said with a smile. "Sorry I startled you."

"But why are you here?" Caleb asked. "Is it safe?"

"Yes, I think it is now quite safe. I would never have put you in danger, Cousin," Judah said. "Over the last three days, there have been no spies around my house. It appears I am no longer being watched. And I heard from one of my spies that I am no longer being investigated for the attack on the soldiers. It appears our friends told the Romans nothing."

"That is incredible news!" Caleb tried his best to act surprised. "You can now return to your family, resume your life!"

"Yes, it appears I can," said Judah quietly.

"But what brought you here this morning?" Caleb asked. "And where is the rest of my family?"

"I came to tell you all the news of the morning's events. Have you not heard?"

"The news of Jesus?"

"Yes!"

"Yes, I am aware," Caleb said quietly. "I was there this morning."

This news seemed to surprise Judah. "You were there? Why were *you* there?"

Caleb realized he needed to be cautious. "By accident, really," he lied. "I woke up early and could not go back to sleep, so I went for a walk. While I was walking, I overheard people talking about something happening at Herod's palace, something about the prophet Jesus. I was curious, so I followed them. I arrived just before Pilate came out to greet the priests who had arrested Jesus."

"So, is it true what people are saying?" Judah asked. "Did Pilate actually find the man innocent? Did our priests protest and demand his death?"

"Yes!" Caleb said. "It is all true."

"Is it true that he even released a Jewish prisoner?" Judah asked.

Suddenly it dawned on Caleb that Judah did not yet know the only good news of the morning. "Yes, it is true!" he said. "They released a prisoner. Judah, it was Samuel!"

Judah's countenance went from confusion to surprise to joy in a matter of seconds. "Samuel?" he sputtered. "Samuel?"

"Yes, Judah! Samuel! He has been freed!" His cousin grabbed him in a tight embrace and swung him once around the room. Then Judah quickly drew back and asked with excitement, "What about Simeon? What about Joseph? Were they also freed?"

Caleb looked down. "I am sorry, Judah. Only Samuel was released. I know nothing of the fate of Simeon and Joseph."

"All right, but there may still be hope!" Judah said excitedly. "Samuel is free. I thought he was dead, but now he is free!" Judah hugged Caleb again and quickly turned to leave.

"Wait," Caleb said. "Where are you going?"

"I have to find Samuel!"

"Yes, of course," said Caleb, "but where is the rest of my family?"

"Oh yes! When I told them the news that Jesus would die, they were heartbroken. They all decided to go to the place of the skull to witness the event. I think they wanted to support him in some way."

This news both frightened and horrified Caleb. He shook his head.

"Don't worry, Cousin," said Judah. "They will be fine!" He ran out the front door.

Caleb was not so sure. He had no interest in witnessing a crucifixion, but he felt he needed to go join his family. He grabbed some bread and dried dates and threw them in a sack. As he headed out the door, the dreadful thought of his destination replaced the joy of his celebration with Judah.

ELEAZAR

As Eleazar watched Pilate enter the palace that morning, he was amazed at how well things had gone. Together, his father and Pilate had orchestrated a convincing display of conflict over the guilt or innocence of the prophet Jesus. The priestly faction of the great council had been successful in creating a crowd of almost two hundred people. They had played their part well in their unrelenting demand for Jesus' death—though some had no idea they were playing a part at all. The fact that they were unaware no doubt made their performance all the more convincing.

And Pilate had even created his own little wrinkles in a light scourging of the prophet and an offer to release Jesus and punish a true insurrectionist in his place. Both acts gave the demonstration an authentic feel and hopefully made the entire scene more convincing to onlookers, of which there were a significant number. Many informants had been tasked with spreading the narrative that Pilate had wanted to release Jesus, but the large number of observers made it even more likely that word of the morning's events would soon blanket the entire city.

As preparations were being made for Jesus' crucifixion, Eleazar noticed that the Roman soldiers were mocking him. One had placed a crown made of some sort of greenery on his head, while another had placed his garment over Jesus' shoulders. Two were bowing before him as if he were a king.

The mockery didn't last long, as the centurion leading these soldiers reprimanded them after a quick word from Caiaphas. The centurion then returned to Caiaphas and spoke to him quietly. Whatever the centurion said did not make his father happy. The centurion simply raised his hands, indicating there was nothing he could do, and walked away. The exchange made Eleazar curious.

As he approached his father, Caiaphas was cursing Pilate under his breath. "Is something wrong?" Eleazar asked. "What did the soldier say that upset you?"

"It's Pilate!" his father said. "He improvised enough earlier and now he lays this on my lap!"

"I don't understand," said Eleazar. "What has he done?" It was rare to see his father this angry.

"We are to be responsible for two more executions today!" his father said in an exasperated tone. "While Pilate has freed one of the three men arrested for the attack on Roman soldiers, the one who is clearly no threat, he has tasked us with crucifying the other two with Jesus."

"Why would we do that?" Eleazar asked. "We did not arrest them or have them tried."

"Pilate doesn't care about that!" Caiaphas said angrily. "And he knows most people won't know that either. They will think we are responsible for the execution of all three for insurrection and disturbing the peace."

"Is there nothing we can do?" Eleazar asked.

His father shook his head. "He is the Roman governor, Son. He appointed me, and I serve at his behest. There is nothing we can do now but follow his order. But we will remember."

A messenger arrived to inform them that preparations had been made and they could now make their way to Golgotha, the place where crucifixions commonly took place. It was decided that Caiaphas, together with Eleazar and Aaron, would lead the processional, and a number of priests from other ranking families would follow. Ezra and Simeon would return to the temple to oversee the Passover preparations of the day. Caiaphas told Eleazar that Annas and his sons had volunteered to take on extra responsibilities in the temple while Caiaphas oversaw the crucifixion.

How gracious, thought Eleazar sarcastically. Annas would not dare be caught playing any more of a public role in the prophet's death than he already had. Eleazar had noticed earlier that Annas did not wear his formal robes to the trial before Pilate, and that he stayed toward the front of the crowd to make it difficult for onlookers to identify him.

Only six soldiers were to accompany them to Golgotha. The Roman presence needed to be as small as possible, but they were needed to perform the crucifixions. The desired image was that of Jesus being executed by Jerusalem's leading priests. While there was certainly a danger of protest from the people, perhaps even violent protest, the hope was that they would be reluctant to stand in the way of their high priest. Ultimately, Pilate and Caiaphas were relying on both a respect for the office of high priest and Caiaphas's own reputation as both righteous and devout.

The procession would not take long. The place of execution was just outside the north wall of the city on a hill that resembled a skull. However, they *would* have to travel through city streets, and Eleazar was anxious about the reception they might receive.

After leaving the courtyard, they entered their first public street. Since it was not yet nine in the morning, there was little traffic. But as they passed by, people came to their windows, balconies, and rooftops to watch. Some ran ahead to tell others of the procession. Eleazar looked around at the faces and saw primarily sorrow. Tears stained the faces of many, and some were wailing loudly. One woman ran forward to offer Jesus a cup of water, and Eleazar was relieved to see that the Roman soldiers allowed it. Anger was on some faces, but ultimately the priests' worst fears remained unrealized. The people threw no stones and formed no mob. In fact, Eleazar was surprised to see that no one even yelled at them. He concluded from this that the narrative of the morning's events had already reached the people. The streets were quiet and somber as they passed, and by the time they reached the north gate the peace had held.

As they drew closer to the execution site, they saw that a large crowd had gathered. Crucifixions did not generally draw many people, as most of the condemned were not widely known. Family and close friends might be present, but few others showed up for such a gruesome event.

But because of Jesus' popularity with the people, this crucifixion was a different story. Many likely came to show support for the prophet they loved, and others no doubt came to confirm the rumors they had heard about the morning's trial. Did they really convict the Galilean prophet? Did Pilate really find him innocent? Would his execution be at the hands of their own priests? Pilate's absence would answer all their questions, as he generally presided over crucifixions.

As the procession arrived, they saw that the other two prisoners were already there, with four Roman soldiers standing guard. They were stripped to the waist, and it was clear that they had been tortured while in custody. Now new lashes from scourging also lay across their backs.

Crucifixion was a gruesome and horrific punishment, one the Romans had perfected. It was a public execution intended to deter anyone from challenging their power. The cross declared Rome the winner, and the crucified, losers. Victims were stripped naked, a humiliation in itself. They were then fixed, usually by ropes but at times by nails, to a wooden cross. Death was caused by exposure to the elements and suffocation.

Eleazar had seen victims writhing in the agony of cramping muscles and gasping for breath as they tried to push the weight of their bodies up for air. Such pushing usually made the cramps worse—it was a vicious cycle and one that was painful to watch. Despite the intense pain, the will to live often led victims to fight for many hours, and at times even days. But the outcome was always the same. No one escaped a Roman cross with their life. Dying quickly was the only mercy a victim could hope for.

Much to Eleazar's chagrin, it appeared these Roman soldiers preferred nailing their victims to the cross. He could not bring himself to watch. The sounds alone, iron crushing through bone and the subsequent screams, were enough to turn his stomach. These preparations brought gasps and horrified cries from onlookers. Even those who were aware of what was coming could never be prepared to see such horrors.

Before the soldiers erected the crosses, signs were made describing the crimes for which each victim was being executed. Above the two who were guilty of killing Roman soldiers, the sign read "Insurrectionists." Above Jesus, the sign read "King of the Jews." Jesus was being executed because he styled himself a conquering figure, a messiah who would lead Israel in overthrowing Rome. It was a warning to anyone who might have such aspirations, and also mocked all who had hoped that Jesus was just such a deliverer. There was little more paradoxical than a crucified messiah.

The crosses were raised, with Jesus placed between the two insurrectionists. Their agony was just beginning, and it brought cries of sorrow and anguish from the crowd. Caiaphas, Eleazar, and Aaron left soon after. Their presence had achieved the desired effect, and it was necessary for them to return to the temple to purify themselves and join in the preparations for the Passover. Caiaphas appointed a handful of priests to stay and oversee the crucifixion, but the rest he gave their leave.

With the sights and sounds of crucifixion in Eleazar's mind, it was hard to take pleasure in the success of the morning. But the plan couldn't have worked better. They had removed the problematic prophet, and at least so far, the city remained at peace. Although not entirely out of the woods, it seemed they were through the most dangerous part.

CALEB

Caleb pushed through the crowd at Golgotha, looking around to find his family. At first his searching distracted him from the fact that there were three crucifixions taking place instead of one. It was not until after he had seen his sister and cousins standing opposite the crowd from him that he noticed there were multiple victims. His eyes were drawn immediately to the prophet Jesus in the middle, but when he looked at those to the prophet's right and left, instant recognition gripped him with paralyzing horror. He was looking into the contorted faces of Joseph and Simeon!

Guilt, shame, and unbearable remorse slowly washed over him. This was his fault! His actions had placed them on those crosses. Almost involuntarily, he fell to his knees and began to convulse with uncontrollable sobbing.

After some time he felt a hand on his shoulder. When he turned around he saw the face of his cousin Judah, whose eyes were also filled with tears. He knelt next to Caleb and placed his arm around him.

"I feel your pain, Cousin," Judah said softly. "These were two of my closest friends, closer than brothers."

Caleb heard the words, but they were untrue in a way that Judah would never know. The pain he felt was pain that

Judah could never feel. His pain was steeped in his own act of betrayal.

"They knew this could happen," said Judah, a hint of strength rising in his voice. "We all did. When you take up arms against Rome, you know the cross might very well be your fate. These men die as heroes. Let that knowledge ease the pain in whatever way it can."

If it was not for my betrayal, they would not have to die at all, thought Caleb, but he said nothing and only nodded.

"Their lives will not be in vain. They do not die like the prophet who dies between them. He promised a coming kingdom and presented himself as a messiah who could bring it, but in the end he did nothing for the cause of our people," Judah said. "Joseph and Simeon die with real Roman blood on their hands. Their faith was true, their zeal unquestioned. It will take more men like them to bring about God's kingdom."

Judah's words made more sense to Caleb than they ever had before. There had been too many like the prophet Jesus who brought hope of a dawning new age, only to die with that hope unfulfilled. Perhaps violence *was* the only way a kingdom of God would ever be realized. But then and there, motivated by both hatred for Rome and himself, Caleb decided to join Judah's cause. He might never see the new and glorious kingdom, but he didn't care. Whatever the result, he would devote himself to shedding Roman blood and the blood of all who aided the enemy. Maybe in such devotion he would find forgiveness for his own betrayal. Perhaps his guilt would drive him to actions that might eventually assuage it. Whatever the cost, his days as an informant were over.

"I need to go to my family," he said softly to Judah.

"Of course," said Judah, who quickly got to his feet and helped Caleb do the same.

They made their way through the crowd to Miriam and Caleb's cousins and aunt. All were in tears, and Caleb's arrival led to many consoling embraces. His cousin Jacob had placed great hope in the prophet Jesus, and the death of that hope was clearly painful. Miriam was fond of the prophet, but it was the deaths of Joseph and Simeon that truly broke her heart. They had played together as children; the boys had pulled her hair and teased her.

The family stood together for a while, unable to look away from the tragedy in front of them. It was Caleb's Aunt Elizabeth who finally said, "There is no more good that can come from remaining here. Our hearts need a reprieve, and the great Passover requires preparation. It will do us good to put our hands to work." No one spoke, but all heard the truth in her words. As she turned to go, the rest slowly followed.

Caleb and Judah were the last to leave. Caleb turned to his cousin and said, "Know, Cousin, that today I am committed to your cause. You have my life to whatever ends you require it."

Judah nodded, a hint of pride on his sad face. They embraced and departed for home. That evening's Passover meal would surely be a somber one.

EIGHT

THE AFTERMATH

PILATE

The cool breeze of the spring evening washed over Pilate as
he sat on his balcony for a private dinner. Tonight, he wanted
to dine alone and in peace. He wanted to reward himself for
the day's triumph. He ordered his cook to prepare a thick cut
of tender beef rib (in Rome it would have been pork, but this
was much harder to find in Judea), a block of fine Italian cheese,
an assortment of roasted vegetables, and a strong red Pom-
peian wine, which many considered the finest in the empire.

As he was enjoying this small feast, he ruminated on the
success of the day. The morning trial of Jesus the prophet
couldn't have gone better. Those present saw a play so convincing it would have entertained audiences in the theaters
of Athens. And while Caiaphas's priests played their part well,
Pilate felt his own performance won the day. The look on
Caiaphas's face when Pilate had offered to release either Jesus
or an insurrectionist was priceless! It was as if the old priest
almost thought Pilate wanted to free Jesus! The image made
Pilate laugh out loud. He did regret losing his temper with the
prophet. Striking him was uncouth and could have been dangerous. His anger could have shown itself during his public
performance, which would have been a problem. But at the
end of the day, the plan went off without a hitch.

Best of all, the people believed it! His soldiers and informants stationed at strategic places around the city had been prepared for violent protest, but nothing of the sort ever emerged. Certainly, there was the danger of a slow-burning anger that might erupt in the following days, but Pilate felt confident that if nothing had happened yet, nothing would happen. The celebration of the Passover feast would distract the people from the morning's events. He would remain vigilant, but for now he felt he could breathe easy.

The clever way he managed to pawn off the deaths of two additional troublemakers onto Caiaphas also brought a smile to his face. The centurion Cornelius, whom Pilate had brought with him from Caesarea, had told Pilate that Caiaphas was quite unhappy to learn he would be responsible for the execution of additional prisoners. This was no surprise to Pilate, and was of course his intention. He respected the old priest and was pleased with the way he had helped solve this Jesus problem, but it was ultimately a problem of Caiaphas's own creation. Pilate was not quite ready to let the priest forget this.

And these men were certainly deserving of execution. There was no doubt they were involved in the attack on the Roman soldiers. But Pilate was troubled by their resolve. Suffering great pain, they had refused to name their coconspirators. Such devotion to a cause was frightening, and death was the only way to end it.

The man Pilate had released was clearly less important than the crucified ones. Although he had given up little information, it seemed that was because he knew little. Before a hand had been laid on him, he whimpered like a baby. Pilate doubted that he had even been involved in the attack. By releasing him, Pilate was able to add authenticity to his verdict on Jesus while releasing only a harmless prisoner.

He said a prayer of thanks to the gods for the great fortune that had befallen him that week. While diligent planning played a significant role, Pilate was not arrogant enough to ignore the role that fortune had played. He knew well that the gods could frustrate the best-laid plans of mortals. When he returned to Caesarea Sunday morning, he would honor them properly. The resolution of this threat was yet one more evidence that Roman rule was a divine gift, and the gods would thwart any and all attempts to resist it.

Shortly before finishing his meal, the through struck him that as he was feasting that night, so were thousands of Jews. But while they partook in a meal celebrating their deliverance from foreign domination, Pilate celebrated yet another thwarting of such deliverance. He took great pleasure in this irony.

Eleazar

It had now been almost two full days since the crucifixion of the prophet Jesus, and the city was still at peace. Today, Caiaphas was hosting his inner circle of priests for a celebratory midday meal, for they had much to celebrate. They had gotten rid of a dangerous threat and had done so without inciting violent protest. At the same time, they led the people of the city in a successful Passover celebration. The lambs had been slaughtered, the sacrifices had been observed, and the people feasted in peace with their families. Moreover, the previous evening, Caiaphas had received a private letter from Pilate giving him significant credit for maintaining the peace of the city. Pilate also assured him that despite any protests that might arise, he had Rome's complete support as Jerusalem's reigning high priest. Less than a week ago, it had appeared that his role, along with the peace of the city he so loved, was in great jeopardy, but now all was well. Indeed, there was much to celebrate!

Spread before them was an abundance of food, including roast lamb, fresh fish, plates of grapes, figs, dates, and olives, and a variety of fresh breads. Flagons of various wines were also present—strong Jewish wines from Corinth, Alexandria, and even the Italian countryside.

When the last guest had arrived, Caiaphas addressed them all with a short speech. "My dear brothers! Two nights ago, we celebrated God's faithful deliverance of our people from the land of Egypt and from slavery. Today we celebrate God's deliverance of a different kind, a deliverance from the misguided and distorted vision of our own people. Their hatred of foreign occupation keeps them from seeing the great opportunity we have set before us—the opportunity to be a witness to our pagan neighbors of the greatness of our God and the way of life he has bestowed on us. If left to their own devices, the people would bring a second judgment of God down on themselves. As God sent the Babylonians to destroy our temple before, he could send the Romans to do so again. But that judgment will not come today!"

With these words, Caiaphas raised his glass high and received a chorus of cheers in response. He continued, "Because of the wisdom, diligence, and hard work of those at this table, and with the help of our God, we have delivered our people once again from foreign oppression and destruction. So today we celebrate!" Again, cheers.

As they ate, stories circulated about the week's events that were known by some but not all. All praised each other for their efforts and accomplishments. Laughter filled the room as they shared jokes and old stories. Success, together with strong wine, had a way of making everything seem funny.

Eleazar took particular joy in seeing his father laugh and celebrate. He was a man of great temperance and dedicated moderation, a man who rarely let himself experience life's pleasures in this way. It was rare that he allowed himself to cross the boundary of sobriety. But Eleazar knew how great a stress Caiaphas had been under for the past months and how much he needed a celebration of this sort.

Aaron was in the middle of telling a joke that everyone had heard a hundred times before when a slave entered the room and handed a note to Caiaphas. Aaron continued with his joke, but Eleazar watched his father read the note. At first a confused look crossed his face, but then he began to smile. After Aaron's punchline brought bellows of laughter, Caiaphas raised his hands and said, "Your attention, please! There is news regarding the prophet from Galilee!" He spoke with sardonic seriousness. "This note I hold has come from the esteemed Pharisee Joseph, son of Isaac. He writes to inform me that the body of the crucified prophet, which Pilate allowed him to bury, is now missing!"

Around the room there appeared confused looks and cautious smiles.

"It appears we have a great crime on our hands!" Caiaphas said sarcastically. "A prophet's body has been stolen. As the keepers of justice and peace in this city, perhaps Joseph feels it falls on us to solve the case. Who among us is worthy to lead such a task?" He paused, looking around the room, then said, "It can be none other than Simeon!" All turned and erupted in laughter when they turned to see Caiaphas's younger brother, who had fallen asleep with his cheek resting in a pile of soft vegetables.

"I will send word immediately to Joseph that we are putting our best man on it!" boomed Caiaphas.

Again, roars of laughter filled the dining hall.

CALEB

It had been almost two months since the Passover. The Feast of Weeks, which came seven weeks later and celebrated first fruits and the giving of the Torah on Mount Sinai, had come and gone, and Caleb's visiting family had returned to Damascus. With the close of these two great festivals, life had resumed its normalcy. The shop continued to thrive, although Caleb had not seen his contact since before the crucifixions. Apparently, the need for information was not pressing. But the continued increase in business, together with his monthly stipend, surely meant that those he had been working for understood him to remain in their employ.

In the days immediately after the crucifixions, Caleb had believed the only way forward would be to cut his ties with the high priest completely. The priests had used him for the benefit of Rome; he saw that clearly now. That would never happen again.

But the more thought he gave to his situation, the more he considered another option. Perhaps remaining an informant could be advantageous. Not only could he control the information he would pass on, but he could pass on misinformation to advance his new cause. He might also be able to gather information for the cause through his connections with the high priest's family. Ultimately, Caleb decided that this approach would be the best use of his position. He would be a double agent, providing innocuous or even misleading information to the high priest and his family while ultimately working for Jewish liberation from Roman power.

So it was that he found himself at the first meeting of like-minded freedom fighters since the execution of Joseph and Simeon, both founding members of this movement. Judah was still leading the group, and he had found a new meeting place. The attention he had drawn for the attack on the Roman soldiers led him to believe that Solomon the Pharisee's scriptorium was no longer a safe place to meet, so now they had gathered in the basement of a small restaurant. The space was smaller than the scriptorium, but safety was a far greater concern than comfort. All present had taken precautions. Though there was no evidence of continued Roman surveillance, all feared they still lived under Roman suspicion.

In light of all that had happened since their last meeting, they had much to discuss. They said prayers for the families of Joseph and Simeon and spent time in silent meditation to honor their lives and sacrifice. They took comfort in the hope that they would see them both again at the great resurrection. The entire group pledged to financially support Joseph's and Simeon's families in order to make up for the hardships their deaths had caused. The amount Caleb pledged was quite significant.

Judah informed them that he had recruited several possible soldiers for the cause, and that he had marked a large number of potential recruits. Others indicated that they, too, had identified potential recruits. Though the crucifixions on the day of the Passover feast had not led to immediate violence, they had stirred up anger and a more intense desire for liberation in the hearts of many. Far more people now talked openly of throwing off the chains of Roman tyranny and striking at the Jewish leadership that was in bed with Roman power. Judah declared that public dissent was growing, and the time to capitalize on it was now. All potential members needed careful vetting, of course, but he was confident that many would be joining their cause soon. They would need to look for a bigger meeting place in the months to come, but this was a good problem to have.

They also discussed a new movement that had emerged in Jerusalem over the past two months. Some of the closest followers of the prophet Jesus had begun to claim that he was no longer dead but had been resurrected. They were claiming that he had appeared to them, that they had touched him, and that they had even eaten with him. They took this resurrection as a sign that he was indeed God's Messiah and that the long-awaited final age of God's salvation had dawned.

Few at the meeting thought this movement posed any sort of a threat, and for the most part they dismissed the group as a misguided sect of fanatics that would soon come to an end. The absurdity of their claims was evident in the simple fact that nothing had changed! Rome still occupied Israel, and everyone still felt its heavy oppression. People still suffered from illness, disease, and financial hardship. If the final age of God's blessing had indeed come, it had fallen far short of all Jewish expectations! But surprisingly, the movement had won over some converts. Not many, to be sure, but it was nevertheless odd that the movement had convinced anyone at all of such an absurd notion.

Judah also noted that this group had been causing trouble for the ranking priests by continually bringing up the crucifixion of Jesus and blaming these leaders for it. Though they were of little real consequence, their constant haranguing was no doubt an irritant to the temple authorities. Judah suggested that the distraction they caused could be a veil of sorts that protected their own resistance movement from the eyes of authority.

The meeting ended with a discussion of plans for striking at Roman power to exact revenge for the executions of Joseph and Simeon. They even talked of attacking the high priest and his family, as most saw them as puppets of the Roman governor who allowed them to do his dirty work. They agreed to gather more information and further develop these ideas at their next meeting. Judah reminded them that an effective strike against Rome would take meticulous planning. No matter how angry they were, he demanded patience from them all.

As the meeting broke up, Judah asked Caleb to stay behind, and he wondered what his cousin might want to discuss. Judah began by talking about potential recruits. He inquired about Caleb's cousin Jacob in Damascus, explaining that it might be important to start developing support for the cause outside Judea. Caleb was uncertain about Jacob, though he said he would consider it. He agreed that expanding support outside the region seemed like a good idea. They also discussed a few workers in Caleb's shop and a couple of other family members.

Caleb thought the conversation was ending when, all of sudden, Judah asked, "So, when will you pass on all this information to the high priest?"

He froze, looking at Judah in stunned silence. He knew he had to choose whether to lie or tell the truth. His instincts told him the truth was already known and that lying would do him no good.

"How long have you known?" Caleb said, his voice thick with defeat and shame.

"Soon after I visited you on the night the Romans arrested Joseph, Simeon, and Samuel. I suspected you immediately, given that you were one of only three new people at the previous meeting. Also, there was the sudden success of your business. When I came to you, I hoped it wasn't true. Your denial gave me hope, but I couldn't take you at your word alone. I had you followed. At first, your actions gave nothing away. You were observed once interacting with a man known to work for the high priest's family, but that wasn't enough to be certain." Oddly, it gave Caleb some comfort to know he had been successful in avoiding detection even when being watched.

Judah continued, "But I was convinced on the night I came to you seeking help for my family."

"When I asked about the prophet and his disciple," Caleb said. He had feared the questions would arouse suspicion.

"Yes. I didn't believe that you were merely curious. You were collecting information, and that could only mean one thing. After that, I followed you myself to confirm. Do you remember that night?"

"Yes, very well. I met with my contact and then with the brother of the high priest himself," Caleb replied.

"I saw both, and then I was certain," Judah said, a sadness in his voice.

"If you knew, why am I still alive?" asked Caleb matter-of-factly. When he decided to tell the truth, Caleb had resigned himself to the fact that this night was not going to end well for him. Judah had let him live to this point for some reason, but now he figured that reason had come to an end. He knew what Judah was capable of and how he handled betrayal.

The question brought a look of pain to Judah's face that said he knew exactly what Caleb was thinking. "I was angry when my suspicions were confirmed," Judah said. "Angry enough to kill you." Tears filled his eyes and began to slowly fall down his cheeks. "It shames me now to say it, because"—he paused— "because you are my *family*." The tears were flowing freely now, and Judah took a moment to gather himself.

"I followed you to the tavern that night with vengeance in my heart. I planned to kill you when you left. Forgive me, Cousin."

"Why didn't you?" Caleb asked, tears now filling his eyes as well.

"Because of what I heard in the tavern," Judah replied.

"You were there?" Caleb asked.

Judah nodded. "I heard your request of the high priest." He paused, sobbing. When he could speak again, he said, "I heard you save my life that night." Another pause as Judah tried to compose himself. "You could have handed me to them. But instead you used the power you had to spare me." With these words, Judah placed a hand on Caleb's shoulder and then embraced him.

"I only wish I could have saved Joseph and Simeon as well," Caleb said.

"I know," whispered Judah.

They separated and Caleb looked at Judah with confusion. His fear that his cousin meant to kill him had largely diminished, but he still didn't know the purpose of this confrontation or why Judah would allow Caleb to come to the night's meeting knowing he was an informant.

"If you knew, why did you allow me to come to this meeting?"

"I am not really sure," Judah replied. "But I felt like something changed in you when you saw Joseph and Simeon crucified. I saw true sorrow. I saw that you loved them, that you were feeling the pain not only of loss but the pain of knowing the role you played in their death. And do you remember what you said to me that day?"

Tears returned to Caleb's eyes. He nodded. "I told you I was committed to your cause."

"You promised me your life that day, and I believed you. I didn't know what that meant for you and your relationship to the high priest, but I wanted to give you time to figure that out. The true reason I asked you to stay tonight was not just to confront you but to ask you where things now stand. Are you still an informant for the high priest, or are you now truly committed to our cause?"

Caleb paused a moment. The answer to that question was complicated, and he hoped his cousin would understand. "Yes . . . and yes," he finally replied. "I will remain an informant, and I will use that position to advance the cause."

The smile on Judah's face took Caleb by surprise. "I was hoping that was the case. I knew you might end the relationship, but I hoped you would not. For the past two months, I have wanted to suggest that you not do so, that you use the relationship to aid our cause. But in the end, I thought it best you come to that decision on your own."

Caleb wiped the tears from his eyes and shook his head. "You are full of surprises, Cousin."

"I think I could say the same thing of you." They laughed.

On their way to the door, Judah said, "Having you as an informant will be a great weapon for us. There is something sweetly satisfying in knowing that our ranking priests, puppets of Roman power, will be financing those who will bring that power down."

As they stepped outside, Caleb breathed deeply of the cool night air and said with a smile, "It is sweet, indeed."

AUTHOR'S NOTE

No doubt after reading this narrative, many readers are left with a variety of questions, particularly given the fact that my depiction of Jesus' death is, in some significant ways, different than traditional understandings. Some might be left wondering how much of what they just read is fact and how much is fiction. Some might be wondering if this narrative contradicts the Gospels of the New Testament. Others might be questioning my interpretation of this detail or that. While I cannot possibly respond to all of the questions this story has raised, here I will attempt to answer some of them.

First, what can be said to those seeking a distinction between fact and fiction in the narrative? It is not as easy as dividing the events in the narrative into two categories: those that are fact and those that are fiction. Such an approach ignores the difficulty of assessing what is indeed fact. When it comes to the historical facts of Jesus' death, there is great disagreement and debate among historians and biblical scholars as to what those facts actually are. While some will simply conclude that all the details found in the New Testament are historical fact, others will not. And for those who accept everything in the Gospels as historical facts, what is to be made of the places where there are apparent discrepancies among the Gospels themselves? Even among historians and biblical scholars, there are wide-ranging opinions regarding the facts of Jesus' life and death. Did Jesus' triumphal entry actually happen? Did Jesus actually disrupt the temple—and if he did, what was the significance of this action? Did Jesus present himself as a "messiah" in any way? Would Jesus have been perceived as a threat to the peace of Jerusalem? Was Jesus actually tried by Jewish authorities or the Sanhedrin? Did Judas actually betray Jesus? The list of debated issues goes on and on. My narrative has woven in my own historical assessment of what is fact and fiction, and to address each disputed issue here would be overly burdensome. Instead, I will here outline for you my own scholarly opinion about the facts of Jesus' death. After doing so, I will be able to more easily identify the aspects of the book that are clearly fiction.

My understanding of Jesus' death begins with the social and political setting that Jesus entered during his final week in Jerusalem, namely the celebration of the Passover. This feast was a celebration of God's deliverance from slavery in Egypt, and given that the Jews of Jerusalem and Judea were currently living under foreign occupation, such a celebration would be of particular relevance to them. Put another way, there is likely no time of the year in which Jews were collectively focused on freedom from Roman occupation more than at the Passover festival.

Compared to the rest of the cities of the Roman Empire, the civil unrest and political tension within Jerusalem was regularly quite high, but at Passover it was even greater. In fact, the historian Josephus tells us that the risks of riot and revolt were greatest during festivals like Passover (Josephus, *Jewish War* 1.88). The feast drew a large number of Jewish pilgrims to Jerusalem; most scholars estimate that the population grew between four to five times its normal size of somewhere between 50,000 and 100,000 people. The crowd-control issues alone would have been enough to give the governing Roman officials a major headache! As the narrative explains, the tension and the crowds put both Jewish and Roman authorities on high alert in the months leading up to the Passover and during the festival itself. I think it is fair to say that during the Passover celebration, the Roman governors of Judea wanted nothing more than for it to come and go without any disruption to the peace. When Jesus came to Jerusalem just before Passover, he entered a political tinderbox that could be set ablaze with the smallest of sparks.

But before discussing Jesus' entry into the city, a few comments must be made about Jesus himself. Though not all historians and scholars would agree, many would contend that Jesus was an extremely popular prophet and teacher, and it is likely that many Jews hoped or believed he was God's Messiah who would deliver them from Roman occupation. As such, I believe Jesus would have drawn the eye of Roman and Jewish authorities long before he came to Jerusalem for Passover. Whether there were any attempts or plans to stop Jesus from coming, as I suggest in my story, is admittedly speculation. But I would contend that, given Roman vigilance in this region, such efforts are highly plausible. Roman authorities would have certainly seen a popular prophet who proclaimed the coming of a new kingdom of God as a potential threat to peace.

Now let us consider Jesus' entry into Jerusalem at Passover. While some scholars reject the historicity of the Gospels' depiction of this event, I not only affirm it but give it great significance in my reconstruction of the political realities that led to Jesus' death. Jesus entered the city of Jerusalem as a conquering king, welcomed by the people's cries of "Hosanna!" (which means "salvation" or "save us") and acclamations of him as Messiah. This entrance is at the heart of church celebrations each year on Palm Sunday, but rarely do Christians pause to think about the political significance of Jesus' actions. In the eyes of Roman authorities, Jesus is committing a capital crime! From a Roman perspective, and the perspective of the crowds, Jesus is entering the city as a messianic king who will save the people from Roman oppression. An entry like this would be extremely dangerous at any time of year, but it would be particularly so at Passover. The Roman governor Pilate would quickly know of such actions and would need no other reason to execute Jesus as a dangerous political threat. To add fuel to the fire, Jesus caused a major disturbance in the Jewish temple. He condemned the temple leadership, which had been appointed by Rome and thus were representatives of Roman power. Such an action could be regarded as a capital crime as well.

Despite both of these actions, Jesus was not arrested, and one must ponder why. In agreement with the Gospels, my narrative suggests that he was not arrested because of a fear that his arrest itself might catalyze what Roman authorities wanted to avoid, namely rioting in the streets that could lead to rebellion. Thus, Jesus presents a Catch-22 for Pontius Pilate. If Jesus is not arrested, he might lead the people to riot and revolt. But if Jesus is arrested, that very arrest might bring about the same outcome. How then can Pilate solve his Jesus problem?

Pilate's solution is at the heart of my narrative. I propose that Pilate colludes with the Jewish authorities of the city to formulate a strategy for eliminating Jesus and the threat he poses to peace. This strategy involves Jesus being arrested and tried by Jewish authorities followed by their formal and public request to Pilate for his execution. Pilate makes a public show of finding Jesus innocent, but ultimately accedes to the will of the Jewish authorities and hands Jesus over for crucifixion. Pilate reasons that if he is seen as executing Jesus, the chances for riot and revolt are much higher than if the people's own leaders are perceived as responsible for Jesus' death.

Thus, I present the Gospels' depiction of Jesus' trial before Pilate and the Jewish authorities' participation in that trial as an act of political gamesmanship. The ruse takes place in the early morning so that the crowds of Jesus' supporters, who might respond violently to a public arrest, would still be in bed or just waking up. But the ruse is also public so that witnesses could spread throughout the city the narrative that Pilate had created. As the people in the city hear this news, there is sadness and anger, but most importantly there is confusion regarding the role Rome played in Jesus' death. This confusion stifles the potential fires of rebellion. In the end, the plan works, and Pilate gets exactly what he wanted all along: the death of a dangerous prophet and messianic claimant without riot or revolt.

The narrative in this book is primarily a way to creatively introduce the reader to this reconstruction of Jesus' death and the political realities that brought it about. Obviously, many aspects of the story are my own creations. The only characters that have a firm basis in history are Jesus, his leading disciples (including Judah/Judas), Caiaphas, and Pilate. Caleb, Caleb's cousin Judah, Judah's coconspirators, and even Caiaphas's son Eleazar are fictional, as are many of the events and interactions they participate in. Even the interactions between truly historical characters such as Caiaphas and Pilate, and Jesus and Pilate, are fiction, although they are grounded in a sound historical understanding of the sociopolitical realities of Judea and Jerusalem under Roman occupation. That is to say, characters *like* Judah, Caleb, and Eleazar did exist, and their actions in the story reflect plausible historical realities, even if such actions are not themselves those realities.

Some might fear that this narrative contradicts the New Testament Gospels or undermines their claims in certain ways. This could not be further from my intended aim. My primary goal is to help readers better understand the social and political realities that provide the proper context for understanding the depiction of Jesus' death in the New Testament Gospels. The Gospels are not exhaustive historical accounts of all the details related to Jesus' death, and they were not intended to be so. Each Gospel has its own purpose in its depiction of Jesus' Passion and death, and thus each depicts Jesus' death slightly differently. Not only is there much the Gospel authors assume the reader already knows about the social and political context, information most modern readers do not in fact know, but also there was at least some information related to Jesus' death that the Gospel authors were simply not aware of. Thus, while the New Testament Gospels are our best historical sources for the death of Jesus, for the history that they depict to be best understood, additional historical analysis and reconstruction are necessary. The narrative I have created reflects just such analysis and reconstruction.

Perhaps an example will best illustrate these claims. The Gospels' depiction of Pilate finding Jesus innocent has long been a thorny problem for historians and New Testament scholars. At least two ancient writers outside the Gospels depict Pilate as quick to shed blood when faced with resistance to Roman authority (see Philo of Alexandria, *Embassy to Gaius* 299–305; and Josephus, *Jewish War* 2.9; *Antiquities of the Jews* 18.35-177). However, the Gospels depict a reluctant Pilate who does not want to execute a troublemaking Jew. That Pilate finds Jesus innocent is particularly perplexing when one accepts as historical Jesus' triumphal entry into the city as a messianic figure, his great popularity with the people, and his harsh critiques of the Roman-backed Jewish authorities. How do we explain Pilate's innocent verdict in the face of such realities? Some scholars have dismissed the Gospel accounts of Pilate finding Jesus innocent as fabrications created for apologetic, polemical, or theological reasons. Others have sought alternate explanations that maintain the veracity of the Gospels' claims. But the point remains that the depiction in the Gospels of Pilate finding Jesus innocent begs for further historical explanation and understanding. The Gospels do not resolve this tension, and it was not their purpose to do so.

I offer my own solution to the problem of Pilate finding Jesus innocent by offering the narrative that while Pilate privately wanted Jesus eliminated, for political reasons he publicly found Jesus innocent. Does such a solution contradict or deny the Gospel accounts? I would propose that it does not. The Gospels depict the public narrative that Pilate wanted people to see and to be reported throughout the city, yet I am proposing that there was a private narrative that was kept secret by the power brokers of Jerusalem. Instead of contradicting the Gospel accounts, my narrative actually affirms the public narrative that the Gospels bear witness to. At the same time, however, it offers a way in which the historical tension present in the Gospels can be explained and alleviated, namely that there may have been a private narrative of which the Gospel authors were not aware.

Another example is my treatment of the character Barabbas, who appears in each of the Gospel passion narratives. In each Gospel, Pilate gives the crowd gathered before him the choice of freeing either Jesus or a man named Barabbas. Many readers have probably noticed that the name Barabbas does not appear in the story they have just read. Instead of Pilate releasing a person named Barabbas, he releases Judah's best friend, Samuel. This name change is related to historical questions that surround the Gospel tradition of Barabbas. Why would a Roman governor release a dangerous political prisoner at Passover? Would this be advisable for a figure tasked by the Roman emperor to keep the peace of the region? The name Barabbas itself also raises questions of legitimacy. The name comes from Aramaic, and literally means "the son of the Father." That Barabbas would be an individual's personal name is quite odd, and there is no evidence of any person with this name in the entirety of ancient literature outside the Gospels themselves. Many have suggested that the name is not a literal or actual name of a historical figure but that it serves a literary/theological purpose in the Gospels. The choice between Barabbas and Jesus is the choice between two "sons of the father," one who is a political revolutionary and sought to bring about God's kingdom by violence and one who is truly God's Messiah and sought to bring about God's kingdom through his own sacrificial death. Some have concluded that the entire episode finds no basis in history, and that it is merely a literary/theological device used to contrast the way of Jesus with the way of zealots and revolutionaries. Others have maintained that the tradition is strictly historical. My narrative provides a compromise of sorts. It offers a historical basis for the tradition, that is, that Pilate did indeed give the crowd a choice between Jesus and another prisoner, though a choice that was part of his larger act of political manipulation. But at the same time, by changing the name of the character to Samuel, I am recognizing that the name Barabbas itself (not the tradition of releasing a prisoner) is best understood as a literary/theological device and not the actual name of historical figure.

But what of other apparent discrepancies between the above story and the Gospel accounts? Why does Judas not kiss Jesus in the garden? Why does the Passover meal come after Jesus' death and not the night before? Why doesn't Jesus stand trial before Herold Antipas? These are all good questions, but people would be asking them even if they never read my narrative and relied on the Gospels alone! While Judas kisses Jesus in Mark and Matthew, he does not do so in Luke or John. While Luke presents Jesus' Last Supper as a Passover meal, according to John, the Passover meal would have been eaten the night of Jesus' death. And while Luke presents Jesus standing trial before both Herod Antipas and Pilate, Matthew, Mark, and John do not report a trial before Herod.

That the Gospels vary in such details should not be troubling given their various purposes and audiences, but the fact is that they do differ from each other both in the details noted here and in many others. In creating historical fiction about Jesus' death, an author has to make the choice to follow one Gospel or another at certain points, and my narrative reflects my own choices in these matters. No single factor can explain all of them. Some choices reflect a move toward narrative coherence and/or consistency, and others reflect my own historical assessment of particular Gospel details. Yet ultimately, all of the decisions I have made have some precedent in the Gospels themselves.

The theory this narrative proposes is only one among many competing theories regarding the political realities that culminated in Jesus' death. All such theories have strengths and weaknesses, with some accounting for certain aspects of the historical data better than others. As noted above, not all scholars agree on what the actual pieces of the historical puzzle are. Even when they do agree, they do not always assemble those pieces in the same way. It is not my intention to debate the merits of my own approach to the historical puzzle over against the approaches of others. Such an enterprise would no doubt require another book! Here I simply throw my own proposal into the ring for consideration, and I will leave the evaluation of its merit to you. For both your praise and criticism I am equally grateful.

THE DEATH OF JESUS AND THE HISTORY OF ANTI-SEMITISM

Traditional Christian depictions and interpretations of the death of Jesus have long been intertwined with Christian anti-Semitism. Given the Gospels' depiction of a Roman governor who finds Jesus innocent and a mob of angry Jews demanding Jesus' death, Christians have long understood Jews to be responsible, at least legally and politically, for Jesus' crucifixion. Thus, throughout the last two thousand years, Christians have destroyed Torah scrolls, burned synagogues, confiscated Jewish property, taken Jewish lives, and even engaged in genocide, regularly justifying such actions by using the epithets "Christ killers" and "God killers."

Tragically, such evil actions persisted even in the face of official teachings from the Christian church that denounced both the actions themselves and this particular justification for them. Even today, many Christians are either ignorant of or simply insensitive to the implications that the Gospel accounts of Jesus' death have for Jewish-Christian relationships. In light of such a history, it would be highly irresponsible to write a book on the death of Jesus without addressing anti-Semitism.

One of the purposes of this book is to demonstrate that the historical realities surrounding Jesus' death are more complicated than what appears in the Gospel narratives. While the Gospels reveal a public narrative that was witnessed by the masses, I propose that a private narrative also existed that the Gospel authors were not privy to and thus did not include. While my imaginative re-creation of this private narrative does not completely remove Jewish involvement from the death of Jesus, I hope that it qualifies Christian perceptions of Jewish culpability in significant ways. First and foremost, my reconstruction rejects the perception that Pilate truly believed that Jesus was innocent, and instead argues that he was the primary instigator and orchestrator of Jesus' arrest and execution from the beginning. Such a move is important, because Jewish guilt for Jesus' death is often magnified when compared to the Gospels' portrayal of Pilate finding Jesus innocent. While throughout Christian history Pilate has often been rehabilitated and sometimes even presented as one who later came to Christian faith, the Jews have been vilified for demanding the death of an innocent man. By strongly implicating Pilate in Jesus' death, I hope readers' perceptions of Jewish guilt will be mitigated.

Second, my reconstruction undermines the belief that the majority of Jews in Jerusalem rejected Jesus and demanded his execution. This belief has been propagated by the misguided yet often-preached message that goes something like, "The Jews welcomed Jesus as a savior on Palm Sunday, but by Good Friday they rejected him and demanded his execution." As my narrative (and any responsible historical treatment of Jesus' death) demonstrates, this belief is grossly misguided. Jesus was apparently highly popular among the people, which in the eyes of the power brokers of Judea made him a threat to the stability of the region that needed to be removed. The crowd that demanded Jesus' death was not the throngs of supporters that Jesus had throughout the city, but likely a small group of leading Jewish priests that were orchestrated by the high priest and Pilate himself. Thus, the Jews involved in Jesus' death were an extreme minority of the population (maybe a couple hundred people in a city of three hundred thousand!) and far from representative of Jewish attitudes toward Jesus.

Finally, I reject the theory that the Jewish leaders involved in Jesus' death knowingly killed an innocent man out of jealousy or hatred. Through my narrative reconstruction of Jesus' death, I sought to present the complexity of political realities facing the Jewish high priest, Caiaphas. The weight of keeping the peace in Jerusalem as well as maintaining the safety of his Jewish brothers and sisters in the city would have no doubt lain heavily on his shoulders. A figure like Jesus would have greatly threatened that safety. His actions would have been perceived as illegal and seditious by Roman legal standards, which Caiaphas was tasked to uphold as high priest under Roman authority. Jesus' entrance into Jerusalem and his temple actions would have, from a Roman perspective, made him guilty of capital crimes. If Caiaphas had refused to play a part in Jesus' execution, he could have been perceived as taking the side of a traitor and rebel, thus aligning himself against Rome. Ultimately, Caiaphas acted in accordance with the legal responsibilities of his office at that time in Jewish history and likely did so out of a motivation to keep the city of Jerusalem at peace and its inhabitants safe. By better explaining the position of Caiaphas and the complicated realities he was negotiating, I hope my readers' perception of Jewish guilt in the death of Jesus (and the historic charge of deicide) is yet further mitigated.

The historical reconstruction I have offered does include the involvement of the high priest and his administration in the death of Jesus. However, it undermines the teaching that "all Jews" were and are responsible for Jesus' death. This claim is central to Christian anti-Semitism, the consequences of which, including the Holocaust, are well known. I hope that the reconstruction provided in this book will have an impact on Christian assessments of the role Jews played in the death of Jesus and that it will provide Christians with a more responsible way to both understand and present that role moving forward. My prayer is that such efforts to more responsibly handle the scriptural traditions of Jesus' death in Christian preaching, teaching, and dramatic depictions will lead to healing and increased trust between Jews and Christians.

QUESTIONS FOR REFLECTION AND DISCUSSION

1. Each main character—Judah, Caleb, Eleazar, and Pilate—has his own motivations for his choices. Did you find yourself becoming sympathetic with any of them? If so, did this surprise you?

2. Numerous stereotypes of the Pharisees, Sadducees, and Zealots exist among Christians. How did this book challenge these stereotypes? How did it help you better understand these Jewish sects and their beliefs?

3. If you were a Jewish leader such as Caiaphas or Eleazar, how do you think you would respond to Jesus and his influence among the people?

4. What stood out to you about the way Jesus and his actions are portrayed in this book?

5. Before reading this book, had you ever considered the political implications of the ministries of John the Baptist and Jesus? How has this book informed or challenged how you understand the way both of these figures affected the politics of first-century Judea?

6. How do different characters in the story understand "the kingdom of God"? How do their views compare to what you know about Jesus' teaching on the kingdom?

7. How does the portrayal of Jesus' entry into Jerusalem (Palm Sunday) in this book compare to the way you have seen it portrayed in Christian teaching and writing?

8. What did you think about Pilate's reactions to Jesus in the story? How do these two men and their conceptions of power compare?

9. In what ways do anti-Semitic interpretations of Jesus' death fail to fit the biblical and historical evidence?

10. How does learning about the political, social, and economic realities of first-century Jerusalem shed light on your reading of the Gospels?

11. What aspects of the author's interpretation of the events surrounding Jesus' death do you find convincing? What do you find unconvincing?

12. What topics or questions raised by this book would you like to explore further?

NOTES

1 A Fragile Peace

10   *upcoming Passover celebration:* The Passover celebration commemorated God's deliverance of the people of Israel from slavery in Egypt.

11   *study of Torah:* The Torah, or "Instruction," refers to the first five books of the Hebrew Bible (or Christian Old Testament). These books are Genesis, Exodus, Leviticus, Numbers, and Deuteronomy. For first-century Jews, these books contained the regulations of their covenant relationship with God, and as such were highly valued—though interpretation of their content varied.

19   *Among the Sadducees:* The Sadducees were a Jewish sect largely composed of Jerusalem's upper class. Many of Jerusalem's leading priests, and usually the high priest and his family, were Sadducees.

22   *Herod the first:* This Herod would later be identified as Herod the Great.

23   *Asia Minor:* Asia Minor refers to modern-day Turkey.

24   *Greek Seleucids:* The Seleucids were a Greek dynasty that emerged from Alexander the Great's empire. They controlled the land of Israel from 198 BC until the Jews revolted against them in 167 BC. This revolt, known as the Maccabean Revolt, resulted in Jewish independence.

2 An Approaching Storm

36   *Herod's unlawful marriage to Herodias:* The Roman-appointed ruler in Galilee, Herod Antipas, married the wife of his

half-brother, Philip, who ruled for Rome in the neighboring regions of Iturea and Trachonitis. Both were the sons of the client king Herod the Great, though neither bore the title "king" but instead were given the titles of "tetrarch," meaning "ruler of a quarter" (both Herod Antipas and Philip ruled a quarter of the region previously ruled by their father).

41   *fifth commandment of the Decalogue:* The Decalogue is more widely known as the Ten Commandments. Here I refer to the fifth commandment according to the Jewish count (and that of most Protestants), but which is fourth in the Catholic count.

46   *Jerusalem cohort:* A cohort consisted of approximately six hundred soldiers. A Roman legion was generally composed of ten cohorts.

52   *client king Herod Archelaus:* Herod Archelaeus was the son of Herod the Great, brother to Herod Antipas, and half-brother to Philip. He was granted reign over half of his father's kingdom, but his failings in this position caused him to be removed and replaced with a Roman governor.

68   *150 drachmas:* The drachma was a common Greek silver coin, which, like the Roman denarius, was worth approximately a single day's labor. While many have assumed that Roman denarii were used in Judea during the lifetime of Jesus, recent studies on Roman coinage strongly indicate that they were not. The fruit of this recent research is reflected here.

4 THE CRISIS

101   *Simeon Maccabeus, entering the city of Jerusalem:* Simon Maccabeus (or Simon Thassi, as he is often called) was the older brother of Judas Maccabeus. Judas led the Jews in revolt against the Seleucid King Antiochus IV, who had outlawed Judaism in Judea and Samaria. In this revolt, Judas had retaken the city of Jerusalem, but he was unable to take the Acra, a Greek military stronghold built by Antioch IV that sat in close proximity to Jerusalem. The Acra was occupied by Greek forces, and for over twenty years was a persistent problem for the Jews in Jerusalem and Judea. In 141 BC, Simon Maccabeus finally captured the Acra (historical sources conflict on whether he destroyed it or inhabited it). In celebration of

this great accomplishment, Simon was welcomed into the city
with songs, praises, and palm branches (see 1 Maccabees 13:51).

114 *latrones match*: Latrones was a Roman board game quite
similar to the game of chess.

THE DEATH OF JESUS
AND THE HISTORY OF ANTI-SEMITISM

227 *"God killers"*: For discussion of this relationship between the
Christian passion narratives and anti-Semitism, see Jeremy
Cohen, *Christ Killers: The Jews and the Passion from the Bible
to the Big Screen* (Oxford: Oxford University Press, 2007).

official teachings: See, for example, Vatican Council II, *"Nostra
aetate*: Declaration of the Relationship of the Church to Non-
Christian Religions"* (1965), section 4; or more recently, *Criteria
for Evaluation of Dramatizations of the Passion*, produced by
the United States Conference of Catholic Bishops' Committee
for Ecumenical and Interreligious Affairs (1988).

ALSO AVAILABLE

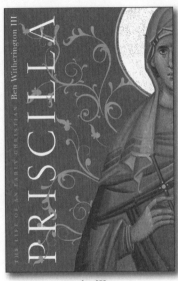

Priscilla
Ben Witherington III
978-0-8308-5248-2

Phoebe
Paula Gooder
978-0-8308-5245-1